EXTREME LOVE

A LOVE TO THE EXTREME NOVEL

EXTREME LOVE

A LOVE TO THE EXTREME NOVEL

ABBY NILES

Entangled Publishing, LLC
2614 South Timberline Road
Suite 109
Fort Collins, CO 80525
Visit our website at www.entangledpublishing.com.

Edited by Liz Pelletier
Cover design by Heather Howland

Ebook ISBN   978-1-62061-247-7
Print ISBN   978-1-62061-246-0

Manufactured in the United States of America
First Edition April 2013

The author acknowledges the copyrighted or trademarked status and trademark owners of the following wordmarks mentioned in this work of fiction: Barbie, Brawny Man, G.I. Joe, Kleenex, MGM Grand and Casino, Michelin Chef, Miss Piggy, MMA, Paramount, Playgirl, Rocky, Superman, Terminator, The Hulk, Thor, U-Haul, Vaseline, Wolverine, YMCA.

To Linda and JJ: Thank you for introducing me to MMA. Yes, I know I spent the first night cringing and covering my eyes, but without you two I would have never grown to love and respect the sport, and the idea for EXTREME LOVE would've never been born.

CHAPTER ONE

Thunderous screams filled the arena as a dark-haired fighter twisted his blond opponent's arm. The man struggled to free himself but only succeeded in cranking the twist tighter. Unable to watch any more, Caitlyn Moore slapped her hands over her eyes.

How could her friend bring her to such a barbaric event?

"You suck," she said to Amy through her hands.

She couldn't watch this. She'd already endured two bouts. Luckily, they'd been quick. Not this one, though. Two brutal rounds in, blood stained the canvas as well as both fighters, making them appear as if they'd emerged from the aftermath of a Scottish war movie.

But with real blood.

She shivered.

Amy laughed. "Jesus, lighten up." Then she gasped. "Oh my God! Bash his teeth in!"

The beefy man to Cait's left roared, "Come on, Majestic! Take him down!"

Droplets of cold beer splattered on Cait's arm. She grimaced.

"Rip him apart!" a woman behind her screamed.

The volume in the arena reached deafening levels. The way the floor shook, she knew even without opening her eyes that everyone was on their feet, jumping up and down, waving their colorful signs.

The crowd booed then roared again.

Cait spread her fingers to see what everyone was excited about.

Bad idea.

The fighters grappled on the mat of the wire-meshed enclosed octagon. The blond on top lifted his elbow high in the air before crashing it into the temple of the poor soul beneath him. The other man's head jerked to the side, his arms splaying wide before he brought them back to protect his skull from the relentless punches raining down on him.

Why didn't the referee stop this?

Cait glanced at Amy, who stood with her hands cupped to her mouth, screaming, "Come on. Choke him out!"

Then Cait peered around the packed arena. As she guessed, everyone was on their feet, arms raised high in the air, chanting for these two men to knock each other out.

How could *any* of these people enjoy watching such violence? It was inconceivable. But if the last hour and a half was any indication, every person packed into the sold-out arena got some sick thrill from watching two men beat the crap out of each other.

Cait turned back to the spectacle just in time to see the blond land a nasty right hook on the jaw of his rival, which sent her friend into another bout of screaming,

"That's my baby!"

My baby?

Cait stared at the hulking man on top. Blond hair? Check. Tribal sleeve on left arm? Check. About two hundred pounds of solid muscle? Check.

No freaking way.

She'd accompanied Amy for one reason and one reason only: to meet her new boyfriend, who just happened to be working at the arena tonight.

Cait had assumed Brad was a security guard, but now everything made sense. The man straddling the other guy, beating him with a left-right combination, was none other than Amy's Brad.

Brad "The Majestic" Sanders.

Oh God.

Cait didn't know much about mixed martial arts—or MMA, as Amy referred to it. The violent sport was too painful to watch, and she avoided the television anytime her friend had the sport on.

From what Amy said—and from what Cait could see with her own eyes—these men were the elite of the elite, warriors in their own right. Some of the most well-defined, tattooed eye-candy a girl could ask for.

She jabbed her friend's side with her elbow. "Why didn't you tell me he was a fighter?"

Amy winced and rubbed her ribs. "Would you have come?"

"Hell, no."

She turned back to the octagon. "Well, there you go."

A grin broke over Amy's face, and she squealed. Not sure what was going on, Cait focused on the ring. A medical team and coaches surrounded the dark-haired man lying on the ground then helped him sit up. Brad stood beside the referee, hands on hips, breathing deeply, satisfaction rolling off him.

A commentator with a microphone strode into the ring. "Ladies and gentlemen, this fight has ended in the third round declaring the winner by knockout, Brad 'The Majestic' Sanders."

As the referee lifted Brad's arm high into the air, the crowd went wild, and a horrifying thought occurred to Cait. Of the bits and pieces she'd caught while trying to avoid the fights on television, she'd heard these men liked to party. Bloody. Bruised. Stitched. The injury didn't matter. There was drinking to be done and they invited the entire arena during their victory speech.

Brad took the microphone and thanked his manager, fans, and God. Then, as she'd feared, "Please join me tonight at the Boot Scoot to help me celebrate my victory."

Their favorite country bar! Oh, this was very bad.

Cait grabbed Amy's arm. "We're just watching the fights, right?"

"No, we're going to the after-party, too."

Cait groaned and leaned back in her seat. As soon as the fights were over, she'd march her ass right out front and hail the closest cab, semi, heck, even U-Haul she could find. She didn't care what the mode of transportation was, just as long as it carried her far away from this overwhelming sense of panic.

Amy sat and took her hand. "These are all great guys. You're really going to like them."

Cait had no doubt they were great. One on one, she

would have been fine getting to know them, but she knew what was going to happen next. She'd be the fat girl in a sea of skinny minis.

The horror.

She rested her head in her hands. Amy, of course, fit right in. Her long, blond hair fell past her perfect, non-double chin. Her tight, black tank top hugged her pert breasts and tiny waist. She'd never known the feeling of being self-conscious around a group of fit people.

Bitch.

"I really want you to go."

Cait remained silent. After a minute, she looked up. "You *will* keep an endless supply of booze in my hand. Got it?"

Amy grinned and hugged her. "You won't regret this."

Cait doubted that.

Music vibrated throughout the country bar. In the corner, Cait sat on a wooden stool, feeling like a fish out of water. She hated being an outsider in her own local hangout, but the crowd was different tonight. The after-party had brought in an influx of MMA followers, some of the prettiest, most petite, flesh-baring women she'd ever seen. She envied their confidence. Every one of these women was comfortable in her own skin.

Maybe one day she would be, too.

Cait snorted and took a swallow of her beer. Not likely, since she wasn't even comfortable in the clothes hiding her skin. Damn Amy anyway for making her wear this stupid outfit. She tugged at the too-tight pink top and shifted on the stool.

Amy bounced up to her. "Cait, come and dance."

"No, thank you. I'm quite comfortable right here."

"Please. You haven't said one word to anyone since we arrived."

Cait held up her empty glass. "You've been slack in your duties."

Amy glanced down at her full bottle, shrugged, and traded beers. "Now, come on. I really want you to meet Brad."

"Fine." Cait slid off the stool. Better to just get it over with. Amy wouldn't leave her alone until she did. She'd do a quick, hi, bye and then get back to her corner. Simple as pie.

Amy grabbed her hand and yanked her along. Moments later, they stood before a group of such hotness Cait thought she might hyperventilate. Testosterone engulfed her while she surveyed the wall of broad shoulders. These men were *men*.

Her gaze landed on the one with the clipped-short brown hair who stood directly before her. All the others faded into the background.

He was watching her, blue eyes alight with curiosity. Unable to glance away, she felt her heart stutter then pound in her breast.

Amy walked in front of her, breaking the man's unwavering gaze. Cait blinked. Where in the world had *that* reaction come from?

Her friend pulled the blond guy from the earlier fight forward. "This is Brad."

He extended a bruised hand, his left eye swollen shut. "It's a pleasure to finally meet you. Amy talks about you all the time."

Unfortunately, Cait couldn't say the same about him. *Thanks, Amy*. She grasped his hand. "Nice to meet you."

She stuffed her hand in her pocket and tried not to study the floor, but the wood planks were too enticing to resist. Could she just go home, for God's sake? She didn't like this feeling of not belonging. Never before had she felt as out of place as she did right now. And it was all because of these overinflated men staring at her, most likely wondering what an overweight girl like her was doing here. She tugged on her shirt.

Amy introduced two other fighters: Mac "The Snake" Hannon and George "The Crusher" Hart. Cait politely smiled. Then Amy introduced Blue Eyes.

"This is Dante 'Inferno' Jones."

"Fitting, since I feel like I've entered the seventh layer of Hell." The words were out before she could stop them. Her skin turned to fire. Damn her mouth.

The man's eyes widened, and he sputtered a laugh. "I can honestly say I've never had a woman react that way to my name before." Amusement lit his face. "It's intriguing to say the least."

His words flustered her, as did the strange interest gleaming in his eyes. The attention was unnerving. Men his type—the type who should never wear a shirt—rarely noticed her. She cleared her throat. "Sorry. Been a long night."

Dante moved forward and offered his hand. Biting her lip, she hesitated. Touching him was a bad idea. If she reacted the way she did with a look, a touch would… She shivered.

But with his hand outstretched, she knew ignoring the gesture would be rude. Tentatively, she slid her palm into his.

Electrical currents zipped up her arm to charge her stomach in a thrilling little quiver. She snatched her hand away.

This was not good. From the jeans hugging his muscled thighs to the gray T-shirt straining against his chest and biceps, he was practically a god. She had absolutely no experience with this kind of man.

Dante moved to stand by her side, making her pulse quicken. "Is there anything I can do to make the night more bearable?"

Seriously? Was he flirting with her?

Oh God. Oh God. Oh God.

"I-I don't think so."

"How about a dance?" he asked.

"Dance?"

She glanced over her shoulder, certain he was talking to someone else.

The breath whooshed from her lungs as those mesmerizing blue eyes snared hers again. "You want to dance with *me*?"

"Yes."

As if it had a mind of its own, her head nodded. What in the hell was she doing? Before Cait could take back the impulsive agreement, he took her hand and led her onto the dance floor. The farther they entered the crush of dancing bodies, the more Cait's nerves pinged.

She was thankful the country hit song "Save a Horse (Ride a Cowboy)" pulsed from the speakers and not a slow song. Then she grimaced. Maybe not. Right now, her body would have more than welcomed taking a ride on this man.

Still, the rocking country tune *was* better than a slow song, where her body would press against his. She trembled at the thought.

They reached the center of the floor and Dante pulled her to his chest. Her nipples hardened on contact. The feel of his hard pecs beneath her palms caused a dull throb between her legs.

Ah, jeez. This was way too close.

He brushed against her as he moved to the beat of the music, taking her with him.

Holy hell, she'd been wrong. Fast and furious dancing was *not* better than slow. Each rock of his hips whipped fire through her lower anatomy. She slid her hand down his bicep—strong, chiseled biceps—trying to create a little distance. The move only brought her pelvis closer to his and increased the throbbing to a full-fledged ache.

Dear God! The song needed to end. *Now*.

He bent close to her ear. "Is Cait short for something?"

Distraction. Exactly what she needed. "Caitlyn."

"Caitlyn. Beautiful."

Spoken from his lips, her name was beautiful. Too bad the name didn't fit the person.

She tensed. Damn it. Why'd she go and do that? She'd promised no more demeaning herself. Yet, his perfectly toned and muscular body made her very conscious of the extra pounds she carried. Made the old securities flare to life even though she'd made progress with the new Cait.

His smile faded. "You okay?"

She forced herself to meet his gaze. "Of course."

He's a fighter. Remember that. These men were used to attention, used to women falling all over them. Skinny, fat, old or young, they all probably swooned when he was near. So it wasn't like this dance was a huge deal to him.

She tried to relax and move with him, but she only felt stiff and awkward. Her face heated in embarrassment. He, however, just smiled and went with it. His tight body was anything but tight as he danced against her. Loose. Flowing. Grinding. Oh, my.

Cait swallowed and stared at his chest. She wasn't used to dancing with a man, didn't know anything about the bump and grind. When she came out on the floor she usually danced with Amy and they just acted stupid. Dancing with Dante was not stupid at all. If anything, it was like a sense of foreplay.

When the song ended, Dante led her back to the group. The feel of his fingers wrapped around hers burned her skin. Panic churned her stomach at the frightening amount of attraction she was experiencing.

Attraction, my ass. Try downright lust. This was so far outside her comfort zone. Hell, *he* was outside her comfort zone. He was more man than she'd ever dealt with and it was overwhelming. She needed to breathe.

As she pulled her hand from his, she whispered, "Excuse me," then pushed through the crowd and headed for the restroom.

She was prepared to spend the rest of the night alone, in a corner, far away from this alarming man who made her body sizzle with one touch.

• • •

What had he done wrong?

Frowning, Dante watched the curvy redhead weave her way to the other side of the bar. Things had been going great, then she tensed, and it felt as if she couldn't get away from him fast enough.

Women didn't run away from him. Ever. They tended to flock around him, whether he wanted them to or not.

Yet, she wasn't like most of the single women who hung around the MMA crowd. There'd been no coy smiles, batting eyelashes, or breasts shoved in his face. Instead of turning him off with the blatant invitation, which happened more and more these days, she'd been shy and standoffish. He liked the difference, the hint of a challenge.

Besides, her "seventh layer of hell" comment had been enough to pique his interest. His mouth twitched at the memory of the shocked surprise rounding her eyes and plump lips when she realized she'd spoken aloud. Yes, the woman was definitely worth getting to know.

Amy came to stand beside him.

"What's her story?" he asked.

She bit her lip then sighed. "Are you interested?"

"Very."

"Be patient, then. I'm not going to tell you Cait's story. But I *will* say she's shy. She gets spooked very easily."

An explanation for her hasty retreat. "How would she react if I asked her out?"

"Spooked times ten. Take it slow, big boy. Get to know her, become her friend, and then she'll open up."

Dante nodded. He'd be around for the next two months, training. He could do slow.

"Excuse me for a minute," he said.

He walked to the bar and took his place at the end of the line. He glanced around the club designed like a saloon. The place was balls to butts tonight. The fighters' presence probably had something to do with the crowd. But even for a huge club the place was overly packed.

Someone jostled Dante from behind and he bumped the man standing in front of him. The guy glanced over his shoulder and did a double take. His eyes widened. "Oh, man."

Used to the reaction, Dante smiled. "Sorry about that."

"N-no worries." He turned around, still staring at Dante as if he weren't real. "I knew there'd be fighters here, but you, wow."

"Just got into town tonight. Thought I'd check the place out."

"John Smith," the man said, thrusting out his hand. "I'm a huge fan, Mr. Jones."

Dante shook the outstretched hand. "No need for formalities. Call me Dante."

John grinned. "So what brings you to Georgia? You're a long way from Connecticut."

Dante blinked then shook his head. It always surprised him when complete strangers knew facts about him, not that a simple Google search wouldn't bring up a variety of "Inferno" fan sites with some of the stupidest things about him listed. It was the way fans said those facts so conversationally, as though they had been buddies for years, that always startled him. "I'm training here for the next couple of months."

"With whom?"

"Mike Cannon."

John's mouth dropped open. "He's one of the toughest coaches out there. He doesn't put up with any bullshit."

The line moved and they stepped closer to the bar. "That he doesn't."

"Look at what he did to Sentori! I mean, wow! That breakup shocked the hell out of me. With Sentori's record, I thought he could get away with anything. It goes to show you Mike's not in it for a paycheck."

"No, he's not." Dante had never met the man he'd hired to coach him, but word had spread quickly in the industry about Mike's rep. The top dog of coaches, Mike Cannon was fierce and extremely picky about the fighters he trained.

"You focused and ready to jump in?" John Smith asked.

"I'm always focused."

Egotistical sounding, perhaps, but the God-given truth.

Over the last ten years, he'd worked hard as he fought his way up the MMA ladder, prided himself on being driven—nothing distracted him. Those qualities as a fighter had landed Mike as his coach. The man hadn't even hesitated when Dante called him, just told him the date and time they'd start.

The person in front of them left and opened up a space at the bar. John squeezed in and placed an order. While he waited for the bartender to return, he turned back to Dante. "It's a huge fight coming up for you."

"The biggest of my career."

The bartender returned with the drinks. John took them. "I hope you kick Sentori's ass. I can't stand the bastard."

Dante stifled a laugh. "You and everyone else I talk to."

Sentori also had a reputation, a bad one. Dante hadn't been subjected yet to the other fighter's idea of games. Time was running out, though. It would happen. Soon.

And Dante was ready.

"Good luck with the fight, man."

"Thanks."

The man nodded then walked off. Dante took his place at the bar and ordered. Thoughts of his upcoming match clouded his mind—Sentori, the cage, and a belt on the line.

He shoved the thoughts aside. Tonight was about relaxing. Tomorrow would be here soon enough and with it, two months of intense training.

The bartender slid a couple of bottles of Select toward him. Dante smiled; he knew exactly who he wanted to relax with. With the beers in hand, he returned to his group and frowned. Caitlyn still hadn't returned. Something wasn't right. Almost twenty minutes had passed. Even for the line to the women's restroom, that was a long time.

He surveyed the area and found her sitting at a table, sipping from a glass. So she was huddled in a corner by herself. This might play to his advantage—alone in a dark nook, a perfect setting for getting to know her. Dante made his way over.

She glanced at him and blinked. "Um. Hey."

"What are you doing over here?"

She blinked again. "It's a little crowded tonight. Just getting out of the way."

"I don't think you could ever be in anyone's way."

She remained silent, brows knitted together. Dante grimaced. She was supposed to respond with some kind of lame answer, like "I'd like to get in your way." To which he would respond with his own lame line. And the ball would start rolling.

Not this woman. She stared at him, then looked away, and it made him feel like an idiot. He cleared his throat. "Er… I brought you a beer." He held out a bottle.

Caitlyn peered down at her full glass, then back at him.

Well, shit.

He set the beer on the table next to her and shrugged. "Well, you can have this after you finish that one."

"Thank you."

Dante pulled a chair up beside her. Her blinking increased tenfold and her gaze traveled frantically around the bar. She seemed panicked, but he planned to stay. He studied her, trying to see behind her stiff posture. Something felt off.

His eyes narrowed on the glass wobbling gently in her hand. Definitely not a sign of someone who was unaffected by him. He heard her take a shaky breath, then release it slowly. She couldn't possibly be nervous, could she?

The woman was simply too gorgeous to be nervous around a man.

Caitlyn continued to avoid his gaze, so he took the time to soak her in. She'd captured his attention immediately. Straight, red hair fell slightly below her chin, framing her oval face with full lips. Kissable lips. The pink top hugged her lush breasts and cinched the curves at her waist. He liked what he saw. Liked what he'd held as they danced.

He leaned in closer. "So, do you watch MMA?"

She tensed. "No."

"Oh. Okay." Strike one. "Did you enjoy the fights tonight?"

"No."

Strike two. He breathed deeply. "What about you, then? Anything you'd like to talk about?"

Her fingers traced the glass. "Not really."

And you're out. He glanced heavenward. *Throw me a bone, please.* He wracked his brain searching for a topic to talk about. He'd never had this much trouble striking up a conversation with a woman before.

Hell, he normally didn't have to strike up a conversation at all. They came to him, even if he warned them off. The groupies didn't do anything for him, which seemed to only increase their interest.

Fate sucked, man. Here sat a woman he'd actually want hanging all over him and she was being difficult as hell.

The longer the silence stretched, the more he felt as if he was royally screwing up. He took a long swig from his beer. Finally, she sighed and her shoulders slumped. He would have said in defeat, but he had no idea what would've defeated her.

Her green eyes made contact with his before she went back to studying her hands. The same jolt from when they'd been introduced hit his crotch. Shifting on his stool, he released a long breath.

"How did you get the name 'Inferno'?" Her voice was soft.

He tried to concentrate on the question when all he really wanted her to do was look at him, but she kept her attention on her glass as her finger slowly circled the rim. The movement captivated him. Images of her making the exact motion on certain parts of his body made him gulp as his body tightened.

He shook his head. *Stay on track. Keep to the conversation.* "I got the title when I was fighting amateur. I had a match against one of my buddies."

Her head jerked up, and she once again graced him with eye contact. His mouth went dry as his gaze dipped to her lips.

"You had to fight a friend? How do you do that?"

With her attention on him, he took a chance and slid his arm around the back of her chair, bringing himself closer to her shoulder. Her eyes widened.

Okay. Trying to get close was a big no-no right now.

He sat back and rolled his shoulders. What were they talking about? Oh, yeah. Fighting friends. "Fighting can't be personal. You lose focus that way."

Caitlyn frowned and sipped her beer. "With what you do, there has to be hostility."

"Between some, yes. I haven't had that happen yet. I've respected every fighter I've fought."

"But it does happen."

Where was she going with this? "Rivalry matches do happen. I have a friend who has a rival." He chuckled. "God, anytime they have a matchup, everything heats up. The tension, the slandering, the bitch talk. Brian, my friend, trains as though he's possessed."

"Then fighting *is* personal."

He laughed and held up his hands. "I concede. In some cases, yes, looking at it that way, I guess the added hostility does help focus."

"I would say so." Caitlyn shook her head. "So your title?"

"The match lasted three minutes. I pretty much beat on him the entire time and finally knocked him out. For days afterward, he talked about the raging inferno who was Dante Jones. And the name just stuck."

"So you didn't pick it to make yourself sound cool?"

A startled laugh escaped his mouth. This woman held nothing back. "I didn't. Some fighters do, though. I'm proud I earned mine."

"As you should be." He thought he heard sincerity in her voice, but she was looking in the opposite direction as she took a swallow of her beer, so he wasn't certain.

Had he impressed her? He wanted to, but he couldn't tell one way or the other if she liked what she heard. He had no idea if he was on the right track or headed for shutdown.

Even if she was trying to brush him off, he really wanted to get to know this chick. He didn't know why; he usually didn't waste his time on someone who appeared uninterested. But his body responded to her in a way it hadn't to a woman in a long time, probably because everything was offered to him freely nowadays. He was damned tired of it.

"Inferno!" Mac, his temporary roommate, waved him over.

She sighed, and Dante frowned. That wasn't a good sigh. She shouldn't be relieved to see him leave. He grabbed a napkin off the table and pulled out the pen he always kept handy for autographs, then jotted down his number. He folded the paper and handed it to her. "Call me."

She stared at it before hesitantly taking it, pushing him to ask, "Can I have your number?"

Caitlyn's mouth popped open. "Umm…sure."

She took the pen from him and wrote down a number on another napkin. He tucked it into his back pocket. "My roommate is ready to leave. I'll call you, okay?"

"Okay."

He walked away from table, hoping she hadn't done the classic give-the-man-the-wrong-number move. He'd soon find out.

• • •

Later the same night in her bedroom, Cait scowled at her image in the oval mirror. What was it about her that sparked his interest? Yes, she'd lost eighty pounds, a feat she was immensely proud of, but she still wasn't the typical kind of girl these fighters hung around. And she knew the type; one glance around the club confirmed the blond Barbie was the preferred woman.

And she was far from the blond Barbie.

Well…she was closer than she'd ever been to being one, but she still had thirty pounds to lose. Turning to the side, she sucked in her gut and pressed the oversized navy shirt close to her stomach. She'd worked so hard. It'd taken her a year to lose that much, but even with the extra weight gone, the mirror refused to get any friendlier. She still felt like the chunky girl all the guys loved to hang out with, but never thought to date. With a disgusted sigh, she yanked the material away from her body.

Dante's attention didn't make any sense.

On rare occasions, a guy would ask her out—guys completely unlike Dante Jones.

Inferno.

Cait still cringed at her remark to his name. But being surrounded by such muscle, such perfection, *in hell* had been exactly how she'd felt.

She turned from the mirror and picked up the folded napkin on her vanity. Opening it, she studied the masculine scrawl. Underneath his number, he'd written his name in sharp block letters. The writing matched the man—strong and commanding.

Two traits she didn't know how to deal with when it came to her limited experience with men. Two traits she didn't *want* to deal with. So she'd tried being aloof with her one-word answers. Anything to give him the impression she wasn't interested. It hadn't worked.

Crumbling the napkin in her fist, Cait walked to her wastebasket. She stood over it and held out her hand. But her fingers refused to cooperate.

Open, damn it.

But they remained firmly locked around the paper. Groaning, she tossed it back on her vanity and slumped onto her bed.

What if he called?

It wouldn't matter if he did. They were not suited for each other. He was a cage fighter. And Caitlyn Moore and violence did not mix.

CHAPTER TWO

Dante slung his heavy gym bag into the corner and studied the facility he'd call home for the next two months. The sheer size of the training center impressed him. It was at least four times larger than the one in Connecticut.

A traditional boxing ring in the center captured his attention. Two men, one wearing red headgear, the other in blue, squared off as they sparred. Dante itched to join them. He wanted to feel the energy course through his body as he calculated his opponent's next move—while formulating the countermove that would shock his foe and lead Dante to victory.

He forced his gaze from the ring. On the left, numerous red punching bags hung unused before bleached white walls. Contrary to his reaction to the ring, the bags sent nervous anticipation traveling through him. The sand-filled canvas bags appeared innocent enough, but Dante knew better. Hours upon hours of grueling, painful torture would take place before them, testing his strength of mind. He dreaded the encounters.

In the right corner, a blue mat was on the floor. Dante sighed and stared at the grappling pad. His biggest challenge. The one weakness that could cause him to lose the most important fight of his life. He shook his head. He wouldn't think like that. Negative thoughts only brought negative energy. That he wouldn't allow.

He swept the facility with one final glance. The only thing missing was the cage.

He'd save the cage for Vegas, when he'd rip Sentori a new one.

A door closing echoed through the quiet room. He turned to see a bald boulder of a man headed his way. Dante recognized the former heavyweight champion immediately and smiled. "Mike."

The man returned the smile and offered his hand. "Damned pleased to meet you, Dante. I'm excited to have a fighter of your caliber under my roof."

"Only the best to help me beat the best." In two months, Dante would have the toughest fight of his career. He would need every advantage he could get, and a coach who'd once trained his opponent would help lead him to victory.

"You said it. Defeating Richard Sentori won't be easy. You're going to have to train your ass off. I've watched your fights. You're good, real good, but Sentori is better. Unless you improve your ground game, you don't stand a chance in hell."

Dante respected Mike's bluntness. This was what he had come for. A kick in the butt, one that would push him into the next realm of fighting, which would end with the championship belt wrapped around his waist. Of course, there was the bonus of being the first to crush the unstoppable Richard Sentori.

Mike leveled him with a stony stare. "Battling Sentori won't happen just in the octagon. He trained here until his attitude got out of control. Quite frankly, he's an asshole. Mind games are his weapon of choice outside the cage."

"Yeah, I've heard of his reputation." "Asshole" didn't begin to cover how the other fighters described the man. "He's pissed a lot of fighters off before their match. How he keeps winning is beyond me."

"Because he's good. But he does enjoy getting under his opponent's skin before a fight."

"I know his game and I'm prepared for it. He won't get the better of me."

Seeing the sparring partners finish their drills, Dante climbed onto the side of the boxing ring, hooked his hand around the ropes, and entered the square. Hopping from foot to foot, he shadowboxed along the perimeter of the stretched canvas floor.

Blood pumped through his body. Adrenaline raced through his veins. He threw his head back, relishing the feeling that always accompanied his entry into the ropes, fight or not. Increasing the momentum of his punches, he exhaled in measured breaths as he pictured Sentori's face before him.

Mike jumped onto the side of the ring and leaned against the ropes. "Those punches aren't going to help you, you know."

Dante lowered his arms. "Yeah, I know. I like to stand up and fight, which will be a problem with Sentori."

"Damned straight it'll be a problem. If luck is with you,

you might catch him with a punch."

Dante grimaced. No fighter wanted to win by luck. They wanted a solid no-questions-asked win.

Mike sighed. "I know Sentori. He's studying your fights, looking for all your weaknesses. As it stands, he'll have you on the ground within seconds. A ground game is what we'll have to work on. We have to make sure he won't catch you in his signature hold once he takes you down."

Dante nodded and resumed his shadow boxing. Sentori's rear naked chokehold was lethal. He was able to snake his arm around an opponent's neck like a python: strong, methodical, and unbreakable. Once he had it locked in, well, his record spoke for itself. Out of twenty fights, fifteen had been won by submission.

Dante, on the other hand, had twelve wins by knockout. Improving his jujitsu was crucial to handling Sentori on the ground.

"We have a lot of work to do, but with dedication and focus, I think you can win this. And I will get my own personal satisfaction at training the man who finally takes down Richard Sentori."

Dante had every intention of delivering. Sentori was the last fighter standing in his way to achieve the one thing he had beaten countless men senseless for: the welterweight championship title.

And he would have it.

Nothing was going to stand in his way.

. . .

"I want the name, Ron," Cait persisted.

For the last hour, she'd been in her boss's office at the

YMCA going over the plans for her new program. Ron had approved everything but the one thing that really mattered to her—the program's name. But she wasn't going down without a fight.

Ronald Bigby—the program director and resident pain in the ass—leaned forward, pushing his glasses up his nose. "I've gave you free rein on this program. All I'm asking for is a different name. Why is that too much to ask?"

She stared across the desk at the balding man and clenched her teeth against rising frustration. This man was the last obstacle to getting her program off the ground—a program she would have given anything to have had when she'd started her own weight loss journey. She refused to let him stand in the way. "Because the name sets the tone for the entire program. Something generic won't do that."

"Cait, the title of a program like this should pertain to the core reason for the class, which in this case is losing weight."

God, he just didn't get it. That wasn't the main reason for the class and she wasn't sure how she'd get him to understand. "What do you suggest, then?"

"I was thinking 'Shrinking Georgia.'"

She suppressed the urge to roll her eyes. How freaking dull. The name held no meaning, nothing to be proud of.

Now "Altering Assumptions"?

That was a chin-held-high title, stemming from the many obstacles she'd faced anytime a new member entered a fitness room. She loved taking the skeptical looks directed at her when she walked into an advanced aerobics class and turning it to an awed "Damn-this-bitch-can-bust-ass" expression.

It hadn't always felt like that for her, though. In the

beginning, just facing the looks had almost been enough to send her scurrying back home. Not anymore. *She* was proud of what she'd accomplished and wanted to help other people struggling with their weight to feel the same.

"My entire program is based around teaching others you don't have to be rail thin to be physically fit, while teaching them to alter their assumptions about themselves, as well as the assumptions of others. It's not just a weight loss program."

Ron lifted his glasses and rubbed his eyes. "You're not going to relent, are you?"

"Not on this."

"I'm going to have to think on it. I'd still like to see a title more directed at fitness."

She fought a smile of victory. At least he was willing to think about it. That was something. "Thank you, Ron. This is important to me."

"Get out of here. I have another meeting in ten minutes."

She left the office with a huge grin, only to freeze mid-step as she heard, "Whale alert. Stand back, the treadmill is about to blow."

The grin slid from her face. Two boys stood pointing at a young, overweight teenaged girl on a treadmill. Cait clenched her hands into fists. She knew the boys well. The arrogant, nineteen-year-old troublemakers were inches from having their membership revoked. Now she'd make sure it happened.

She glanced at the girl, who couldn't have been more than sixteen. Tears shone in her eyes, but she lifted her chin and continued her walk.

Teens could be the meanest creatures on earth.

She stalked over just as one of the little bastards said,

"This isn't Sea World, Shamu."

"You two should be ashamed of yourself."

The boys turned and eyed her with disinterest. "What are you going to do about it? Take away our memberships? Ohh!" They waved their fingers in a mock gesture of fright.

Brats!

The brown-haired one raised a brow. "It's not like you can talk. You need to be on the treadmill beside her."

The hurtful words only fueled her anger. This was why she wanted to name her program "Altering Assumptions." "You think so, huh? I could run circles around you without breaking a sweat."

The boy snorted.

She spread her arms wide. "I'm dressed for it. You're dressed for it. Come on, take on a fatty."

He waved his hand. "I don't want to humiliate you."

"Oh, honey, the only humiliation will be yours and you need a huge dose of it."

The girl had stopped walking, her fingers pressed to her lips, eyes wide. "You don't have to do this."

"Oh yeah, I do."

Cait jumped up on a treadmill and started to warm up. When the boy didn't move, she glanced behind her. "Scared?"

He scowled. "You asked for it."

He climbed on the treadmill beside hers and started his warmup.

"Here's how this'll work," Cait said. "Every two minutes we increase pace by point five until the other can no longer hang on. Got it?"

Sneering, he said, "Got it."

"Starting at five."

The treadmill began to beep as she increased speed. The treadmill sped up under her feet and she started to run. Exhilaration filled her as her legs pumped beneath her. She loved to run, loved the feel of energy flowing through her body, the feel of her heart beating hard against her chest.

Two minutes passed quickly, and she increased to five point five. She glanced at the boy. A smidgeon of guilt hit her. He had two more minutes, tops. Once they hit six, he would be finished. Sweat poured from his beet-red face. Labored gasps came from his mouth.

She'd give him credit, though. Determination still filled his face as he struggled to keep up. What nineteen-year-old boy wouldn't try his damnedest not to be beaten by a woman, especially one who was overweight?

For two more minutes, he hung on. Then they increased to six. Thirty seconds passed before he slipped off the back of the treadmill and landed in a heap on the floor.

He sat up, dazed and gasping. Cait stopped her treadmill and faced him. "I hope you learned a lesson to never assume. Overweight doesn't mean out of shape."

She hopped to the floor. The win did nothing to ease the anger still gripping her stomach. She glanced at the girl, who exclaimed, "That was awesome!"

Not sure how to respond, Cait extended her hand. "Cait Moore."

The girl grabbed her hand and shook it. "Becky Morris. Thank you. It's hard enough coming in here, much less being heckled while you work out."

"No thanks necessary. I was proud of how you handled the situation. Instead of leaving, you kept going. You have the drive. And it makes me proud to see it."

"Do you work out here?"

"Everyday."

"Do you mind—I mean, maybe…"

Cait studied the girl and saw a reflection of herself, an insecure, overweight woman wanting nothing more than to change her life but unsure of how to do it, or even if she could. She reached into her purse and took out a sheet of paper and a pen. Jotting down her name and number, she handed it to her. "I'll be starting a program soon. I'd love for you to join."

Becky gazed down at the paper. "I will," she said, then hugged her.

Emotions hit Cait, and she blinked back tears as the girl pocketed the information and ran off toward to the locker rooms.

Cait turned to leave and spotted Ron leaning against the wall.

He smiled. "You have your name."

"You okay?" Amy asked.

Groaning, Cait placed her tray on the table and sat across Amy and Brad. "Been a long morning."

"Wanna talk about it?"

Cait glanced at Brad. The thought of talking about her encounter at the gym in front of him didn't appeal to her. "Not right now."

Every time she thought of those two boys, her anger flared again. She really needed to let it go. She'd proven her point. But the memory of Becky's large green eyes filled with tears infuriated her. Why were people so cruel?

"How'd the meeting go?" Amy asked before she shoved a spoonful of broccoli and cheese soup in her mouth.

"Good. I got my name."

"That's wonderful! I knew how important it was to you."

Brad leaned forward. "What's wonderful?"

Amy quickly filled him in about Cait's program.

"That's awesome," he said.

Cait picked up her club sandwich and took a tiny bite. "Yeah, well, we'll see how it pans out. I'm hoping for a good turnout."

She studied the couple across the table. Brad had a muscular arm slung around the back of Amy's chair, her friend pressed close to his side. The perfect couple: blond, fit, and gorgeous, complementary to the other.

No one would ever underestimate them, unlike Cait, who fought every day to prove there was nothing she couldn't handle.

A movement to her left caught her attention. She glanced over and froze.

Except him.

The constant chatter in the small deli faded away as the blood roared through her ears. *He* was the last thing she needed right now. Today had been tiring enough without dealing with the man who hadn't called. Four days. Not one ring.

Cait whipped her head around and stared at Amy. "I can't believe you."

"What?"

Dante strolled toward them and sat in the vacant seat next to hers. Awareness overwhelmed her. Even with a gaping space between them, he was too damned close.

She pressed against the wall, avoiding eye contact with his unnerving blue eyes. Why did she have to react this way to a fighter? She hated fighting, wanted nothing to do with the limelight following them. It so wasn't fair.

"Hey, guys," Dante said. "What are we talking about?"

"The YMCA has agreed to sponsor a program Cait's formed," Amy said.

"Congratulations!"

The smile he sent her caused her heart to stutter and she jerked her gaze back to her plate, rattled at how her body responded to him just from his simple smile.

"What's the program about?" he asked.

"I'm leading the new weight loss program," Cait whispered, never taking her eyes off her plate as she reached for her unsweetened tea. Was he sizing her up? Seeing she wasn't the image of a typical fitness instructor and wondering what she could possibly have to offer anyone who struggled with their weight?

She lifted her chin. Well, she had a lifetime of experience with it.

Dante made a derisive noise. "I don't understand the need for weight loss programs. Cut calories and go to the gym. How hard is that?"

She lifted her head and met his gaze, unflinching. "Are you serious?"

"It's simple math. Burn more calories than you take in. Not too difficult."

Cait twisted to face him. "Tell me, Dante, have you ever had a weight problem?"

Amy moaned and covered her eyes, shaking her head.

"No, I haven't," he responded, shooting a glance at Amy

with furrowed brows.

Cait kept her voice calm, even though her anger was quickly resurfacing. "Do you know what it's like to walk into a gym with a bunch of fit-looking people and feel like everyone is staring at you? To have to overcome your fear of being made fun of in order to participate in a class?"

"Those are excuses. If a person wants to lose weight, they will. If they don't, then they'll use those fears to stay at home. It's all a matter of self-control."

"You tell that to the sixteen-year-old girl I just rescued from two vicious teenage boys. How is being called 'Shamu' while she worked out making her want to return to the gym? How does heckling help her get past the insecurities she's already feeling? It *doesn't*."

Dante's mouth snapped closed, and his head jerked back.

"Here's some food for thought. Until you've hauled around an extra eighty pounds most of your life and then struggled to lose it, maybe you should keep your opinions to yourself."

Images of the boys taunting the poor girl flooded her mind. Tears burned the back of her eyes. "I've got to go."

She pushed back her chair avoiding any and all contact with his shoulders as she brushed past and hurried from the deli.

"Hey, wait. I'm sorry." She heard him call after her, but she kept going. Amy chastised Dante with, "Nice work, bonehead," before she pushed through the double glass doors and into the hot July air.

Dante's opinion wasn't anything she hadn't heard before. Every day, Cait dealt with people who couldn't comprehend what she and people like Becky had been through and struggled against. Normally, she didn't react, knowing it was easy for people to judge something they knew nothing about. But hearing the same ignorance spewing from Dante's mouth had lit a ball of fury in her that only added to the anger those boys had kindled.

Add in the raging ball of hormones she became when Dante was around, and keeping *her* opinions to herself became impossible. What was it about the man that caused all these festering emotions? And, boy, was there a wide range of them. Distaste for his career choice, paralyzing insecurities when he was near, anger at his uninformed opinion, and desire...so much desire.

She hurried across the parking lot to her car. Desire didn't matter. He was Dante Jones, fighter extraordinaire, surrounded by cameras, screaming fans, and violence. She wanted nothing to do with it.

Why was she even thinking about this? It wasn't an issue. He hadn't called—heck, he'd probably stumbled across their table by accident in the first place.

She climbed into her car and sat behind the wheel. Glancing back at the deli, she took a deep breath. Dante stood on the top stair with his long legs spread, hands on his hips, watching her.

In response, her heart stuttered.

Distance.

She had to keep her distance.

• • •

Nice going, idiot.

Dante watched Caitlyn make a left onto the busy highway and cursed. What was it with this woman and his inability to connect with her?

He should have called her. He'd wanted to. But Amy believed face to face would be better than calling. So he'd gone with her suggestion and waited. Fat lot of good that had done.

At least his appearance had been enlightening. Caitlyn's shyness was a façade. One wrong comment from his mouth created such spitting passion, he believed he'd gotten a glimpse of the real Caitlyn. And all that fire was enough to incinerate him.

He chuckled. They called *him* the Inferno. He was sure he'd found the female equivalent to his name. But what held her back, though?

A mystery to unfold, one he was certain he would enjoy every minute of. Besides, Caitlyn challenged him. She didn't agree with every word that came out of his mouth like the Stepford wife types who threw themselves at him, who stared at him adoringly even though they didn't know him. He smiled. Caitlyn could give two shits he was a MMA star, and she had no issue putting him in his place when she disagreed with him. He liked the change.

It'd been a long time since he'd pursued a woman—a very long time. The idea of chasing Caitlyn energized him.

Dante smiled. And on the day they finally kissed, he'd know it wasn't because of his celebrity status or his hefty bank account. No, when they kissed, it would be because she wanted him.

He returned to the table. He sat down and took a huge bite of his BLT.

Amy tilted her head, her gaze never leaving his.

He swallowed. "What?"

"You like her."

Dante shrugged. "She's interesting."

"Yeah, 'cause you've learned so much about her to make that assumption."

He lowered the sandwich to his plate. "What are you saying?"

"If this is some sort of hard-to-get game that has you all turned on, I'm warning you, look elsewhere. Cait doesn't need that, and I won't let it happen."

With her arms crossed and her lips pinched together, Amy was closer to the truth than he cared to admit. Admitting the reason Cait piqued his interest would be a bad idea.

"It's not a game for me."

And it wasn't. It was a challenge with a woman he found insanely attractive.

Amy relaxed, a small smile coming to her lips. "Then I'm willing to help."

"How?"

"I'll tell you the one place you can get to her where she can't hide."

CHAPTER THREE

Two days later, Cait rushed through the doors of the YMCA with Amy. As she passed the counter, she grabbed two white towels. Tossing one to her friend, they hurried down the hall, knowing if they didn't speed it up, the equipment would already be claimed.

The moment Cait stepped over the threshold of the group fitness room, she stopped dead. Amy slammed into her back. "Cait, what in the world?"

Cait gasped and spun around. "I've been a member for three years and I've never seen *him* here."

Amy peered around her shoulder. "Oh. He asked me where we worked out."

"I thought he had a training facility to use. Brad has one."

"Well, yeah, he does."

Cait turned. Dante stood with one foot propped on a two-riser step, talking to Brad—someone else Cait had never seen here. She glanced down at her sloppy clothes, a huge oversized shirt, and baggy cut-off gray sweat pants.

For the first time ever, she wanted to change into a tighter workout outfit.

Amy moved past her toward Brad. Cait slunk around the perimeter of the polished floor, trying to stay out of sight. She couldn't face this man, not after everything she'd said to him, not dressed the way she was now.

"Caitlyn!"

The deep voice froze her in her tracks. Dante trotted over, a grin splitting his handsome face. Her heart did that jackhammer thing as she smoothed her hand down her sweat pants and gave him a strained smile. "Dante. I didn't know you were a member here."

"Just joined, actually. I needed a place to do my cardio. I get tired of looking at the same walls as I train."

She exhaled. "Listen, I'm sorry about the other day. I had a bad day, and my mouth got away from me."

"No. *I'm* sorry. I made a harsh judgment I shouldn't have. I didn't mean to touch on a hot button."

"We all have those, don't we?" There was a tremble to her voice and she bit her bottom lip, uncomfortably aware of him.

"I have a few."

Needing to put some distance between them, she moved into the supply closet and collected a platform and risers. Dante entered the small space behind her. It felt as if he'd sucked all the air from the room and replaced it with his heavenly, clean scent. She tried to ignore the smell, but God help her, it was impossible. Standing ramrod straight, she turned and faced him.

Immediately, she wished she hadn't.

His massive body filled the door frame, his broad

shoulders blocking her only means of escape. With him towering over her, she couldn't fight the desire she tried so hard to suppress. She ached to run her fingers over the thick, black lines of the tribal tattoo that decorated his exposed bicep, then trail down the tight, black workout top clinging to his chest. She clenched the equipment to her suddenly heavy breasts.

"Here, let me take that." Dante smiled, then took her step and risers and strode away. Stunned, she stood there staring after him. Slowly, she came out of the closet to find he'd set up her step right beside his.

She closed her eyes and sighed. She didn't want to work out beside him, but going to the back of the room as she had intended would be rude. She could move it back, though.

After she reached her step, she bent and moved it back about two feet. When she straightened, Dante had a brow quirked at her.

She tried for a polite smile. "I like to keep the area to my left and right clear."

Which was the partial truth—she always staggered her step so no one was on either side of her, but in this case, the idea of working out beside him terrified the crap out of her. At least this way she was behind him and he wouldn't have a clear view to her every move, or any jiggles she didn't want him to see. Because nothing on this man jiggled.

"I can get that. I hate running beside someone on the treadmill."

A bubble of amusement filled her chest, stunning her, and she busied herself with her step, making sure the equipment was locked into the risers.

Cindy, the bubbly brunette session leader, walked in.

"Sorry I'm late, guys. I had a long night."

Within minutes, upbeat music bounced around the room and the class started to move in unison. As the class progressed, Cait tried to focus on Cindy, but the mirrors surrounding the room were too much of a temptation to resist. She glanced at Dante's reflection.

Ah, hell. She shouldn't have done that. The mirror gave her an amazing view, although the reality would be ten times better.

What would it hurt to take a quick peek? Just a simple little glimpse, for curiosity's sake?

She stole a glance.

Oh, dear God.

No man should be allowed to look so good. Sweat glistened on his smooth, tanned skin, giving him an oiled godlike appearance. Not an ounce of fat resided on the man's entire body. Each tendon and muscle flexed with every movement. Completely mesmerized, she couldn't drag her eyes away.

As she crossed the top of her step, she caught his gaze in the mirror. He winked with a crooked grin on his lips. Her stomach flipped and she landed on the side of the step, stumbling. Heat flamed her face.

"You okay, Cait?" Cindy asked.

Could she die now? Please?

She nodded to the instructor and spent the rest of class avoiding the gaze of the man whose presence bothered her more than she wanted to admit.

After class, she put the equipment away and stood to the side, waiting for Amy to finish talking with Dante and Brad. When all three headed her way, she sighed.

"Cait, I've invited Dante and Brad over to our place to watch a movie tonight. We're talking takeout. Is there anything you're interested in?"

"Uh." She cleared her throat, scrambling to find an out. The idea of being trapped in a room with Dante and all the unwanted desire he brought to life inside her terrified her. "Yeah…see, I-I've already got plans tonight."

Dante huffed out a breath as if she'd disappointed him. Unnerved by his reaction, Cait kept her attention on Amy.

"Really? You didn't mention that."

"It just came up, actually." She patted the side of her purse. "Text message. Already said yes, so I can't back out." The smile she forced felt too bright. She cleared her throat again. "You guys have fun."

Cait hurried from the gym without glancing back.

Once she made it to the front of the Y, she fished her cell phone from her purse. Pressing six on her speed dial, she waited until a familiar male voice answered.

"Hey, what're you doing tonight?" she asked.

. . .

Dante arrived at Caitlyn's at precisely seven.

Caitlyn's.

Getting to know her was proving to be more difficult than he'd imagined. He'd thought the four of them watching a movie together would offer an opportunity to spend time with her without the pressure of being alone with him.

Wrong.

She'd already had plans. With whom? Amy hadn't been any help in answering the question. She'd just muttered, "That's weird," as they'd watched Caitlyn stalk away.

And he'd been disappointed, especially after catching her watching him.

He'd seen her desire, her appreciation, her longing as their gazes met in the mirror, and fuck, if it hadn't hit him in the gut in a very exciting way.

He knocked.

A few seconds later, Amy opened the door. "Hey. Come on in."

"Caitlyn here?"

"It's good to see you too, Dante. And yes, she hasn't left yet."

He stepped inside. A counter was the only thing separating the small kitchen from the living room. The tiny space reminded him of his first apartment. Neutral walls, beige carpet, and white trim: typical apartment décor. The girls had brought some color into the room by using crimson curtains to cover the two windows in the living area and added red accents throughout the space. It was definitely better than the milk crates and blow-up mattress he started off with.

Man, he didn't miss the days of living off ramen noodles while he fought to be noticed—literally. It felt like another lifetime ago when he worked whatever part-time job he could get just to pay the bills, so he had all the time he needed to train and realize his dream. The sacrifices had paid off and he was reaping the rewards now, but he'd never forget his struggles to get here.

He walked farther into the living room. On the far wall, a hallway led to two closed doors. Caitlyn was behind one, perhaps changing. Just not for him.

"Who's she going out with?" he asked.

"Honestly, I don't know. She's been tight-lipped about her plans."

Dante sighed. He didn't like that she had plans. Another man would only complicate his attempt to get to know her better.

"Go and sit. Brad should be here in a minute." Amy hurried down the hall and into one of the bedrooms.

He'd just made himself comfortable on the red faux-suede sofa when footsteps padded on the hallway carpet behind him. He twisted to see Caitlyn enter the room. The first thing that grabbed his attention was her baggy clothes. The black slacks had to be two sizes too big and the button-down, shapeless red blouse hung off her frame. It did nothing to flatter her figure, and damn, but she had one. He'd held those full hips in his palms, felt them sway under his hands.

So what was up with this outfit?

Her eyes met his and she tugged the bottom of the ugly blouse. "Hi."

"Hey."

"Just getting ready to head out." She offered an apologetic shrug and hurried past the couch. "Enjoy the movie."

"Caitlyn."

She stopped but didn't turn. "Yeah?"

"I'd really like for us to be friends."

Finally she faced him, head tilted to the side, curiosity brightening her eyes. "Why?"

Because you excite me. But he couldn't say that, so he shrugged. "There are not too many people I meet nowadays willing to get up in my grill after I spout off my opinion. Mostly they just smile and nod, no matter how much they disagree. You had no issue with setting me straight. I respect that." He paused. "I *miss* that. So, I thought maybe you and I could hang out some. You know, so you can keep me straight."

It looked like her gaze softened a touch. She opened her mouth to respond, but the doorbell chimed.

"That's probably Paul." She rushed to the door.

Paul?

Seconds later, a tall, dark-haired man with small round glasses walked into the room. Not exactly what Dante would consider Caitlyn's type, but the man was good-looking, in a dainty sort of way. He rose from the couch.

"Paul, this is Dante. Dante, Paul."

Dante forced himself to offer his hand as *Paul* snaked his arm around Caitlyn's shoulder and accepted the handshake with the other. Dante didn't like the possessive way Paul held the woman *he* wanted to pursue.

"Ready, babe? Movie starts in twenty minutes," the other man asked. "I can't wait to get you alone in a dark theater."

Dante scowled. Caitlyn gave an overly loud startled laugh and pulled away from Paul. She stumbled to a side table and picked up her purse. Dante narrowed his eyes. How well did she know this guy? She sure wasn't acting like she was receptive to the man's suggestions.

"Now, Paul. Behave," she said as she turned to face them.

"I'm done behaving." Paul strode up to her. "It's time for action. Lots of action."

She froze and stared at the man, her mouth opening and closing. "W-what?"

Her alarm made Dante stiffen. If she didn't want to leave with this man, he'd throw the ass out. Her head snapped toward him, and her eyes widened as he began to rise. She grabbed Paul's hand and ran out the door.

Dante frowned. Could he have misread her cues? That was possible. God knows, she was a complex woman. One moment she was shy, the next her eyes blazed with indignation, the next desire. A paradox of emotions that made her all the more intriguing.

Figuring out what made Caitlyn Moore tick was turning out to be his favorite puzzle.

· · ·

When the door slammed behind her, Cait smacked Paul's arm. "What the hell was *that*?"

"Jeez, Cait, what did you expect? I'm supposed to be your date." He linked his arm with hers and walked her toward the parking lot. "I about wet myself when he came off the couch. Let me tell you, girl, that is one fine piece of man flesh and I think you're crazy for discouraging him."

"Then *you* take him."

"Gladly, but I don't think he swings that way. But he's exactly what I like. All man."

That he was. Scrumptious. Hard-bodied. Man.

As she started down the cement steps, Paul grabbed her hand and yanked until she looked up at him. "Why don't you give him a chance? You can't hide behind me forever."

She sighed. "Because he's not attracted to me."

"Why do you think that?"

"He had four days to call and he didn't. That says a lot." She turned and made her way down the rest of the steps. "Besides, men who should be on the cover of *Playgirl* have never glanced my way. And there's no reason for them to start now."

"You also don't look the same as before."

True. Being overweight and playing the friend role to guys all her life, she tended to forget that fact sometimes. Either way, attracted or not, that didn't take away from their one huge problem. "He's still a fighter."

"So?"

"I hate the sport."

"Maybe you could learn to like it?"

"You think?" She couldn't keep the sarcasm out of her voice. "I can't believe people are paid to do that."

"I don't know much about it, but I do know these guys take it very seriously. I heard they train about eight hours a day when a huge fight is coming up."

"To get beefed up and knock the crap out of someone. No thanks. Not interested."

"Your loss. If he even batted an eyelash at me—" he snapped his finger—"look out."

She couldn't help but laugh. "You're crazy." Her humor faded.

Paul didn't get it. Dante wasn't interested. He hadn't called. Simple as that. A man like him knew what he wanted, went after what he wanted. She couldn't see him being hesitant in anything he did, particularly with a woman.

Even if he were interested, her aversion to the violence he willingly engaged in turned her off. She just wished her body would agree.

"By the way, you look like shit in that outfit."

She pointed at him over the hood of the car. "Don't start."

He opened the driver's side door. "What size are you now?"

"Twelve."

"And what size are you wearing?"

She rolled her eyes as she slipped into the passenger seat. "Eighteen."

He slid into the seat and inserted the key into the ignition. "I'm not Amy. I don't play passive aggressive. Get ready, honey, we're going shopping."

"You can't be serious! There is no way I'm going to wear this." Cait pulled at the tiny black skirt showing way too much of her thighs.

Paul sat in a cushy chair, his ankle resting on his knee. "You're no longer wearing those rags. I've tolerated it long enough. No more."

"What are you going to do? Burn my wardrobe?"

Paul pursed his lips and arched a brow.

Well, hell.

"This thing barely covers my butt. I can't wear this."

He shot to his feet, grabbed her by the shoulders, then turned her to face the mirror. "Look at yourself. I mean, really *look* at yourself. Not as you see you, but what's actually reflecting back at you."

She still saw the heavy woman she had always been, but deep down she knew the size twenty-two woman no longer existed. Why couldn't she let her go? Why did she cling to this image that held her back? It should be easy to embrace the new Caitlyn. But letting go of the past was harder than losing the weight.

Paul turned her to face him. "I see a breathtaking woman scared to death to see how beautiful she actually is, a woman refusing to live because she has spent her entire life feeling inadequate in her appearance, a woman who has nothing to be ashamed of."

He whirled her around to face the mirror again. Reaching in front of her, he waved his hands in front of her breasts. Breasts now showcased in a new pushup bra and low-cut shirt. "And these. Girl, please. Women will be jealous as hell of your cleavage if you show it off."

She studied her reflection. She felt awkward in the getup. But if she was honest with herself, the outfit wasn't half bad. The material fit like clothes were meant to, hugging where it accentuated her better features, and loose to hide the not-so-flattering ones. And her boobs were well displayed. What would it hurt to buy something to show herself off? She'd never let the old Cait go if she didn't try to move forward. She wanted to move forward. It was past time to do that.

"Fine, I'll take the skirt."

• • •

Where was she?

Dante tried to concentrate on the second movie of the night, vaguely aware of some kind of mist and creatures terrorizing a small town. At the moment, though, the digital readout on the DVR clock held his attention.

11:01.

He'd wanted to ask Amy about Paul, but she hadn't returned to the living room until Brad showed up, and then he had a hard time getting a word in edgewise with their lovey-dovey cooing. It was sickening, really. He did finally get to ask who Paul was between a "snugglebunny" and a "pookie." Amy's response calmed some of his worry at

Caitlyn's less-than-eager reception to the man's forward advances.

Amy's comment—"Paul? Good Lord, why did she keep him a secret? They've known each other for years"—could only be taken one way: Caitlyn had known she wasn't in any danger from this man.

Still, it was pretty damn clear *Paul* wanted to take things to the next step with her.

Dante reached for the popcorn on the coffee table. He'd just popped a handful into his mouth when the door opened. The popcorn turned to dust as Caitlyn stepped over the threshold.

Where were the damn clothes she'd left in?

"Cait?" Amy bolted upright beside Brad, her mouth ajar.

Caitlyn lifted her head and looked straight at Dante. His heart picked up speed until he was sure it would burst from his chest.

She glanced away, clearing her throat. "Hey, guys, enjoying the movie?"

No one answered. Dante jumped to his feet, offering his chair. "Why don't you sit? You can watch it with us." He scowled when Paul walked in behind Caitlyn.

"No, thanks. We—uh—have something we have to do."

She hurried from the room with Paul right on her heels.

What the hell was their "something-to-do"? Had the man convinced her to take their friendship to the next level? Had Dante lost any chance at solving the Caitlyn puzzle?

That would *blow*. Finally, a woman had entered his life who fascinated him. After almost three years of having sex handed to him, Dante found himself revved up with Caitlyn's detached attitude, especially after seeing she *was* attracted to him. Women never fought their attraction for him. Why was she?

Damn it, he had to know if she would still be able to fight the attraction if he added a little pressure.

But right now, there was another man in her bedroom, mostly likely applying his own pressure.

He didn't like that idea.

"He's gay."

"What?" Dante blinked, looking down at Amy, who cuddled into Brad's side on the couch.

"Gay," she repeated. When he just stared at her, she added, "as in show tunes and Judy Garland."

"Oh." That explained Caitlyn's shocked reaction earlier, but what was up with the "get you alone" crap? Was Paul warning Dante away from Caitlyn like a brother would?

Seemed reasonable, but it wouldn't work, not unless *Caitlyn* made it abundantly clear she wasn't interested.

Dante sat back down, his gaze drifting to the hallway. He needed to get her alone, see how she reacted without the safety of her friends around her, see if the desire he'd witnessed in her eyes at the gym could be set free. The idea of being on the receiving end of her passion pumped him up. But with her camped out in her room with Paul, how could he manage that?

CHAPTER FOUR

"That's it! I'm no longer your beard. That man was about to tear me apart."

"You're overreacting." Cait glanced at Paul, who sat on her bed, his foot dancing a frantic rhythm.

"Did you see the way he glared at me? It wasn't with daggers, Cait, it was fists. That fine piece of man-meat has staked a claim on you and he's going to pummel anyone who stands in his way, including my gay ass. My face can't handle that. After tonight, you're on your own."

She unfastened the heels Paul had made her buy and groaned as the torture devices popped off her feet.

What Paul said was true. Before they'd left, she'd witnessed Dante buck up with an impressive amount of testosterone. The way his body had tensed and his eyes turned fiery had reminded her of a Spartan warrior and scared her to death. Not a psychokiller scary, but a stole-her-breath-until-she-felt-like-she-would-keel-over scary.

Not a promising reaction for a woman trying to convince

herself she didn't want him.

To make matters worse, she saw the way Dante had watched her when she'd come in, with narrowed eyes and disapproval bracketing his tight lips. Instinct told her his displeasure had nothing to do with her and everything to do with Paul.

Apparently, Dante didn't believe in hiding his emotions. Was she wrong about him not being interested in her? If so, why hadn't the man picked up the phone and called? His actions were so confusing, making her feel even greener than she had before she'd met him.

The big question was, did she even *want* him interested in her?

She really wasn't certain. Yeah, she was attracted to him, but he was a whole new world of scary that she'd never dealt with before and had no clue how to handle.

Cait sighed. Enough thinking about the baffling man sitting in her living room.

She yanked open her closet door. "We came in here to do a job. Can we get this over with before I change my mind?"

"Gladly." Paul rose from the bed and crossed the room. Tsking, he studied the hanging clothes with horror. "Cait, really, I thought you had better fashion sense than this."

He plucked a green shirt off its hanger and dangled it from the tip of his finger. "A turtleneck?"

"Shut up, I like turtlenecks." She jerked the shirt from his grasp.

Paul shrugged before turning to grab an armful of clothes and throwing them on the floor.

"Hey! I might want to keep some of those."

"Like what?" He picked out a heavy sweater and held it

against her body. The material could now be used as a towel to wrap around her.

"Fine. Point taken."

She thought of the shopping bags still sitting in Paul's SUV. So different from what she was used to. "I take it back. I *need* to keep a couple of items." At Paul's perturbed look, she added, "I've made leaps and bounds tonight. All I'm asking is to keep a couple of pieces."

He sighed, shaking his head. "Four things."

She sifted through the material and grabbed a pair of red and white striped pajama bottoms, her favorite Rodney Atkins T-shirt, worn jeans, and a pair of khaki shorts. Then she spotted her pink hoodie peeking out from beneath a blue blouse. She reached for it.

"Uh-uh. I said four."

She snatched the hoodie and held it close to her. "I can't even wear it. It's July, but I love this thing."

"No more." He put his hands on his hips. "I'm going to get some bags to toss this junk in."

He left the room. Cait knelt beside the pile of clothes and removed the hangers. It would be odd opening her closet tomorrow and not seeing her old favorites hanging there. In their place would be fitted shirts, some so sexy she had a hard time imagining where she'd actually wear them, jeans that hugged her bottom, and shorts a little too short. A new wardrobe for her new body. Step one to forgetting old Cait completed.

Footsteps sounded from the hall then her door clicked shut.

Cait removed another hanger. "That was quick," she said without looking up.

"Not two words a man likes to hear."

She gasped and jumped to her feet. Self-consciously, she tugged at the skirt, which drew Dante's eyes to the material.

"I like the skirt. I like seeing your legs even more."

She gaped at him. Was he serious?

He glanced at the pile of clothes. "Spring cleaning?"

"More like summer," she croaked out.

Please don't see the sizes. Please don't see the sizes.

He dismissed the clothes as his gaze landed on the chocolate-brown comforter with pink accents that covered her queen-sized mattress. His attention lingered there for a moment before he lifted his gaze to the shelves that held an assortment of her favorite books and movies. "What do you like to do, Caitlyn?"

How could a man come across so damned relaxed? Especially when she was wound so tight she felt ready to shatter any second.

"Do?" She actually squeaked her question.

"You know. Read? Watch movies? Shop?"

A conversation? The man walks into her room, disrupts her perfect little world, and he decides to have a conversation? "All of the above."

Dante's smile sent her heart into a frantic staccato. He moved closer, and she retreated until her butt touched the wall. Her breath came in short, erratic spurts. His gaze started at her legs and raked upward over her body. "I like all of the above, too."

Ah! She liked that response. A little too much. Her heart pumped even faster. She had to escape.

Now.

As if reading her thoughts, Dante blocked her by bracing

his arms against the wall on either side of her body.

She couldn't swallow, couldn't breathe, couldn't do anything but stare into gorgeous blue eyes belonging to a gorgeous man. He leaned closer, his chest brushing against hers. Lord, she *felt* the strength of his body.

"So pretty." He ran his fingers across her cheek.

The desire in his eyes confirmed his statement. Could this be real? Could this man truly want her? Everything he did screamed *yes*.

"W-why did you come in here?"

His fingers paused on her skin. "Isn't it obvious? To be near you. Would you rather I leave?"

Yes. No. Hell, she didn't know.

"Maybe," she finally decided on.

"Maybe?" One masculine brow lifted. "A very indecisive answer. *Maybe* we should kiss and see if it helps you make a firm decision."

She swallowed, a response completely lost to her. Flustered by her inability to come up with her own flirtatious, witty comeback, she felt greener than ever. "I think that would be a bad idea."

"Give me one good reason why."

She opened her mouth, but no reason emerged. Instead, she murmured, "Me and you…we don't fit."

"Oh, I think we'd fit very nicely together."

Her mouth popped opened, shocked and alarmingly delighted by his words. "T-that's not what I meant." But now that he'd taken their conversation in that direction, it was all she could think of. She shook herself. "I meant we're too different. We don't have any chemistry."

Amusement filled his eyes. "No chemistry, huh? I'll

have to disagree." He placed his lips against her ear and whispered, "Do you remember when our eyes met in the mirror this morning? That punch of lust that socked us both? *That's* chemistry, Caitlyn."

He'd felt it too?

He lifted his head, and his gaze lowered to her lips. "Just one kiss. Nothing more." He eyes met hers. "Consider it an experiment."

He lowered his head, and she stiffened.

"One," he said.

Yes, just one kiss.

"Two."

Counting? Why was he counting?

His breath warmed her lips. "Last chance."

He paused, and she realized he was giving her time to say no. Why didn't she? She could stop this so easily.

"Three."

Thank God, she didn't have to make a choice.

The first touch of his lips sent electrical currents pulsing through her body and she jerked. He didn't deepen the kiss as she suspected he would. Instead, he steadily brushed his mouth against hers. Sweet caresses that caused thrills of excitement to scurry down her spine. She moaned and slid her palms over his chest. Fisting his shirt in her hands, she pulled him closer. A low growl rattled in his throat as his lips continued their teasing pursuit.

"You really need to clean out from under your kitchen sink. It took me forever— Oh, shit."

Dante shuddered and broke the kiss. Dazed, she turned her head to find Paul standing at the doorway, trash bags in his hand.

She looked back at Dante, very aware his arms still trapped her between the wall and his body. He didn't move. "I'd say this experiment has just proven that we do indeed have chemistry." A slow, wicked smile curved his lips. "Tons of it."

Damn it all to hell. She'd just ruined every attempt at the distance she'd tried to keep.

She released the wadded material in her hands and pushed at Dante's chest. "Please leave."

His arms dropped away. "Now that was a serious request. So I will. For now."

Dante strode to the door. Paul plastered himself against the wall, arms up in surrender as Dante passed. A trembling hand pressed to her lips, Cait stood frozen. She stared wide-eyed at her friend, whose mouth hung open.

He snapped it shut. "Damn girl, I feel like I've been kissed breathless. Was that as hot as it looked?"

All she could do was nod.

"You've surprised me this morning," Amy said.

Cait paused, a forkful of egg whites on its way to her mouth. "Why?"

"I thought last night was a fluke. I expected to walk in here and see you back in your rags."

Cait shoved the eggs in her mouth. Amy had no idea how close she was to the truth. If Paul hadn't taken every stuffed garbage bag with him, she would have ripped open the plastic and dug out a more comfortable outfit to wear. Instead, she'd been forced to wear her new clothes. Oddly enough, they weren't as horrible as she'd thought they'd be.

Definitely clingier than she was used to, but she had to admit the light-green shirt and fitted jeans showed off her curves and made her walk a little taller.

"Paul took all my old clothes."

Sputtering her coffee, Amy squealed, "He did what?"

"Took. Them. All."

"Why didn't I think of that?"

Cait gave a begrudging smile. "Because you're not as mean as he is."

"I wondered what you guys were doing in there all night. Honestly, though, it was past time for you to toss those things out."

"I know, and I'm glad I finally did."

"Did she tell you about the kiss?"

Paul's voice sounded from behind her. Cait closed her eyes and groaned. *Here we go.*

"Kiss?" Amy's eyes grew owlish. "With whom?"

Cait glared at Paul, who shrugged. "How was I supposed to know you didn't tell her?" His gaze lowered to her shirt. "Oh! Nice!"

"It should be. You picked it out." She glanced back at Amy. "Dante."

Amy's fork hit the plate with a clatter. "Dante? I wondered where he'd gotten off to last night and why he looked so pleased with himself when he came back."

Cait's cheeks heated. She guessed he had a reason to be satisfied. He'd gotten the answer he'd wanted: they had chemistry.

"I didn't tell you because…" She flicked her hand toward Paul. "He knew. He's enough to deal with, but both of you can be overwhelming. I should've known Big Mouth here would never stay quiet."

Paul grinned then grabbed Amy by the arm. "Girl, let me tell you about this kiss. It was *hawt*. He had Cait pressed against the wall, I mean, total dirty movie pressed." He pulled out a seat and sat at the table. "She was so into it too."

When Amy's brows shot to her hairline, Cait said, "Paul, enough."

Amy leaned forward. "How into it were you?"

"She wasn't asking him to leave, if you get my drift."

Cait sighed. "I liked it when I shouldn't have."

"What in the hell is that supposed to mean? The man is to die for, why shouldn't you like kissing him?"

"You know as well as I do I don't have experience with men like him."

Amy grimaced. "Yeah, you're a little green in the men department, but it's nothing that can't be learned."

Yeah, right. The last date she'd been on had been six months ago with an accountant at a law firm. The most *experience* she'd needed was keeping up a steady stream of chatter, easy enough since he did all the talking.

Dante would be much more difficult to entertain. And he wouldn't sit there and hog the conversation. No, he'd pry and dig, then smile and make her heart melt. Too dangerous.

"Do you like him?" Amy asked.

"I hardly know him."

Amy rolled her eyes. "Good God, you do need help. You don't have to know a guy to like him. The *like* starts the know. How about this? Would you like to get to know him?"

"He flusters me, Amy. He's so overwhelming. So big and—there."

"And how is that bad?"

"Yeah, I'd like to know the answer to that one myself," Paul piped in.

When Cait remained silent, Amy said, "Brad says Dante is into you."

Cait blinked. "What?"

"Yep. Totally entranced. My words, not his."

Hadn't she gotten a taste last night of exactly how into her Dante was? And how that one kiss had kept her up all night fantasizing about doing it again?

Paul pointed a fork at Cait. "See. I told you Brawny Man was interested."

"He didn't call." Yet the man had turned out to be interested in her. But how was she supposed to know when he'd fallen through on the one thing he'd promised?

"That was my fault," Amy said.

"What?"

"I thought his seeing you in person would be better. Even as your best friend, I find a conversation on the phone with you is like pulling teeth."

"I don't like to talk on a phone."

"Yeah, I know. That's why I gave him the advice. He wanted to call you."

He hadn't fallen through. He'd wanted to call her. What excuses was she supposed to hold onto now?

Fighting, fighting, fighting. His attraction was evident now, but his career still hadn't changed.

"You just need to let him in," Amy continued.

"Not happening. I feel like a goob when he's around."

"You feel like that because you want him." Amy studied her. "More so than any other man you've ever met."

"No, I don't."

"Whatever you say." Amy shrugged. Then her expression softened. "It's okay to be scared. Just don't let the fear ruin your chance."

"I'm not scared. I'm overwhelmed. There's a difference."

"True, but I can help lessen that feeling." Amy speared a piece of pancake and winked.

Oh, no. Cait knew that wink.

"Don't worry. I have a plan. I'll get you comfortable around the hotter versions of the opposite sex if it's the last thing I do." Her friend shoved the pancake into her mouth.

Amy and plans equaled chaos.

Joy.

• • •

Dante strolled on his way to the training facility. Caitlyn hadn't been far from his thoughts since their kiss three days ago. Amy had advised him to move slowly, but slow didn't work for him. Nothing about him was slow. It was time to do things his way.

Besides, Amy was wrong. Slow wasn't the way to deal with Caitlyn. She responded to his forward advances. Dante smiled. She responded nicely against his lips.

"Jones!"

Surprised to hear his name, he turned. An immense man sat outside the coffee house he'd just passed, foot resting on his knee, conceit in his relaxed expression. Shocking purple hair jutted in every direction from his head. Blue, pink, or green, Dante would have recognized the man anywhere.

Sentori.

With one leap, the man vaulted over the twisted wrought iron fence. The distance between them vanished.

Sentori didn't stop moving until they were eye to eye. "You don't stand a chance in hell against me."

Dante forced himself to relax. "We'll see in two months."

"Pack your shit and leave now. You're always going to be second best, always looking up at me with the belt around my waist."

Dante laughed. "You're going to be the one looking up, bitch. Right after you tap out."

Sentori lifted a brow. "'Tap'? You think you can beat me on the ground and force me to tap? Think again, little boy, you'll need a better game plan than that."

"You're too much of a chicken shit to stand up to me."

Sentori shoved Dante. "Who the fuck are you calling chicken?"

The sound of chairs pushing back at the coffee house filled the air. A group of men started toward them.

Dante rose to his full height and pressed his nose against the other fighter. "We're not in the cage, asshole. Don't. Touch. Me."

"Or what?" Sentori jabbed Dante in the shoulder with his pointer finger.

Dante worked his neck back and forth to suppress his rising anger. He'd known Sentori would eventually make an appearance, but he hadn't realized how easily the guy would be able to piss him off. Instead of hitting the man's smug face, he wheeled around and started back up the sidewalk, only to have "Pussy!" called after him.

Dante's shoulders tensed but he kept walking, refusing to entertain the man's taunts. If Sentori wanted to make a spectacle of himself, fine by him. Dante, however, wouldn't be a part of it.

Once he entered the training facility, he strapped on his gloves then went to work, furiously hammering the hanging red leather bag with punches, kicks, and elbows.

Crack, crack, crack, his fists hit like a machine gun. A roundhouse kick toward the head of the bag boomed throughout the room.

"Who pissed you off?"

Dante turned to see Mike leaning against the wall.

"One guess."

The older man walked toward him. "Don't let him get into your head. Sentori is going to do everything he can to ruffle your feathers. Anything to get you off your game."

"He's a prick." Dante used his forearm to wipe the sweat on his forehead.

"I won't argue. But whatever confrontation you had with him, just remember he can and will do worse. He likes to play mind games."

"I don't have anything he can play with."

"You better hope so. Once he finds your weakness, he'll exploit it."

Dante nodded and turned back to the bag. Nothing Sentori could do would ruin his concentration.

He had one goal and one goal only.

Win the championship.

CHAPTER FIVE

Cait glanced around the packed Boot Scoot.

It was official.

She'd finally lost her mind. Since the day she'd met Dante, she'd worried over her sanity, and now it was confirmed. She needed to be admitted to the closest psychiatric ward.

What had she been thinking to go along with Amy's crazy plan?

Men loitered around the club. From time to time, their gaze rested on her, appreciation in their eyes. She'd never noticed the admiring glances before, but she couldn't pretend they weren't there anymore. Men were actually staring at her. She sat up a little straighter, a small smile playing at her lips. Not that she really wanted to encourage any of them, but it felt good to be noticed. Damn good. But what would she do if one of the guys actually walked over and talked to her? She didn't know the first thing about flirting. Maybe Amy's plan wasn't crazy after all.

She bit her lip.

"Would you stop?"

She glanced at Paul, who sat across from her. "Stop what?"

"Acting like you're the fox in a fox hunt. If anyone should be cowering in a corner, it's me."

"It's your fault I waltzed in here in these tight-ass jeans and a shirt that makes my boobs look two sizes bigger than they really are."

"Oh, Cait." Paul shook his head sadly. "Your boobs have always been that big."

She smacked at the air in front of her, a laugh escaping even though she tried to suppress it. "Shut up."

Paul was outside his own comfort zone. The fact that he was willing to accompany her for support meant the world to her. "Will you dance with me?"

Paul shook his head, holding up his Sex on the Beach drink. "Ask me after a few more of these." His lips twisted in a wry smile. "Don't look now, but Amy has wrestled up a few wannabe cowboys for your little assignment."

Cait glanced over her shoulder. Sure enough, Amy was walking toward them between two beefy men, coming straight for them. Nerves hit her full force and her stomach clenched.

No. Amy's plan was pure crazy.

Practice flirting?

The suggestion had made perfect sense a few days ago. Now? Not so much.

She inhaled deeply as Paul did the same.

"This is crazy," they both muttered.

Lifting her drink, Cait asked, "In this together?"

He clicked his glass to hers. "Together."

A large shadow fell on the table. With one more calming breath, she twisted to look at Amy.

Her friend slipped an arm through each cowboy's elbow. "Cait, I have a couple of friends I'd like you to meet." Amy released her hold on one of the men and placed her free hand on the other's bicep. "This is George."

In simple terms, George was a blond giant. Although he wasn't bigger than Dante, his size still intimidated her. She sent him a tentative smile. "Hi."

He winked. "Hi, yourself."

His gaze roamed boldly over her upper body, coming to rest on her cleavage. Though Dante had done almost the exact same thing a few days ago when he'd allowed his gaze to slowly travel the length of her body. Her reaction to this man wasn't the same. Her body didn't heat, heart didn't flutter, stomach didn't grip. Instead, she recoiled.

"And this is Jack."

This man wasn't so intimidating. Warm brown eyes met hers and a real smile, not a leer, curved his lips.

All three took a seat at the round, wooden table. George sat next to her, his jean-clad thigh pressed into her leg. He leaned close. Distaste rose in her mouth, but Cait swallowed it. Paul sat back, frowning. Jack was studying Paul, and Amy had a satisfied glint in her eyes.

This would be a long night.

"So, beautiful, how about I buy you a drink?" George asked.

Amy motioned for her to accept.

Flirt? With this? *I don't think so.*

Cait held up her half-empty Tequila Sunrise. "I'm good, thanks."

A scowl crept over the man's features.

Yeah, she didn't like this guy one bit. She turned her attention to Jack. "I haven't seen you in here before."

Well, that sounded plain stupid. There had to be about two hundred people in here on any given night.

Amy shook her head, dismayed. Cait glared at her. What did she expect? She was new to all this, for freaking sakes.

But Cait didn't get the oh-aren't-you-pathetic reaction from Jack she expected. Instead, his lips twitched at the corners. "I could say the same about you."

His brown eyes met hers. All her worries faded away.

She could "practice" with this man. There wasn't one hint of attraction in his eyes. The indifference relieved some of her worry of coming across as a tease, or having to pretend interest in a man who did nothing for her. Unfortunately, only one man did anything for her these days— and she still wasn't sure what to do about him.

"I'm out here a few times a month with my friends."

Jack leaned forward, resting an elbow on the table. "I've found it hard to meet anyone in here. How about you?"

"I really don't come here to meet anyone. Just hang out, dance, and do a little drinking. Release some stress."

George slid his arm around the back of her chair, the beefy appendage touching the back of her shoulders as his thigh pressed harder into hers. "I have a method for relieving stress and you don't even have to leave the bed."

He danced the tips of his fingers over her bicep, a suggestive leer curling his lips.

Gag me. "My current methods work just fine, thank you."

She scooted her chair forward until his arm fell off the back of her chair. Either he was completely unaware of her disinterest or didn't care, because he slipped his arm under the table and laid his hand on her thigh, squeezing. Cait tapped the top of his hand.

George laughed, removing his hand. "You're feisty. I love feisty."

Cait was about to tell him to screw off when Amy's eyes widened at something behind her. "What?"

Amy's mouth opened and closed before she gave a shaky breath. "Um, tall, dark, and extremely pissed just walked in the door."

Cait followed her friend's gaze and clashed with Dante's piercing blue ones. *Pissed* was an understatement; raging mad was more like it.

Dante was standing at the entrance, eyes locked where she'd just smacked George's hand. Her heart beat frantically. Damn, she loved it when he did the whole puffed-up defender thing—over her, of all people.

Cait jerked her head to glare at Amy. "I thought you said he wouldn't be here tonight."

"He who?" Jack asked.

"Brad said he wouldn't be. They had plans. Cait, I'm sorry. I'd never have suggested this if I'd known he'd show up."

"Why is that asshole glaring over here?" Jack asked.

George jumped to his feet. Even over the thundering music, the chair scraped noisily across the wood floor. "What kind of game are you two playing?"

The venom in his voice made the table fall silent. Cait wrung her fingers together, unsure how to respond.

Paul finally broke the silence. "That's Cait's boyfriend. I suggest you hightail it out of here before he arrives. He has rage issues."

At a loss for words, Cait stared at Paul before sneaking a peek at George.

Anger came off the man in waves, his fists clenched tightly at his sides. "Boyfriend? Bitch, do you have any idea what kind of trouble you're getting me into? That's the Inferno." He shot a nasty sneer at Amy. "You knew this and brought me here anyway?"

With a muttered oath, he stalked from the table.

Cait returned her attention to Paul. "What were you thinking?"

"He's gone, isn't he? Dude had a serious creep level I wasn't comfortable with."

Yeah, her too.

"So he's not your boyfriend?" Jack asked.

She sighed. "No."

Paul leaned forward. "He wishes he was, though."

"Hush your mouth," she said.

Jack leaned forward too. "So what's wrong with him?"

"What do you mean?"

"I'm no expert on men, but he's a good-looking guy and definitely appears interested—if the way he's glaring over here is any indication. So what's the matter with him?"

"I keep asking her the same thing," Paul muttered.

Jack eyed Paul. "And you are?"

"The beard."

Cait rolled her eyes. "Paul, shut up."

Paul shrugged. "I am, but if the other night says anything, the man could give two shits we're dating."

"He knows," Amy said.

Jack's brows rose. "Knows what?"

"What? That I'm as straight as a fruit loop? Well, that

makes more sense. I was slightly offended at how easily I was brushed aside. Not saying he couldn't knock me out with a simple bitch slap, but still."

Jack watched Paul closely, then he looked back at her. "Are you trying to discourage his attentions?"

Since her entire life had just been laid on the table for a complete stranger, why not add to it? "I have no idea what I want."

"Do you want to dance?"

Cait studied the man before her. If she said yes, she'd be all but telling Dante to back off. If she said no, she might as well go sit on Dante's lap. And she wasn't close to being ready for something like that.

What did she want? Lord, what could she handle?

She threw a quick glance over her shoulder. Dante sat on a stool, a beer bottle in his hand, mouth tight, eyes not wavering from her table.

Excitement gripped her belly and she squashed the feeling. Why was it this hard? Most people felt an attraction and went with it. Would she still hesitate if he weren't a fighter? She wasn't sure. All she knew was Dante made her extremely nervous.

She closed her eyes and turned back to Jack. "Yes, I'll dance with you."

A little piece of her scolded her for her decision.

. . .

Dante frowned as the cowboy led Caitlyn onto the dance floor. Tight jeans hugged her luscious ass as she walked away from him and into the arms of another man.

She was giving a clear back-the-fuck-off message. One

he had no intention of taking. Not after that kiss. He'd proven she wanted him and she couldn't take that back now, no matter how hard she tried.

The more she denied her desire for him, the more determined he was to prove to her the combustible heat between them was undeniable.

Fuck, was it combustible. The moment her low moan of pleasure had swept across his skin, his cock had gone rock hard, driving him to coax more unquestionable signs of her desire out of her.

And damn, if she hadn't responded to the pressure of his mouth and complied with his unspoken request.

First, by running her hands up his chest, then fisting her hands in his shirt, then tugging him closer. But the most telling of all had been the unmistakable lust darkening the green depths of her eyes after Paul interrupted them. Irrefutable responses to *him* no matter how much she wanted to do-si-do around a dance floor with another man.

Now he needed to figure out how to get past her defenses again and elicit those sweet moans again.

"I told you to take it slow," Amy said as she appeared by his side. "You've spooked the hell out of her."

"How? All I did was kiss her."

"You have a funny definition of slow, Dante." Amy sighed. "Listen, Cait isn't used to this, okay?"

"What? A man being attracted to her?"

"Yes." Amy stared him square in the eye. "Especially a man like *you* being attracted to her."

"That's not possible." He gestured to the dance floor. "Look at her."

"Just trust me on this. Back off. Get to know her."

The sincerity in her voice grabbed his attention. There were more layers to Caitlyn than he'd realized. "What's her story?"

"She'll tell you if you let her get to know you. I shouldn't even tell you this much. I really shouldn't. I'm going against every best friend rule in the book here, but I want to see Cait happy. She feels it, Dante. The attraction. It's there and she's denying it with everything she has in her. So if you really want to make a go of this, *back off*."

He already knew that.

Amy patted his shoulder and walked away.

Slow?

How was he going to do that?

The cowboy leaned in close and whispered to her. Caitlyn stiffened, her cheeks flushing more, but this time Dante was positive it wasn't in excitement. Her throat worked back and forth as she nodded. The cowboy smiled, wrapped his arms around her waist, and brought her close to his chest.

Her gaze met Dante's. For a long moment, she stared at him. Indecision and regret reflected back at him before she sent a brilliant smile to the other man. Jealousy churned in his stomach, a foreign emotion he was unaccustomed to. When she laughed at something the man said, Dante snapped. Without thinking, he stalked over to the couple and placed a firm hand on the cowboy's shoulder. "I believe you're dancing with my girlfriend a little too closely for my liking."

A bold statement to make, but a man's got to do what a man's got to do.

The cowboy turned, took one look at him, and held up his hands, backing away. Dante drew Caitlyn into his arms.

He loved the way she fit so snugly against him.

Or would, if she'd just let go. "Would you relax?"

She glared at him. "Girlfriend? Who the hell gave you the right to call me that?"

"Seemed appropriate. You didn't seem to keen on dancing with the man." At first. "Thought you could use some rescuing."

She tensed even more. "So is this how it works? You barge into my room, kiss me, and now you get to dictate who I dance with? I don't think so."

She pushed out of his arms and left him standing in the middle of the dance floor alone.

Okay, lesson learned. Fuck, he had to learn to control himself with her. Pulling the jealous boyfriend card didn't work on Caitlyn Moore.

Maybe Amy was right.

Slow was the way to get those sweet, sassy lips on his again.

• • •

Girlfriend.

She'd liked the word coming from Dante's mouth way too much, which freaked her out. Dante Jones was not the kind of man she wanted to be a girlfriend to. Everything about extreme fighting turned her stomach. Cait still remembered the way Brad had looked after his fight the night she'd met him: blackened, swollen eyes, one so damaged, it'd been days before the swelling had receded enough so he could squint through it, bruises on his face, and a split lip.

Training didn't seem to spare the fighters from injury either. She'd noticed small places on Dante's face as well: a shadowed area on his cheekbone, a puffy area at the corners of his eyes, raw knuckles—a constant reminder of violence.

Though his wounds convinced her brain she didn't want to be involved with a fighter, her body didn't seem to mind his career choice and responded to his presence.

Cait stirred her drink with a thin, red straw before taking a sip, only to stop mid-draw as a thick man with purple spiky hair made a beeline for her. She swallowed, not sure if the reflex was because of the liquid in her mouth or the determination etching the man's face as he approached. Gaze locked with hers, he stopped at the edge of the table.

"Richard Sentori," he said, extending his hand. "But you can call me Sentori."

His eyes bored into hers and she got the feeling she was supposed to have recognized his name. Too bad Richard Sentori didn't ring any bells.

She took his hand. "Cait Moore."

"Cait? Would that be short for something?"

"Caitlyn."

"A beautiful name, for a beautiful woman."

Crap, this was all she needed. At least he wasn't crowding her like George had. "Thank you."

"I saw you dancing with Dante a little while ago."

"You know Dante?"

He slid into the seat beside hers and slung his arm across the back of her chair as he leaned in closer, his face inches from her ear. Cait shifted away. Why did men think crowding a girl made her aware of them? It didn't work.

"I make it my business to know the men I'm about to fight. It's the little things that let you know the kind of fighter he'll be in the cage."

"Oh wow. You're his opponent."

"Yep, Dante's a big name among the up and comers. He's a damned good fighter with a great reputation in the ring, and a not so great one outside it."

"Really? Dante? Are you sure you've got the right guy?"

Surprise flicked across his face. "I know who I'm defending my title against."

Touché. "Of course you do. Sorry, I just have a hard time believing Dante has a bad reputation."

"It depends on what you consider a bad reputation. Dante likes women, but he likes the chase more. With the way you left him standing in the middle of the dance floor, you're going to become his next conquest."

She already was, but this information definitely explained a lot.

"So he's a womanizer?"

"I don't want to bash the guy, since I've never officially met him. But the guys talk in the locker room. Conversations involving Dante tend to revolve around how quickly he goes through women. He finds one, pursues her, then grows bored once the chase is over."

She studied Sentori. She didn't see any malice toward Dante as he spoke, just honest concern for her. "I'm no one to you, so why tell me this?"

"I don't know why you left Dante on the dance floor, and frankly, I don't care, but I thought I'd offer some basic information so you weren't blindsided later. He can do what he wants in his home town, but in mine I'd prefer not to have any tears shed over him."

"I appreciate your concern." Now she had to digest the information. Her mind grabbed onto the loophole Sentori had given her and wanted the rest of her to not care about Dante's career and jump at the attraction she felt.

"Don't mention it."

A movement to the left caught her peripheral vision.

Dante stormed toward them. Cait tensed before jumping to her feet. "I'm sorry, but would you excuse me?"

Now was not the time to deal with Dante. She needed to think rationally—something she had a hard time doing anytime he was near.

. . .

Dante didn't slow his steps as Caitlyn bolted in the opposite direction. He was glad she left, even if the reason was because of him and not the prick sitting at the table. The farther away she was from Sentori, the happier *he* was. He placed both hands on the table and leaned into Sentori's face. "What'd you say to her?"

Sentori leaned back in his chair, resting an ankle on his knee. "Nothing she didn't need to hear."

"I swear to God you better not say anything to upset her."

"What? You have a soft spot for the fat girl?"

Dante jerked back, stunned by the cruel question. "What the hell did you just say?"

"Oh, come on, Inferno. You seriously think she's hot? Man, I think you've been hit a little too hard in the head."

"Your reputation knows no bounds, does it, Sentori? You really are complete slime."

"If being a slime is speaking the truth, then so be it."

Dante straightened, pointing a finger. "Stay away from her."

"I'll let her make that decision. Besides, your knight in shining armor act has me even more intrigued about Miss Piggy. Even after she rejected you in front of the entire club, you came to her rescue. What am I missing out on? Maybe there is something under all the extra flesh."

"You disgust me." Dante turned away from the delight in Sentori's eyes. The ass was enjoying every minute of getting under his skin. Mike had warned him, but Dante had never imagined Sentori would use Caitlyn to make him see red, and in such a cruel manner. He wouldn't rise to it, though. He knew Sentori's game.

Even as he reminded himself of that, he spun and said, "Caitlyn is breathtaking, one of the most gorgeous women I've had the pleasure of meeting, and I pity you for being so wrapped up in shit-talk you'd stoop to the level you just did. But you've given me all the more reason to beat your ass come September."

As Dante strode off in search of Caitlyn, he took satisfaction in the scowl he'd left on Sentori's face.

CHAPTER SIX

Cait hurried into the bathroom. If Sentori told her the truth, and she didn't see why he'd lie, she'd given Dante all the more reason to pursue her. Why *her,* though? Why not one of the bombshells frequenting the club who could meet him one flirting line after another?

He had to know she was awkward around men, had no finesse. Hell, she'd only had sex with two men. Once. Each. In the dark. So why her inexperienced ass? *Was* it her inexperience that attracted him? Did she represent more of a challenge?

She wasn't sure how she felt about that possibility.

A cluster of women gathered around the sinks, most applying lipstick or fluffing their hair. Cait waited until a space became available to wedge herself in. After dampening a paper towel, she wiped her face, cooling her overheated skin.

"Did you see the Inferno out there?"

Cait froze. Her gaze darted down the long mirror and

focused on the speaker two sinks over.

A tall, slim, strawberry blonde smudged the eyeliner under her eyes with her fingertip as she talked to the shorter brunette beside her.

"I swear that man puts other extreme fighters to shame," the dark-haired woman said, lust dripping off each word. "Did you see his match a few months ago? Damn, that man is completely lickable."

The blonde turned to face her friend, a smug tilt to her bright red lips. "And I plan to lick every inch of his hard body."

Cait's stomach knotted with violent jealousy at the thought of anyone else licking Dante. Then she started. What was she thinking? Here she was ready to claw this woman's eyes out over a man who might have only been interested in her because she *hadn't* thrown herself at him.

She needed some perspective. After pushing her way out of the crowded bathroom, she searched for any place to get some quiet. An open door provided a current of fresh air and she hurried toward it. Once outside, she inhaled deeply. July humidity filled her lungs.

She gripped the white railing of the tiny deck, the dull thumping of the music in the background her only companion. As much as she hated to admit it, Dante was worming his way past her resistance and she was damn close to crumbling. Should she go with it?

Sentori had pretty much guaranteed nothing serious would come out of her seeing Dante, so the pressure was off. She wouldn't have to deal for very long with a career she couldn't stand.

But could she sleep with Dante? He was already far

outside her comfort zone in the man department. She had no doubt that sex with him would be, too. He'd want the lights on and a woman with no inhibitions. She wasn't certain she'd come far enough to stand in front of Dante Jones naked and allow him to see her imperfect glory while he stood before her completely perfect.

"If it's not the Inferno's bitch."

Icy fear washed over her and she froze, her grip tightening on the railing. The planks creaked as someone stepped closer. The stench of rum invaded her nose.

She whirled to find George looming over her. Tall. Muscular. Menacing. She stepped back.

"I don't like being made a fool of, even if you're some fighter's girlfriend."

Cait brushed past him. He grabbed her arm and slammed her against the wall. A cry wrenched from her throat as she stared at the inebriated man.

"I-I didn't have anything to do with that. I'm sorry for the confusion." Her voice trickled out a bare whisper as she tried to yank her arm away.

His grip tightened, his strong fingers digging into her flesh. Pain lanced up her arm and into her shoulder.

"Let me go!"

He laughed, a cold, frightening sound. Terror climbed into her throat. Her lips parted to scream, but before she could release it, he clamped his hand over her mouth and slammed her into the wall again.

She twisted, using her free hand to push against his massive chest. He was like a wall of iron, immovable, impenetrable. God, she couldn't get him off her! The thought paralyzed her and her mind shut down.

He pressed closer and her back bit into the wood. A large hand ran down her shoulder toward her waist, stopping just under the curve of her breast. Cait whimpered.

"I've never had an MMA star's woman before. What would it be like?"

Please, someone help me!

His hand inched upward, leaving a blazing trail of disgust. She tried to jerk away from the offending touch and tried to slap his face. Sneering, he snatched her wrist and brought both arms above her head. The odor of liquor fanned her face. She gagged, closing her eyes.

"Get your fucking hands off her!"

Relief crashed into Cait at the furious growl behind those words.

Dante.

One moment she was flattened against the wall, the next she stumbled forward as the weight of the man's body lifted from her. She opened her eyes in time to see Dante punch George.

The man's eyes rolled back and he crumpled to the ground. Dante whirled toward her, charging forward. Rage twisted his features and made him look so frightening any sensible man would be terrified to fight him. His fierce reaction gave her a sense of safety.

He stopped in front of her, his expression gentling as he cupped her cheek. His hand trembled against her skin. "God, Caitlyn. Are you okay?"

She laid her fingers on top of his. "I am now. Thank you."

"Damn it, that scared me to death."

Her eyes widened. It was hard to believe anything scared this man.

"Are you sure you're okay?"

She nodded.

He kissed her forehead then took her into his arms. She went willingly, resting her cheek against his chest. The rapid beat of his heart sounded in her ear, calming her, and she took a quivering breath.

His arms tightened around her. "Woman, you have no fighting sense. Have you never taken self-defense?"

She couldn't help a shocked laugh. Leave it to a fighter to be pissed she hadn't known how to fight. She pulled back from his embrace. "No."

A frown marred Dante's mouth. "Everyone should know basic fighting, Caitlyn. Especially someone as beautiful as you."

It was the second time he'd called her beautiful, and for the second time, her heart skipped a beat at the sincerity in his voice. She'd only been called beautiful by her daddy and Paul. To hear it come from this gorgeous man left her awed.

His gaze lowered to her lips and he swallowed, then he released her and stepped back. Why did he retreat? It wasn't like him to back away.

"I want you to meet me at my training facility on Monday."

"Why?"

"For your first self-defense class."

Cait stood outside the glass door to the training facility, butterflies fluttering in her stomach. She reached to open the door, then snatched her hand away.

Inside, a shirtless Dante ran on a treadmill. Sweat coated

his tanned back. The tribal tattoo on his bicep ran over his shoulder blade in sharp, curved, thick black lines, disappearing over his shoulder. Cait wondered if the ink continued onto his chest. The tat only intensified her attraction. It made her body quiver in odd sensations as she followed the intricate design with her eyes.

Lickable was an understatement.

She soaked up his masculinity while he continued to run, unaware of her attention. His muscles flexed and moved as his feet glided over the moving track. Effortless. He made running seem effortless.

She glanced down at her attire. She'd gotten up first thing this morning and bought a pair of black yoga pants and a fitted v-neck T-shirt. It was the first time ever she'd dressed in something fitting to work out in. And she was proud of herself of doing it on her own without goading from Amy and Paul.

She reached for the bar and stopped.

Why couldn't she open the blasted door? It wasn't as though this was a date. Dante was simply worried for her welfare, wanted to help her protect herself. She should be grateful, not stand there quaking like the high school geek facing the class quarterback.

"Can I help you?"

Cait whirled to find a bulky, bald man towering over her. She stepped back. "Um, I'm supposed to meet Dante."

No turning back now.

The older man scowled. Shifting from foot to foot, she bit her lip.

"You're pretty nervous for a chick who's supposed to meet someone. You're not a groupie, are you?"

"No!"

"You better not be. Dante doesn't have time for a fan club."

"No, sir. I swear I'm supposed to be here." Why hadn't she opened the door when she had the chance? "He's supposed to give me a self-defense lesson."

"Why don't we go inside and see what he has to say?"

Cait swallowed, nodding. The giant reached around her and opened the door. When he raised a brow, she bolted inside.

Heat flamed her face, whether in embarrassment or anger she wasn't sure. This man thought her one of those pathetic fans who stalked their heroes. It didn't even occur to him that what she said was true. "Dante!"

The heat in her cheeks intensified when Dante's head snapped up and his eyes met hers in the mirror. He grinned and waved before hitting the emergency stop button and trotting over.

"Caitlyn, I'm glad you came." He wiped sweat off his forehead with a white towel. The tattoo did indeed creep along the top portion of his smooth chest, stopping just above the nipple of a well-defined pec.

Ah, hell.

"You know her, then?"

"Yeah, she's Brad's girlfriend's roommate."

"My apologies, miss. I have to stay on the lookout for fans. They clog up my gym something awful, especially with a big name like Dante in town."

Cait waved away his explanation. "No worries, I understand."

"Caitlyn, this is my trainer, Mike Cannon. Mike, Caitlyn

Moore."

He offered his hand. "It's nice to meet you."

She shook his hand.

"I'm going to show her some self-defense moves. She had some drunk bothering her Saturday night."

Mike nodded. "I'll leave you to it, then. I have some business to take care of." He walked into an office and shut the door.

Dante looked at her. "You ready to start?"

He seemed so distant, not like the Dante she'd come to expect. "If this is a bad time, we could do this later."

His gaze flew to hers. "No!" He stopped, clearing his throat. "No. This is a perfect time."

"If you're sure." An awkward silence enveloped them. She bit her lip as Dante pulled a shirt over his head, trying to contain her disappointment at him covering his exquisite chest.

"I guess it would be best to do this in the grappling area."

She turned in the direction he pointed. A large blue mat covered the floor in the far left corner.

"Okay," she said.

He grabbed her hand and pulled her behind him. The feel of his fingers wrapped around hers sent little shocks pulsing up her arm. She closed her eyes. Agreeing to this had been a bad idea. If holding his hand caused this kind of reaction, what would happen once he started teaching her?

When they reached the mat, he released her hand and faced her. "What we'll go over today is very basic self-defense, enough to give you some protection."

He grabbed her shoulders and moved her so she stood directly in front of him. "It's really simple. There are four things to know. Groin, eyes, throat, feet. Groin is self-explanatory, but never kick. An attacker can grab your leg if you do. Instead, use your knee. You had the perfect opportunity to do that, but you froze."

"He surprised me."

His brows rose. "Most attackers don't warn you before they attack, Caitlyn. You always have to be prepared."

Dante lunged forward and pushed her against the wall, his body flush against hers. He grabbed her hands and raised them over her head, bringing him even closer. This was a lesson and he'd just told her how to defend herself, but all that held her attention was his face buried in the curve of her neck, his breath heating the sensitive skin behind her ear.

He released her then stepped back. "You froze again."
Not for the reason you think.

"I want you to try and knee me."

She finally found her voice. "I don't want to hurt you."

"I didn't say to do it, I said to try. I'm prepared for it. I'll be able to deflect you."

Without warning, he lunged again. This time she brought her knee up. Dante twisted his body, her knee catching his hip.

He grinned. "Nice." And he patted her on the shoulder.

A pat? Really?

What was going on with him?

She stepped in front of him, confused by his behavior. Dante pointed to his eyes with two fingers. "Now we move here. The eyes are vulnerable."

She squared her shoulders. Maybe they *could* start a friendship. A friendship would be nice.

"Last night, that guy grabbed you, which meant his hands

were occupied. Come here."

With one hand, he gripped her waist, pulling her forward. The closer he brought her, the tighter her lungs squeezed. He slid the fingers of his other hand into the hair at her nape. Tingles spread from her head all the way to her toes. She stared at his face, so close to hers that if she leaned forward the tiniest fraction, their lips would meet.

"Use one hand to grab the back of his neck and pull him down." He gently placed his thumb in the corner of one of her eyes and moved it back and forth. "Here's where you want to grind down with all the pressure you can."

Again, he released her and stepped back. Cait wanted to stamp her foot in frustration.

"Now your turn," he said.

She moved close to him, sliding her fingers around the back of his neck. The clipped short hair felt rough against her palm. He suddenly wrapped his arms around her body and pressed her back against the wall. She had the urge to pull his head down and kiss him, to go with the incredible need, but she needed him to make the first move, especially with the way he was acting today. Instead, she placed her thumb by his left eye and copied the movement he'd shown her.

Dante stilled, his jaw working back and forth. He shook his head and jumped back. "Good."

Why had he moved away? But she cleared her throat and said, "Next?"

Dante cleared his throat. "Right. Next." He inhaled then finally glanced at her. "The windpipe. One open-handed strike to the front of the throat can cause serious damage."

He hesitated, working his head back and forth before he

walked over to her.

"Take your hand and make a C. Then strike at the neck like you're trying to push the windpipe out the back of his throat. Or you can sink your thumb and fingers into the voice box and squeeze, pulling out. I'll let you decide which one you want to try."

He made no move to touch her. Fine. A spark of irritation lit her small fuse.

Her hand shot out and gripped his throat, squeezing a little more than necessary. When he stumbled backward, coughing, she realized what she had done.

She clapped her hands to her mouth. "Oh my God, I'm sorry."

Dante's eyes watered as he gasped for breath. He waved his hand. "You've got that one down pat," he rasped. "We can move on."

It took him a full two minutes to recover. The entire time he eyed her warily. "Did I piss you off?"

She about spit out the water she'd just sipped from her water bottle. She swallowed. "No, not at all. I didn't realize how easily I could do that."

"You ready for the final lesson?"

He sounded like he was ready to get her out of there. He had every right to be a little angry—she'd done that with way more force than necessary.

"Yeah, I promise to be more careful."

He nodded. "The foot. Stomping is your friend."

She moved close to him. At the same time Dante grabbed her hips, she lifted her leg. She teetered for balance but fell anyway, flailing her arms. She grabbed the front of his shirt. Fabric tore.

He scrambled to stop her descent then lost his footing. The soft mat cushioned her fall, but an oomph of air escaped as Dante fell on top of her. He landed on his forearms, his head directly beside hers, his long, dominant body stretched over the length of hers. A peek of tanned skin stared at her through the rip at the neck of his T-shirt. She fought the urge to shift her legs and bring him closer to the area now throbbing for his attention.

Dante lifted his head and stared down at her. She stopped breathing, his lips holding her mesmerized.

He muttered words distinctly sounding like "Fuck slow," before his mouth closed over hers.

Not soft and teasing like last time, but hard and demanding. She went with it, wrapping her arms around him and pulling him closer. Dante tilted his head, deepening the kiss. The first feel of his tongue made her skin pucker in goose bumps. The entire time he ravished her mouth, a sense of disbelief gripped her.

He kissed her like he still meant it, like he still wanted to strip her bare and lick every inch of *her* body. The thought was thrilling.

"Dante 'Inferno' Jones, what in the hell do you think you're doing?" Mike barked.

CHAPTER SEVEN

Dante jumped off Caitlyn as quickly as a teenage boy turns off the TV when caught watching porn. Raking both hands through his short-cropped hair, he stared at the blue mat.

What the hell *was* he doing?

He glanced at Caitlyn, who'd pushed up onto her elbows, her eyes wide, face pale. He offered his hand. She stared at it before taking it. Her fingers shook as his wrapped around hers. He hoped she'd meet his gaze, but her eyes focused anywhere except on him as he helped her to her feet.

Damn it.

Amy had said Caitlyn wasn't used to men like him being attracted to her. And the way Caitlyn clammed up right after she left his arms confirmed this, but the woman who came alive in his arms, the one who kissed him back fiercely, was another story.

Caitlyn was brimming with passion he'd only just tapped into, and it was begging to be released. And he could if they'd stopped being interrupted. Interruptions gave her time to think. Caitlyn didn't need to think, she needed to let go and feel—with him.

He turned to face his coach.

Fury drew Mike's normally relaxed features into harsh lines. Dante grimaced. There was nothing to say to justify his actions. He was wrong in starting anything here. Period. The tongue-lashing coming was warranted.

Mike stormed forward, pointing his finger at Caitlyn. "You. Out."

Dante tensed and stepped in front of her with his head held high. Mike could speak to him anyway he wanted, but he sure as hell couldn't speak to Caitlyn with any disrespect. "Watch your mouth, man."

Furious eyes swung to his. "I'll deal with you in a minute. First, I'll deal with her."

Caitlyn pressed against his back. "Jesus Christ, he's scary," she whispered.

He reached back and placed his hand on her thigh to reassure her. Wanting her to understand nothing bad would ever happen to her as long as he was around. He'd make damn sure of it. "Leave her out of this, Mike."

The other man stopped and clenched his fist. "You're right." Through gritted teeth, he said to Caitlyn, "Would you please excuse us?"

"Absolutely," she responded. No hesitation, no quivering, just a matter of fact "I'm getting the hell out of here" tone.

Dante turned to find her already across the mat, fumbling with her purse as she swung the strap over her shoulder. He stepped forward. A firm grip on his bicep stopped him.

"Don't you move," Mike said.

Caitlyn raced through the center, never looking back.

Tinkling bells signaled her exit. The second the door closed, Mike spun on Dante. "What in the hell are you doing?"

Dante sighed. "Not thinking."

His coach cuffed the back of his head. "Damned straight."

"Look, Mike, I'm sorry. What I did was inexcusable."

"This facility is not your personal bucking room. Do you understand?"

"It won't happen again. I swear. I don't think when I'm around Caitlyn. I react." Reacted more to her than any other woman. And he liked it.

Mike groaned and pinched the bridge of his nose. "The last thing I need is a fighter in training who's distracted while he sniffs up some gal's skirt."

Dante stiffened, not pleased with his interest in Caitlyn referred to as "sniffing," but he forced himself not to overreact. "It's not like that."

"It's *always* like that." Mike leveled him with a steely glare while he cracked his knuckles.

The action made it clear his coach was resisting the urge to literally knock some sense into him.

As far as Dante saw it, priority number one was the championship. That hadn't and wouldn't change. It didn't, however, mean he couldn't date Caitlyn in the process.

"You don't have anything to worry about. I want this title. I've always wanted the title. She won't change that. If anything, she'll push me to work harder."

"How so?"

"Would you want to lose in front of a woman you're into?"

Mike groaned. "This isn't good. I hope you're aware of that. When I took you on, I did it knowing you took your training seriously. Your other coaches spoke highly of your concentration, claimed you were never distracted." Mike pointed to the glass doors. "That's a distraction. She'll cost you this fight."

"She won't come between me and my training."

"I can't tell you what to do outside this facility, but you need to think about what you want. You're less than a month and a half from the championship fight. A woman is only going to stir trouble. Trouble you don't need."

Dante stared at the double doors. Mike was wrong. Caitlyn wasn't trouble. Oh no. She overflowed with passion she fought to keep contained. But she lost that battle every time she was in his arms. Now he wanted to make it explode. God, he loved a good fight.

Caitlyn Moore had met her match.

. . .

Unable to go home and face Amy's twenty questions, Cait detoured to the Y instead. She grabbed her gym bag and hurried through the entrance. Taking the stairs two at a time, she headed for the women's locker room. Only one place soothed her when she was as scattered as she was right now.

She ducked into a dressing room and closed the curtain. After stripping, she stared at her naked body. She had so much to be proud of. She wiggled her red-tipped painted toes. Toes she hadn't seen in years.

Yet so much of her body still dismayed her. She pinched the fat around her midsection. A midsection that never got any tauter or flatter, no matter how many crunches she suffered through.

She wrapped a beach towel around her and headed to

her sanctuary. As she stepped inside the sauna, clouds of hot steam rolled out. The humid air soaked her skin, welcoming her. She sat on the white tiled bench and inhaled the vapors.

She wanted Dante with everything in her. There. She'd finally admitted it to herself. She wanted him and she could have him, easily. So why didn't she call him up and get things rolling?

She looked down at the towel covering her body.

One thing.

The door opened. A naked woman entered the steam room. Cait watched her through the foggy haze, fascinated at her confidence. The auburn-haired woman was short and far from skinny. If she had to guess, she'd put the other woman about sixty pounds overweight. Yet, she walked with a self-assurance that outdid that of most thin women.

The woman jumped when she realized she wasn't alone. "Excuse me. Normally, no one's in here at this time of day."

Cait smiled. "Spur of the minute decision on my part."

The woman folded her white towel on the bench then sat. "Do you mind?" She gestured to her body. "I can wrap in a towel if you do."

"No, please, I envy your confidence."

"Why be ashamed? It's the body I have."

Why, indeed?

Cait stared down at the wet floor tiles. "Can I ask you a question without you taking offense?"

"Sure, sweetie, ask away."

"Have you always felt like that or did you have to learn to think like that?"

A thoughtful expression crossed the woman's damp face. "I used to beat myself up over my body. What woman doesn't?" She paused, as if thinking about her words. "I finally decided I'd had enough. It was time to believe in me, without shame. I still slip up and have doubts. But for the most part, I take pride in who I am."

Cait mulled over her words, knowing they were the same things Amy and Paul had repeated to her over the last year. Somehow, coming from this woman, it felt different. Truer.

"What did you do to make it happen?"

"Small stuff at first. Nice clothes, got my nails done, bought pretty panties. Anything that made me feel good about myself. It wasn't overnight. Like I said, I still struggle with it. I figure I will until the day I die. But I made a decision, and I plan to stick with it." Then a wicked smile turned her lips. "And guess what?"

"What?"

"The men like the confidence, too." She laughed. "I mean, *really* like it."

The words reached somewhere deep into Cait's soul. "Thank you."

"You're a pretty little thing. You shouldn't be self-conscious."

"I think you're right." Cait stood and started for the door. "I've made a decision."

If she wanted to have Dante in her bed, and she did, she had to let go of her insecurities.

She grabbed the knot and let the towel drop away as she opened the door. The cool air kissed her skin.

The other woman clapped and hollered, "You go, girl."

Cait closed the door behind her. Looking down the long corridor of lockers, she inhaled deeply. She thrust her shoulders back, tilted her chin forward.

Then, for the first time, she walked through the women's locker room naked.

Surrounded by racks upon racks of nothing-there panties and bras, Cait fingered the black lacy underwear. The woman had said to buy things that made her feel good about herself. As she studied the thin wisp of fabric, the last thing she felt was good. She felt horrified. The images this simple piece of material created were something compared to a slasher flick—gruesome, grotesque, and terrifying.

"Oh Cait, butt floss? Really?"

She gave Paul a wry smile. She'd called him about twenty minutes ago to come and help her shop. "So even this horrifies you?"

"Two words. Hairy ass." He shuddered. She laughed.

He plucked the panties from her hand. "This is so not you. I can't even believe you're looking at it."

Paul stepped a little farther down the racks. "Now this I can see you in." He held up a pair of pink boy shorts.

Cait eyed the material. They were cute. She'd never shopped for pretty panties, just reached for her old faithful, a four-pack of cotton underwear. She ran her thumb over the shorts.

Soft.

She liked.

As she drew her hand back, Paul snatched her fingers, staring at them in amazement. "Girl, did you get your nails done?"

"Don't look so shocked."

"Seriously?" He held up his hand, shaking his head.

"Did you seriously just say that to me? I've tried for years to get you to go with me to get a mani-pedi. But you called it frivolous. Who's being frivolous now?"

Words always had a way of coming back and biting her in the ass. "I have no problem admitting when I am wrong."

She studied the shiny tips. She *had* thought it frivolous to get her nails done, but ever since she'd waltzed inside the salon and had her fingers pampered, she couldn't stop admiring them. The French-manicured tips made her hands look feminine and pretty.

Paul narrowed his eyes as he studied her. "What's going on with you?"

"What?"

"Cait Moore does not willingly go shopping."

"Let's just say I had a fairy godmother give me a little advice."

"And what advice was that?"

She grimaced. "To accept myself for who I am."

Paul gasped, his hand flying to his throat. "I've been telling you that *forever*." He gave her a snotty look, then whirled and stomped off.

"Ah, Paul." She ran after him and grabbed his arm. "I know you've told me that over and over again." He crossed his arms, nose in the air. "It was good advice. It was just different coming from this woman. She's been there. It was like talking to myself."

"And it sank in?"

"Yes."

"Good." He smiled. "It's about damned time."

"This isn't going to be some magic turnaround. You understand that, right?"

"The fact you came here by yourself without any encouragement is a huge step and I'm proud of you." He wrapped an arm around her shoulder and led her back to the underwear. "Besides, now I have a shopping buddy. Amy can be such a drag."

Cait laughed.

"Does Mr. Ripples have anything to do with this, too?"

She should've seen that coming. "Maybe. We'll see."

"Give it time, Cait."

Time. How much time did she really have? If he planned to go back home after his fight, she didn't have much time and it was slipping away. Could she overcome her fear before it was too late?

She pushed the thoughts aside when Paul thrust a pair of red panties at her. Lingerie now, worrying later.

By the time they finished, she clutched six pink bags in her hands—a complete new wardrobe of underwear, ranging from sexy to fun. Each pair camouflaged enough of her stomach to make her comfortable, yet still feel flirty. What was it about panties that made a girl feel good?

At Paul's urging, she bought a white camisole with his instructions to wear it with the pink boy shorts. Why, she didn't know and really didn't care. His taste was impeccable, and she trusted his judgment.

Cait smiled as she left the mall. She had a long way to go, but she was on the right path.

• • •

Dante knocked on Caitlyn's door. A surprised Amy answered.

"Sorry to come by without calling first. I need to speak

to Caitlyn."

"No worries, come on in," Amy said, waving him inside.

He entered. No sign of Caitlyn. He'd hoped to catch her by surprise, catch her with her guard down. Now Amy would traipse back to her room and warn her.

"Hey, Amy…" Caitlyn trotted into the living room and stopped cold.

He couldn't tear his eyes away from her. More of her skin than he'd ever been privileged to see was displayed before him. Silky pink boy shorts hugged her hips, defining their fullness with articulate care. The hem rode high on her thighs, revealing muscular legs. They weren't beanpole thin with no shape, like some of the women he knew.

His gaze roamed the white camisole molding to her like a second skin, skimmed full breasts trying to spill out, traced along her delicate collarbone, then up her long neck before finally meeting her eyes.

Dante's heart thudded, and he was perilously close to embarrassing himself like a thirteen-year-old boy. He took a deep breath, trying to control the blood roaring in a downward spiral.

Caitlyn grabbed a pillow off the couch and held it in front of her. "Dante. I wasn't expecting you."

"Obviously." Even to his ears, the words emerged like a croak. He cleared his throat. "I wanted to make sure you were all right."

She moved behind the couch, blocking his view of her legs, the damned pillow still clutched to her chest. "Yeah, I'm fine."

An awkward silence fell around them. Amy darted glances between the two. "Well, this has been fun, but I've got to go." She was out the door before either could say anything.

The temperature rose twenty degrees. He was alone, with Caitlyn, in her apartment. Everything he wanted, but her frightened fawn look kept him planted.

"I wanted to apologize for Mike."

She waved, dislodging the pillow. She juggled, then righted the barrier once again.

"Put the pillow down, Caitlyn."

"Ain't no way in hell that's happening."

"Then change into something else." He turned his back. Right now, a clothed Caitlyn was a much better idea than a partially naked one. Her exposed skin was too much of a temptation, and he doubted he'd be able to resist.

Who was he kidding? There was no way he could resist. He'd proven that this morning.

He heard her pad down the hall and when the door closed, he stepped into the living room and sank on the couch. The silence disturbed him. It brought an awareness of her he needed to keep under lock and key, at least for now.

Picking her up and taking her back to her room—or hell, laying her right here on this couch—wasn't an option. Yet.

She returned, plopping on the chair across from him. He frowned at her clothing choice. The floppy shirt and jogging pants said "Stay back" as clearly as any blinking neon sign. Dante sighed. Yep, she'd had time to think. It was time to do things his way.

"Like I said, before you dashed out of here like a scared rabbit—"

"I didn't dash." She stiffened, her shoulders going straight.

"You could've fooled me."

"I was in my nightclothes. It was inappro—"

"I liked it." He scooted to the edge of the couch and leaned his elbows on his knees. "A lot."

Her face went fiery red.

The magnitude of what Amy told him hit home. Caitlyn truly was inexperienced. Had no idea how to handle a guy giving her a compliment or expressing how fucking hot he found her. How was it possible?

The woman drove him crazy. Men should be lining up at her door.

"Listen, Caitlyn. Amy has told me to take it slow with you. To get to know you and let things happen naturally. That doesn't work for me. It's more frustrating to pretend I want to be a friend than to just ask you out." He met her eyes. "So here it is. Caitlyn, would like to go on a date Wednesday night?"

He held his breath while he waited for her answer. He'd gone against everything Amy had advised, but it was time to put the cards on the table.

Silence stretched between them…and then stretched some more. The grandfather clock in the corner ticked like a time bomb. He finally exhaled and scowled. Why was it taking her so damned long to answer?

She sat in the chair, twisting her fingers together as if this was the hardest decision of her life. Inexperienced or not, was it really that hard for her to go out with him?

He slapped his hands on his thighs. She jumped.

"Okay, I guess I have my answer. I won't bother you anymore." He stood and stalked toward the door. At the same time his hand closed around the doorknob, he felt a light touch on his bicep.

"Don't go."

The whispered words hung in the air. Dante glanced over his shoulder. She wasn't looking at him. Instead, she seemed to find the floor fascinating. He turned and lifted her chin with his finger.

He searched her green eyes, finding vulnerability and unmistakable desire that caused his heart to skip a beat. "Why is it so hard to say yes?"

She swallowed. "You're more than I'm used to, Dante. I'm not sure if I find the idea scary or exciting."

The raw honesty in her confession allowed him a glimpse into Caitlyn Moore. He saw a woman desperately wanting to say yes but... A fierce need to protect her both overwhelmed and stunned him.

"I'm still just a man, Caitlyn. A man insanely attracted to you. And I would really like to take you out." He kissed her tiny nose. "What do you say?"

She inhaled a quivering breath. "Yes."

"See? That wasn't so hard now, was it?"

"No, that wasn't so hard." She shivered.

He kissed each corner of her mouth then lowered his forehead to hers. "We'll have fun. I promise."

With one last chaste kiss, he opened the door and left. Sticking around her apartment would only increase her anxiety. She needed time to absorb what had changed between them.

Wednesday night, however, all bets were off.

CHAPTER EIGHT

What had she done? That was the question of the day.

Day? Ha! More like week. No, year. Heck, lifetime.

Cait stepped around the cars in the parking lot as she headed toward the YMCA. The promise of a killer headache whispered at the back of her eyes. A headache would be welcomed. It'd give her an excuse to cancel this outrageous date.

She snorted. Dante would never buy that. Knowing him, he'd show up on her doorstep with a glass of water in one hand and two ibuprofen tablets in the other. The ailment would have to be more serious. Something not so easily remedied.

Flu?

Stomach virus?

Bubonic plague?

No, none of those would work. Cait snatched the sunglasses off her nose and stuffed them in her purse before she yanked open the door.

Her stupid sensitivity. One glimpse of hurt in Dante's expressive blue eyes and she'd crumbled. She'd wanted more time, time to stand in front of the mirror naked, to accept herself, to be ready to handle this very fine man and give him everything he deserved *when* they finally slept together.

Yet here she was, two days later, a date planned, with him. She had no other option but to say yes. Not after his reaction to her silence. He'd been hurt, which confused her, but she'd had to make a decision. So she'd made one. She only hoped it wouldn't blow up in her face.

She hurried down the long corridor toward the fitness room. In ten minutes, her first class would start, which she was emotionally unprepared for. The Dante distraction couldn't have come at a worse time. She needed to focus on her program and on helping others. Not on an overdeveloped muscle man.

Oh, but what an overdeveloped muscle man.

Ack! No more!

Cait mentally slammed the door on all thoughts of Dante. Stopping outside the fitness room, she peered inside. Twenty-five people—ranging from thirty to one hundred and fifty pounds overweight—waited.

She spotted Becky talking to another woman, and Cait smiled. She'd been worried those heckling boys had run her off.

Clapping her hands, Cait walked into the room. The crowd stilled and went silent, watching her every move. A moment of nerves fluttered in her chest, and she hesitated in her opening speech.

They struggle the same as you. They are not here to judge.

The reminder calmed her and she took a deep breath.

"Welcome to Altering Assumptions! I'm Caitlyn Moore. You can call me Cait. I'm very happy to see you all here today. You've taken the first step to a new you. Everyone here deserves a pat on the back. I'm going to open today's session with questions. Anyone?"

A man with glasses stood in the back and timidly raised his hand. She read the white nametag stuck to his green shirt. "Yes, Doug?"

He fiddled with his glasses. "Why did you start this program?"

"For a couple of reasons. I've always been overweight." She held up her hand when grumbles started. "Before some of you get too carried away in your 'What does she know about being overweight' rant—I've lost eight pounds. So trust me, I know the struggles."

Eyes widened around the room. Hands flew into the air. Cait shook her head. "One question at a time. Let me finish this one first. One of the hardest things I had to learn to conquer was the assumptions I had about myself. I'd tried every diet in the book and always failed. Why would this time be any different? It was hard in the beginning. I felt so alone, and building the confidence that I *would* succeed wasn't easy. I would've given anything to be a part of a group that truly understood. I started tossing around the idea for a program like this about two years ago."

"What made you finally do it?" Doug asked.

Cait smiled. "My second reason clinched it. About a year and half ago, an incident occurred that stayed with me. I'd come to the gym for a run. I stepped up on a treadmill next to this super skinny chick I'd never seen here before. We exchanged smiles, and I started my warmup."

She started to pace the room. "The chick beside me was walking at a slow pace, *until* I finished my warmup and booted up to a run. Next thing I know, she's running beside me. The poor thing probably had never run a day in her life. Her form was all wrong with her arms flailing, legs all over the place as she tried to keep up with me. She made it about a minute. Then she stopped the treadmill and took a walk around the gym to catch her breath."

Cait stopped. "You'd think this was the end of my story. It's not. I do intervals when I run, two-minute run, one-minute walk. That day, I'd powered down to my walk, then I went back up to my run. I kid you not, the chick saw me running again. She hopped back up on a treadmill, a different treadmill from before, mind you—and broke out into a sprint. She made it about thirty seconds before she had to hit the emergency brake on the machine and leave the gym. She assumed because I was overweight, she should have been able to keep up with me. She was wrong. I may still be overweight, but I *am* physically fit. There are two types of assumptions—the ones you have about yourself, and the ones other people have about you. We're here to change them both.

"This room is a place of camaraderie, where everyone has the same goal, has had the same struggles. There will be no judgment in this class. We are here to support one another and if we never find our way to skinny, at least we'll find our way to fit."

Applause erupted from the members. Her heart hammering, she looked at each individual. Hope and determination shone back at her.

She'd done this. She'd given them reason to be here, to

want to be here. It was everything she'd dreamed of when she'd created this program. She refused to fail them. And the more encouragement she gave them, the more she realized she needed to do the same for herself.

• • •

The sound of Caitlyn's voice drifting out of the fitness room stopped Dante in his tracks. He slowly stepped backward to peer inside. She stood in the middle of a group of people. Her eyes were bright, tension absent from her face. It was the first time he'd seen her with her guard down and what he saw awed him.

He remained behind the door so he wouldn't be seen, but could easily watch.

"Who has ever felt uneasy coming to the gym? Ever felt like a class was judged as easy just because you were in it?"

Dante's brows furrowed. She'd said something similar at the deli.

A majority of the hands went up.

"Who has felt embarrassed to go to a class concerned they wouldn't be able to keep up or be forced to walk out?"

The hands stayed in the air.

"Who is tired of feeling this way?"

The hands rose higher, fingers wiggling.

"That, class, is what we're here for today. Now let's get down to business. Everyone grab a step. No risers."

Once the class had their platforms on the floor, Caitlyn arranged her microphone around her head, then started the music. Upbeat 1980s rock and roll filled the room. Dante stood mesmerized at her take-charge attitude. There was no hesitance, no shyness, no vulnerability. The woman before him was completely confident in her ability to lead this class. It was the most erotic thing he'd ever seen.

Hands on her hips, she stepped from side to side. "Let's get your heart pumping."

The class mimicked her movement, and Dante lost his view of Caitlyn behind the jostling bodies. He shifted, careful not to be discovered and ruin her mood.

Finally, he found a spot that made her the center of his observation, and he soaked up every relaxed feature, every genuine smile, and every sweet laugh. How he wanted her to be like this with him, so carefree and full of life.

Would he ever get past the barriers she erected any time he was around? He wanted a chance, a legitimate chance, to win her over. Hopefully, tonight he'd get the opportunity.

As the hour progressed, her personality became stronger, more dominant. Dante found it hard to stay concealed. Everything in him wanted to stride over and kiss her senseless. This Caitlyn was a dangerous turn-on. Someone he'd find it hard to take it slow with. Hell, he was already having problems with that as it was.

He watched as she pushed her attendees. At times, she reminded Dante of how Mike pushed him to the point of collapse. Never relenting, and expecting everything in return. But unlike Mike, her energy was so high and enthusiastic she carried the class along, pushing them harder that they realized.

"Can you feel it?" she yelled.

No answer.

"I can't hear you! Can you feel it?"

She received mumbles.

"You can do better than that! Yell if you can feel it." The

whip-like authority in her voice shot a bolt of lust through him, and he stifled a groan.

The class hollered. God knew he wanted to holler, too.

A young woman in the back of the class stopped, hands on her abundant hips, chest heaving, frustration clear on her beet-red face.

Caitlyn focused on her. "Don't you give up. Keep moving. I know you're tired, but dig deep. You can do this."

The girl inhaled, nodded, and with determined steps, continued her workout.

As the class drew to an end, Caitlyn become more aggressive. Energy zinged in the room—and through him—but he could tell that despite her whooping and hollering, the members were drained. Some barely kept up the relatively slow pace that Caitlyn had set, while others simply stopped, bent over at the waist as they dragged in huge mouthfuls of air.

Dante felt bad for them. From what he could see, the participants in this room didn't exercise much, if at all. Caitlyn's workout hadn't been easy by any means. These people should be proud of themselves for hanging in for as long as they had.

"This is where the real work begins! You're tired. You want to give up. Never give up. Don't let your mind stop you."

How true those words were, and as she intended, her comment had an impact on the class. Every member got their second wind, straightening and doing as she demanded.

She was so motivating, inspiring, as if she knew exactly what each person in her class was struggling through. How could she be so in tune with them?

Dante observed the remainder of the class. The woman never ceased to amaze him. He knew two different people: the shy, vulnerable Caitlyn, and the confident, leader Caitlyn. Both drew him. Both sparked desire he found exciting. But which persona was the real Caitlyn?

When the class ended, the members hung around to ask her questions. Dante impatiently waited as she smiled and gave encouragement. He wanted to see what would happen when she became aware of his presence. Would she withdraw, or was she so pumped from her class that he'd get a taste of this Caitlyn?

Finally, the last member left the room and Dante emerged from his hiding place. Her eyes rounded, and she stopped wiping sweat off her chest with a towel.

"How long have you been watching?" Her gaze darted around the room, never truly meeting his eyes.

So she'd reverted. He swallowed his disappointment at being the cause. No. *He* wasn't the cause. There was another, deeper reason. Could he coax her to finally share her story? Let him understand what made her so hesitant to get to know him? "Most of the class, honestly. Caitlyn, you're a fantastic instructor."

Red flamed her cheeks. "Thank you."

The way she'd expressed that, as if she was unsure he meant it, pushed him to make her understand. "I'm not blowing smoke here." He stopped in front of her. "You were fantastic."

The corners of her mouth twitched, and Dante saw a glimpse of the other Caitlyn. His heart stuttered. He chucked her under the chin. "Smile. You know you want to."

One corner of her mouth lifted, her eyes brightened with

amusement. Oh, he liked her gazing up at him like this.

"I've never seen an instructor so in tune with her class. It was like you knew what they were thinking."

Her smile disappeared.

What had he said now? He reviewed his comment in his head. No, there was no way that could've been taken wrong.

Caitlyn gave a long, drawn out sigh. "It's because I *do* know what they are thinking."

"How so?"

"Lord, Dante. Are you going to make me come out and say it? I used to be extremely overweight." She squared her shoulders and met his gaze dead on. "Obese."

Shock was his first reaction.

Seeing her now, it never occurred to him she'd had a weight problem. However, as the information sank in, everything started to make sense—the big clothes, the shyness, the hesitation, Amy's warning.

Why she had such a hard time coping with the attraction sizzling between them.

"Wow." What should he say? "Congratulations" sounded completely stupid. So he went with, "That's awesome." Dante grimaced. That sounded dumb as well.

Caitlyn shrugged off his words. "Yeah, well, I'm still working on it."

He frowned. She didn't need to lose another pound. She was gorgeous. Inside and out.

Dante studied her. Other than the direct eye contact when she said the word "obese," she had avoided meeting his gaze. Instead, she scuffed her sneaker on the floor. Judging by her bowed head, he assumed the motion fascinated her.

The conversation with Amy came back. Caitlyn wasn't

just dealing with insecurities; she was dealing with a whole new her. From everything slowly becoming apparent, she was having a hell of a time dealing with her new life and her new body.

Dante fought a smile. He'd help her find herself, and in the process, show her how beautiful she was through his eyes.

. . .

When Dante remained silent, Cait peered at him, searching for any sign of disgust or withdrawal. She saw neither. She'd dreaded the moment she would have to inform him about her weight problems. Not that she was ashamed of it. Far from it. But telling someone who'd never had a weight issue, who'd made it his life to be physically perfect, that she struggled every day to do the same was daunting.

He regarded her curiously. "How much weight have you lost?"

"Eighty pounds."

Other than the widening of his eyes, he gave no reaction. "Impressive. How'd you do it?"

"Hard work and determination."

He smiled, drawing her attention to the slight tilt of his lips. Memories of his mouth on hers, soft and caressing, were an aphrodisiac and she prayed he'd kiss her again tonight.

Damn it, she'd spent the last hour not thinking about him at all, and now all she could see were images of them doing some heavy petting on a couch, floor, table — heck, she'd take the top of the washing machine. Spin cycle.

"I guess you'd know a little about hard work, wouldn't you?" she asked.

A full smile split his lips, and Cait thought she'd melt into a puddle at his feet.

"Just a little." He caressed her cheek. "I loved your 'Don't let the mind stop you' comment, by the way."

Pleasure rippled in her chest. He hadn't just watched, he'd listened. And he'd picked up on the one line she tried to adhere to daily—unless Dante was involved. Her mind was her worst enemy there, but she'd beaten the can't-do-it thought process before, and she would again.

"I had an instructor say that in one of my classes about three months after I joined the Y. I was so close to quitting again and his words inspired me." She started toward the exit. Dante fell into step beside her. "It's amazing how much your mind can work against you. But those words reached deep inside and made me determined to succeed. I stopped worrying about what everyone else thought when they saw me work out. Instead, I concentrated on me and my workout. My intensity level went up after that, and I started to love working out."

"So you decided to start a fitness program to help other people who are trying to lose weight?" He kept his attention on her while they walked through the Y and outside.

"It wasn't just to help them lose weight. I wanted to give them a place to go so they don't feel dissected by everyone around them. Everyone in the class is facing the same struggle, so I'm hoping my program will give them an environment to succeed from the get-go instead of having to wake up everyday and talk themselves into going to the gym."

He grasped her hand and tugged her to sit beside him on a bench by the entrance. She stared at his thumb rubbing up and down on hers, feeling the warmth of the movement heat her skin.

"Did you want such a place?"

Inhaling, she dragged her gaze from their entwined fingers up to his eyes. "I did. I even tried working out at home, but I needed guidance, so I forced myself to the gym every day and never felt comfortable."

"Why?"

"It felt like everyone who looked at me was thinking I didn't belong here. It took me a long time to accept that it wasn't *them* thinking that, it was *me*."

"Do you still feel that way?"

"No, not anymore. Occasionally, an incident will knock my confidence, even as far as I've come, but it's much easier to let it go now than it was before."

"Like what?"

Was she really telling him all this? Why was it suddenly so easy to open up to him and let him in?

"A few months ago, I took a class given by a new instructor. It was only her second day, so we hadn't crossed paths yet. After the class, she came up to me, patted me on the shoulder, and congratulated me on how well I'd kept up. She then proceeded to tell me if I kept up the good work, I'd be thin in no time."

Dante reared back, scowling. "Are you kidding me?"

"It's the honest to God truth. She didn't say it out of malice. I knew she was trying to be encouraging, but I was stunned, so all I could do was smile and thank her. A couple of days later, after she realized who I was, she apologized." Cait shook her head. "I'm not sure which was worse, what she said or her apologizing for what she thought."

"I'm sorry." He squeezed her hand.

"Hey, you have nothing to be sorry for. In the end, the encounter gave me even more validation that I was doing the right thing by starting this program."

"How's the program set up?"

"Right now, I have two beginner classes five days a week. One in the morning and one in the evening. In twelve weeks, I'll add a more advanced class."

"What about diet plans?"

She shook her head. "I decided against that. We'll have biweekly meetings with a Q&A session afterward. I'll give them the basics, and for those who want to be in a program, I'll offer some options, but which program they choose is up to them."

"Wouldn't it be easier having them all on the same plan?"

"Does every fighter follow the same training workout?"

"Well, no. Every fighter has a different area he has to focus on more."

"And that is why I decided against a structured diet plan. What worked for me might not work for them. They need to find the diet that fits their lifestyle. If I give them the plan I followed and they hate it, I'm setting them up for failure. God knows how many I tried before I found one I wasn't miserable on. They have to do the same."

"How many had you tried?"

"Dante, I've always been overweight." Sighing, she gestured at her body. "This is the smallest I've ever been. How many do you think I've tried?"

"It's a big change for you, isn't it?"

Cait laughed. "That's an understatement. I'm starting over, especially with—" she paused, then sighed—"men. I haven't dated much."

There. She'd said it. It was out.

He remained silent, studying her intently. What was he thinking? Was he realizing just how green she was? Did he regret asking her out now?

His grip on her hand tightened, his face serious. "Thanks for letting me in, Caitlyn."

He leaned closer to her, and just like that the ease she felt talking to him combusted to an all-out awareness. The side of his thigh and hip pressed into hers. Their shoulders brushed. When he tugged her hand to turn her upper body toward him, her breath caught.

"It means a lot to me that you shared this with me."

He brushed his lips against hers before leaning his forehead against hers. "I have a sparring session with Mike in twenty minutes. I have to go, but I don't want to. I want to stay here with you."

Her breath seized tight in her chest. Oh, man. "It's okay. I understand. You have to train."

He squeezed her hand before capturing another brief kiss. "I'll pick you up at seven."

As he walked away, she rubbed her bottom lip. She could get very used to kissing Dante. She only hoped kissing was all he had in mind tonight.

CHAPTER NINE

"What do you think?" Cait turned uncertainly, viewing every angle in the mirror. The light jeans skirt hit her mid-thigh while the black halter-top showed way too much of her upper body. She felt virtually naked, and she didn't like it at all.

She threw up her hands. "I'm not ready to wear something like this!"

Groaning, Paul shook his head and shifted on her bed. "Sure you are. You're gorgeous."

"I shouldn't have allowed you to pick my outfit."

"Why? Scared you'll get laid tonight?"

Cait whirled. "I most certainly will *not* get laid tonight."

She refused to consider the possibility. So many different emotions tore at her at the mere idea of sleeping with Dante. Fear. Horror. Excitement. Want. She couldn't even think about the last two until she eliminated the first two. Hopefully, tonight would help.

"Whatever you say, Cait. My guess is Muscle Man will

be itching to get into your pants the minute he sees you." He waved toward her. "Therefore, the skirt. It'll help him reach his goal more easily."

"Is that seriously why you have me in a skirt?"

"What can I say, it's been a long time and a good fu—"

"Don't you even say it!"

She didn't want to think about the word, let alone the actual physical act.

But it was too late. Images she had no business picturing slammed at her mind. Dante behind her. Dante between her legs. Dante inside her. Lust pooled low in her stomach and sent tingles racing into her lower anatomy. Oh, she was doomed.

"You're thinking about it!"

Paul's accusation snapped her out of her fantasies. "Shut up." She undid the button on her skirt. "I'm not wearing this."

"Oh, yes you are."

"You can't make me."

"You wanna bet? Don't wear it, and I'm parking my ass on your couch until lover boy gets here. Then I'll let him make the decision."

"Come on, Paul. Let me wear jeans."

"I thought you were trying to change."

"I am! But that doesn't mean I have to flaunt my butt in 'A come and get it' skirt. I'm not ready to encourage that. Just the other night I wore baggy sweats and shirt to *discourage* him. Now I'm wearing this. Talk about sending mixed signals."

"Trust me. He's going to like this signal. A lot."

A lot. Dante had said the same thing. She glanced at the mirror and recalled the desire she'd glimpsed in his eyes as he took in her night attire. More skin was visible then than what she showed now. So Paul was probably right. He'd like this, too.

"Hey, Cait—" Amy rushed into Cait's room and stopped dead. "Oh my God, you're gorgeous."

Well, that clinched it. Cait faced her friend. "You think?"

"Jeez, Dante won't be able to keep his hands off you."

"Told you," Paul said with a smirk.

Cait bit her lip. Her attraction to Dante was fierce, but what if her insecurities won out when things got heated tonight? And she didn't doubt things would get heated. Was it fair to him to wear a tempting outfit, then beg off when the passion got too hot? Would he think her nothing but a tease?

The fates decided for her. The doorbell rang. Her gaze flew to the radio clock on her nightstand.

6:58.

Oh, God. Dante. She fumbled with the button on her skirt.

"Oh no, you don't." Paul jumped to his feet at the same time Amy rushed to her. The two grabbed her arms and dragged her from her room. Paul slammed the door behind them and braced his body against it.

"Come on. Please."

"Not on your life. You're wearing the damned skirt."

The doorbell rang again. A heavy sensation squeezed her chest and made it difficult to draw a breath.

Paul rolled his eyes. "For God sakes, Cait, it's just a skirt, not the end of the world."

The doorbell rang with more persistence, as if Dante were holding down the buzzer.

"He's going to leave, thinking you ditched him," Amy said, crossing her arms. "You want that? 'Cause I don't think you do."

No, damn it, she didn't.

"Fine." Cait pushed past her friends and walked to the door. She would pretend their date was no big deal. That she was cool as a freaking cucumber and nothing fazed her. As she reached for the doorknob, she closed her eyes and inhaled. The piercing sound of the bell jerked her into action, and she opened the blasted door.

"Hey—" All thoughts of feigning nonchalance died on her lips. A bouquet of beautiful daisies greeted her.

Don't you cry.

Dante stepped over the threshold. Confidence oozed from his relaxed posture. Damn him.

"My gut told me you would prefer these over roses." He held out the flowers.

His gut was right. She hated roses. They were fancy and frivolous, but daisies, flowers that could be picked in a field of wildflowers, were something different. Something special. His ability to pick up such a detail about her, after only a short acquaintance, unnerved her.

She took the flowers. "Thank you. I'll get a vase."

Cait turned and spied her friends standing in the hallway, their arms crossed, happy smiles on their faces. Amy mouthed, "Have fun." Then she and Paul disappeared into Amy's room.

Dante followed her into the kitchen and leaned against the door frame. "You're breathtaking, Caitlyn."

Desire flared in his eyes. He meant it. This wasn't a comment to calm her frazzled nerves, but an earnest statement of truth. She fought a smile. "Thank you."

He pushed off the door frame and came to stand in front of her. The combed cotton fabric of his black shirt molded to his chest, clearly defining his broad shoulders and narrow waist. His biceps bulged beneath the straining fabric of his short sleeves. So big. So overwhelming. Cait swallowed.

Dante caressed her cheek with the backs of his fingers. Heat fired her skin, and she couldn't help but rub against his hand. "God, Caitlyn. You're making it very hard for me to be gentlemanly."

His words startled her. She stepped away from him, confused at her easy surrender to his touch. "I'm sorry."

"I'm not complaining. I just don't want to push you for more than you're ready to give."

That comforted her. "Let's see where the night takes us. No promises, no commitments. Just get to know each other."

A slow grin spread over his lips. "I'd like that."

"So where are you taking me?"

Once in a blue moon, Cait went on the traditional boring date that an average Joe took a girl on. Restaurant. Movie. Maybe a peck on the lips at the door.

Why she'd expected the same from Dante, she'd never know. Dante was anything but average or traditional.

Cait squealed as a man picked up his opponent and dropped him on the canvas with a booming thud. Squeezing her eyes closed, she blocked out the awful sight. She hated this.

"You okay?" Dante asked.

"No."

He cupped the back of her neck and rubbed the muscles. The sudden touch made her tense even more. He paused in his motion, then pulled his hand away.

"No, don't stop." She sent him a shy smile. "I liked it."

His pupils dilated as a crooked grin curved his lips. "Yeah? Well, I like touching you."

Wow. A stuttered breath shot past her lips as her heart thumped. When he replaced his hand, she closed her eyes and relaxed into his palm, enjoying the feel of his fingers kneading her nape. Sighing in pleasure, she craned her neck to the side, allowing him better access.

She heard a harsh breath from Dante. "Jesus, woman."

Her eyes popped open. His face was dark with a fierce expression she couldn't decipher. "What?"

Dante shook his head. "You really have no clue, do you?"

"About what?"

He leaned over and whispered in her ear, "How fucking hot you make me."

Her nipples immediately puckered, and an ache pulsed to life between her legs. No one had ever said anything like that to her. And it was thrilling.

Dante straightened and returned his attention to the fight as he continued rubbing her neck.

"Remember, these guys love to fight," he said.

How could he think about the fight after what he'd just said? Her attention was still focused on his whispered confession and the memory of his warm breath heating her ear. *Girl, focus.* She forced her gaze back to the cage. "But why? It has to be painful."

As if to prove her point, the fighter in red shorts twisted the leg of the guy in black shorts into some kind of pretzel-looking move. At any moment, Cait was sure his leg would rip right off. Talk about a mood killer. She slapped her hands over her eyes, then peeked through spread fingers. "See!"

Dante chuckled and pulled her hands from her face. "These guys love every second of what they're doing. Trust me. They want to be in that cage."

Cage. So that was what they called the fence surrounding the octagon-shaped ring. Fitting.

"Watch them," Dante insisted. "Tell me what you see."

Both fighters were on their feet exchanging punches to any open body part. Disgusted, she winced. "Two men beating the bloody crap out of each other."

A slight smile tilted his lips. "You know what I see?"

"What?"

"A fighter challenging himself against another highly trained opponent, just like any other sport."

"Why not play baseball, then?" A sport that didn't involve so much blood.

Dante laughed. "I can't hit a ball to save my life, but I can throw a punch."

"But it's so violent."

"To you it looks brutal and bloody. It's not for the fighter. What you see as violent, I see as heart. The will to survive. The sport we play challenges a man in the most extreme way."

Cait stared at the octagon. That made no sense. Maybe she wasn't meant to understand. She was a woman. And, heaven help her, he was all man. Two very different mind frames.

The red-shorts fighter jabbed and caught the other on the chin. His head snapped back and he stumbled before catching his balance. Good God. She winced. "Doesn't it hurt?"

"Well, yeah. Depending on the fight, I can be pretty beat up afterward."

The black-shorts fighter retaliated by landing a kick to the other's head, which knocked the red-shorts guy to the canvas. Cait's stomach knotted at the brutality and the way the crowd cheered them on. "Why do people want to watch this?"

Dante quirked a brow, amusement dancing in his eyes. "I can explain that. You're at a football game and a fight breaks out in the stands."

When he paused, Cait lifted her own brow. "Okay."

His grin turned mischievous. "Which are you going to watch?"

All right, she got his point. "The fight."

"Correct."

Put that way, the huge fan base for MMA made sense. Not that she intended to join the ranks—she couldn't even watch the men circle each other without flinching. Just the anticipation of witnessing a bone snap was too much to handle.

Cait pointed to the cage. "How do you feel when you're in there?"

"Alive."

And she sensed he did by the way he gazed longingly at the ring. Was he thinking about his upcoming fight?

"Are you ready for your match?"

His gaze swung to meet hers. "I still have some work to do with my ground game—"

"Ground game?"

"What they're doing right now." He jerked his head toward the spectacle in front of them.

Black shorts was sprawled across the upper chest of red shorts, who held his barely gloved hands up to protect his head from the blows his opponent was delivering to his temple.

"That's called a half guard."

Dante's breath brushed her cheek. She brought her gaze back to his. He'd snaked his arm along the back of her stadium seat, leaning forward, their faces inches apart. Oh, man. Her breath caught. Dante crowding her definitely made her aware of him, especially when his eyes dropped to her mouth. Her tongue slipped out to wet her lips. A growl came from Dante.

Damn, but she loved that sound.

Clearing his throat, he glanced forward again. "That right there is called a guillotine choke."

Cait followed his gaze and recoiled, shattering the moment. Red shorts had turned the tables and was sitting on his butt with black shorts' head caught in a tight headlock. "He's going to break his neck."

"Nah, just cut off his oxygen. He's either going to tap or pass out."

"Are you serious?"

Dante chuckled. "Yeah."

Sure enough, not five seconds after Dante's prediction, the man whose head was caught in a vise slapped his opponent's bicep with his hand. The referee intervened and quickly separated the two.

That must have been a tap.

The poor half-suffocated guy lay back on the floor,

staring at the ceiling. Even from their seats, Cait saw him struggle to catch his breath. And Dante did this for a living?

The man was crazy.

He rubbed one of her bare shoulders with his warm palm. "You look a little shell-shocked."

"It's hard to believe you do this and you don't even wear gloves."

"We wear gloves."

Her brows rose. "You call that measly padding around your knuckles gloves?"

He shrugged. "We're not traditional boxers. There's more to MMA than seeing who can throw the strongest punch. You have so many different types of martial arts your hands have to be available. Heavier gloves would interfere."

Dante spent the next hour explaining his world to her. By the time the fights were over and they were back in his truck, her mind was in a whirlwind. There were so many different terms for the torture these men inflicted on each other—the Kimura, the knee bar, and the triangle choke, just as a start. The list went on and on, and Dante enjoyed every minute of it.

A few times he'd been on his feet screaming with the fans. Phrases like "choke him out" and "crank the twist tighter" came out of his mouth as easily as "Oh my God, I can't watch this" came out of hers. This lifestyle was a part of Dante, and she didn't like it one bit. Was everything about him centered on fighting, or was there more to him?

She guessed it didn't matter. Dante was a temporary fixture in her life, so the fighting would be, too. She couldn't imagine doing this day in and day out like he did.

"Penny for your thoughts. You're awfully quiet over

there."

She looked away from the passing buildings to him. *Was his life how she pictured it?* "Is fighting and training all you do?"

He shot her a glance. "What do you mean?"

"You haven't mentioned a career, and you spend a majority of your time at the training facility — training. It's a little excessive, don't you think?"

"Would you ask the same question to a surgeon who spends all his time at the hospital or an archeologist who spends months or even years at a dig?"

"That's not the same."

"Why? Because you say it isn't?"

He hadn't asked the question harshly; he'd used a calm I'd-like-to-hear-your-opinion tone, but she got the feeling she had ventured onto a touchy subject by the way his hands tightened on the steering wheel. She bit her lip. "It's not exactly a traditional lifestyle."

"Neither is a surgeon who works thirty-some hour shifts, or an archeologist who jets off to Egypt and is gone for a year at a time. Just because it's not a career you'd spend your life doing doesn't make it any less a career. I train hard. I've busted my ass to get where I am, like every other person aiming to make something of themselves in the field of their choice. The only difference is I do mine with gloves on my fists and not a scalpel or shovel in my hand."

Yep, definitely a sensitive topic. Better to steer things in a different direction. "Does the training interfere with hobbies?"

He relaxed against the car seat. "Right now? Yes. With working with a new coach and my fight only being a few weeks away, my free time is limited, but once it's over, things will calm down until I have another match scheduled."

"How long do you have between fights?"

"About five months. Intense training usually picks back up about two months before a fight. By then, I know who I'm scheduled to go up against, and I spend the time forming a game plan and working to strengthen my weaknesses. Each fighter is different, has different techniques, so that makes each fight unique."

So this was like a full-time job. "What do you do when you're not training like you are right now?"

"If I don't have a scheduled fight but one of the guys in the training facility does, I become his sparring partner to help with his stand-up. I also volunteer a few nights a week at my local rec center. I've coached everything from T-ball to basketball."

She blinked. "You work with kids?"

"I love kids. If the rec center is struggling to fill a coaching slot, and I have the time available, I always offer."

"That's really nice of you."

He shrugged. "Growing up, I spent a lot of time at my local rec center. It was like a second home for me. I want it to feel like that for another kid."

She guessed there was more to Dante Jones than just fighting. "Where were your parents?"

"Dad's a surgeon and Mom's an archeologist." He sent her a half-smile. "The reason for the little rant earlier. Sorry about that."

"I take it they don't approve of what you do?"

"To say the least. I'm the polar opposite of both of them. If I weren't the spitting image of my father, I'd question my parentage." He chuckled. "The man hates sports, especially MMA."

"How in the world did you get into the sports industry, then?"

"Easy. Rick Pruitt."

"Who?"

"The kid who lived next door to me growing up. The two of us were inseparable until he moved away when I was eleven. When Rick turned six, his dad signed him up for football at the rec center. I begged my father to let me sign up, too. Of course, he said no, but he eventually caved when I reminded him I hadn't seen Mom in months and he was always at the hospital. I needed something to do other than being stuck at home with the nanny. After that, he pretty much let me get into any sport I wanted. I wasn't above using their guilt for being too busy to spend time with me."

"Oh. Dante, how awful. My mom and dad were always there. I can't even imagine growing up like that."

"It really wasn't *that* bad. Yeah, it would've been nice if my parents had come to a game or a school play, but if my childhood had been any different, I might never have started playing football, which led to wrestling—which I still suck at, by the way—which led to basketball, which finally led me to Frank's Gym when I was sixteen."

"I assume Frank's was your introduction into MMA?"

"Nope, that came two years later. I learned to box at Frank's. There is a reason I am the knockout champion, you know." He smiled again. "Frank was a retired professional boxer. He actually fought against Sugar Ray Leonard back in the 1970s. For some reason he took a liking to me and even gave me a part-time job. I spent every afternoon after school there. Those were some of the happiest days of my life."

The wistful tone he used made her heart catch. "What happened to him?"

"He died from cancer a few years ago. Right before I made it into the professional MMA circuit. Man, I wished he'd gotten to see me get there. I could still hear him barking orders from the side of the ring. But I know he's looking down at me, proud as hell."

She reached over and squeezed his arm. "I'm sure he is. I'm glad you had someone who supported you."

"He didn't just support me, he believed in me. He'd tell everyone who came into the gym that I'd win a division belt someday. That I was the next Mike Tyson—of course, he'd said that *before* ol' Mike started biting ears off."

Cait chuckled. "He meant a lot to you."

"I had a father who gave me everything I needed except attention. Frank was my dad. He was the one at my high school graduation. He was the one I called if I did some stupid teen stunt that landed me in hot water and who'd set me straight afterward. My life could have turned out a lot differently if I hadn't met him. I had no supervision at home. Even if my father grounded me, he wasn't there to enforce it. Frank was." Dante laughed. "And boy, did he."

"How did he punish you?"

"Once he made me scrub the locker room. That doesn't sound too bad, but I don't think that room had been cleaned in months. It was *rancid*. Took me all day to clean it. I must have taken three showers afterward to wash the smell off. To say the least, I kept my nose out of trouble for a good while after that."

"He sounded like a great guy, Dante."

"He was." He inhaled. "Damn, I haven't talked about him in years. Feels good to speak about him again."

"Thank you for sharing it with me. It means a lot."

The warmth in his eyes made her insides flutter. He reached across the seat and took her hand, entwining their fingers together. "It means a lot to me that you were willing to listen. I don't talk about Frank much. There's a part of me that still can't believe he's gone. I miss him."

She rubbed the top of his hand. "But like you said, I'm sure he's looking down on you, proud as hell."

"Whew." He let out a breath, and shook his head. "Enough heavy stuff. You ready for some fun?"

She took his cue to change topics. "Where *are* we going, anyway?"

"I thought we'd stop by the after-party for a while. One of the fighters we watched is a good friend of mine and part of Mike's crew. Tommy's win was huge tonight. I wanted to show my support."

"A-after party?" Her stomach dropped to her feet.

Good Lord, the man was taking her straight into Barbie hell.

CHAPTER TEN

Cait stood against the wall beside Dante and tried to calm her growing unease. Things were great at first. When they'd arrived, the host, Tommy "Lightning" Sparks, had made her feel both welcomed and flattered. Normally, compliments from a man flustered her, but Tommy had flirted in a lighthearted way that had only made her blush and feel appreciated as a woman. She wasn't the only girl he made feel that way, either. The fighter was constantly in the middle of a flock of women.

Afterward, she and Dante had gone out onto the dance floor. Their dance this time was the complete opposite from the night they'd met. She'd still been uncomfortable as Dante bumped and ground against her, but instead of focusing on her awkwardness, she embraced it and laughed each time their moves didn't synch together. Each time she'd laughed, Dante's smile grew wider and he edged closer, until it seemed as if only two of them existed. Then he'd kiss her, a deep, thorough kiss that had left her breathless and throbbing. If the harsh exhale he'd given afterward had been any indication, he hadn't been unaffected by the kiss either.

It wasn't until they'd left the dance floor and taken up a place against the wall that she noticed the stares. She tried to ignore them at first, but over the last hour, it became increasingly obvious the Barbies were on the prowl—for Dante. They circled Cait like vultures, waiting for their moment to strike.

She'd been pulled into a feminine game she was unprepared for and had no idea how to handle.

She caught sight of a black-haired woman devouring Dante with her eyes. The short, black leather skirt she wore showed endless tanned legs. The nothing tank top was molded to her had-to-be-fake boobs. Cait gritted her teeth.

The Barbie's gaze flicked to Cait and turned cold, her crimson lips twisted into a sneer as a perfectly plucked brow lifted. Cait held steady eye contact, lifting a brow of her own, hoping her expression conveyed what she felt: *Back off, bitch. He's here with me.*

The woman tilted her head back, squaring her shoulders, and Cait mimicked her.

She couldn't think of any another way to respond to the nonverbal challenges. So if they curled a lip at her or sent her a dismissive look, she copied them.

The woman's attention returned to Dante, and Cait peeked up at him. He stood nodding his head to the beat of the music, sipping his beer, oblivious to what was going on. When he caught Cait watching him, he smiled. Her heart did a flip as he pulled her closer to his side and kissed the top of her head.

The woman had left by the next time Cait looked over.

Good. Another confrontation averted. Dante's lack of awareness seemed to keep the women at a distance. She had little doubt it'd take just one acknowledging glance from him and the cats would climb all over each other to stake their claim.

He squeezed her hip. "You need another beer?"

She held up her half-full bottle. "No, I'm good."

"You having a good time?"

"Of course I am." Just a small fib. She *was* enjoying his company.

Now if someone would write a "How to Date an Uber-Hotty" guide that informed her how to deal with aggressive wants-to-steal-your-date women, the night would be even better.

Dante released his hold on her to put his empty bottle on a nearby table. She stepped aside to give him room, and a buxom brunette shoved between them. Cait stared at her.

"Dante! Hi!" the too-skinny, completely proportional ninny exclaimed. Cait blinked at the breathless, come-and-get-it tone.

He turned. His eyes widened momentarily before all emotion left his face.

Interesting.

"Amanda. Didn't know you'd be here. If I had, we would've skipped the party."

" 'We'?" She gave Cait a dismissive once-over before turning her big-ass, toothy smile to Dante.

Of all the glances Cait had received during the evening, this one pissed her off the most. She curled her hands into fists and opened her mouth to tell the woman off, but Dante slid past the bitch and came to stand behind Cait. She snapped her mouth shut as he snaked his hands around her waist, and pulled her against him. She leaned into his chest and fought a smirk. Maybe she didn't have the know-how these women did, but Dante made up for it.

"I don't think you've met my date, Caitlyn Moore."

Disgust curled the woman's lips. "You're kidding, right? What's this? A pity date?"

The words sent horror piercing through Cait's heart. This couldn't be happening. She was having a nightmare. She had to be. God, please wake up.

Horror became reality when Dante went rigid behind her. His chest no longer gently brushed her back, and he seemed to stop breathing. His loose embrace became steel. This was no dream.

Tears of anger and mortification blurred her vision and she wanted to scream at the cruelty. Why her? Why anyone? No one should ever endure such humiliation.

She blinked furiously, refusing to give the woman the satisfaction of seeing her cry.

"Caitlyn, go to the car."

She glanced over her shoulder. Rage pulsed on Dante's face and drew his features into a terrifying scowl. Cait swallowed.

"What?"

"Go to the car." He met her eyes, his expression softening as he kissed her gently on the lips. "Please."

She nodded and extracted herself from his embrace. She walked toward the exit numbly.

"What the hell is the matter with you?"

Dante's outraged voice carried to her ears. Curiosity made her turn. Anger jerked his movements as he swiped his hand through the air. The woman studied her nails, smirking as if she were pleased in a job well done.

In truth, the woman had. If this was an example of what spending time with Dante meant, it was a deal breaker. Cait refused to endure this kind of treatment from anyone—no matter how much she wanted Dante in her bed.

• • •

Every muscle in his body trembled from trying to control his anger. He could still feel the way Caitlyn's body shuddered against his, still see the glisten of tears in her eyes when she looked up at him. She didn't deserve to have anyone speak to her that way. Ever.

Amanda glanced at him. "I hadn't realized your taste had shifted to fat women. Makes sense why we broke up now."

"We weren't together long enough to break up. You can't hide trash, Amanda, and you're overflowing with it."

A nasty sneer turned up her lips. "So you decided to date a woman with an overflowing muffin top? Not sure you've traded up, Dante."

If these were the type of comments Caitlyn had dealt with most of her life, it was no wonder she felt inadequate. A protective instinct overwhelmed him. No one had the right to make her feel that way.

"You know what? Fuck this."

He hoisted Amanda over his shoulder. Squealing, she pounded her fist against his back. "Put me down."

A couple of fighters stood as he stormed past. "What's going on, Dante?"

"It's time to take out the trash."

"Hey, Dante, wait up!" Tommy and a few others followed

him down the hall and outside.

Why had he ever wasted time on this woman? Yeah, she had the perfect outer appearance, but it hadn't taken him long to realize she was one of the ugliest women he'd ever met. He hated that Caitlyn had been a target of Amanda's malicious mouth, and her foul words would fuel the insecurities he now knew Caitlyn had. Insecurities that were completely unfounded.

Caitlyn was the most beautiful woman he'd ever met— both inside and out. Sweet and innocent with a little feisty added in for spice. Amanda couldn't hold a candle to Caitlyn.

He strode to the lip of the pool and tossed her in, watching her disappear under the water.

She surfaced, sputtering. "You bastard!"

He pointed at her. "Don't ever come near me or my girlfriend again."

How easily the word "girlfriend" had come out of his mouth. Not because he was trying to run off another man, but because Caitlyn brought forth a fierce need to protect he'd never felt for a woman before. This was no longer about a challenge, but a woman who'd gotten under his skin. She deserved to feel as beautiful as he saw her.

Dante spun. Five men stared at him, their mouths hanging open.

"Damn, Dante, what happened?" Tommy asked. "I've never seen you like this."

He wouldn't repeat the foul words. He jerked his thumb over his shoulder. "Make sure this *thing* stays out of my sight."

"Sure, Dante. Whatever you want."

Now he had to face Caitlyn. Damn it, the night had been

perfect. They danced, laughed, kissed. He'd finally succeeded in getting her to lower her guard, and the woman behind all those barriers had forced him to lower his own.

He hurried to the parking lot. Talking about Frank, his past, and the way she'd tried to comfort him with those small touches to his arm, had been amazing. She might not have understood his sport, but she was compassionate and caring. It'd been a long time since he'd connected with a woman on a deeper level. Most of his *relationships* had been superficial with superficial women. At the time, that had been enough. Now it no longer was.

Dante wanted the openness he and Caitlyn had formed today. He'd let her in, and she'd done the same. He refused to lose that.

He neared his truck, but Caitlyn was nowhere to be found. A knot formed in his stomach. She wouldn't have left.

After digging his cell phone out of his pocket, he called her and it went straight to voicemail. He sent a text asking her where she was.

A few seconds later, his phone chimed with a return text. *Took a taxi. It's over, Dante.*

• • •

Caitlyn quietly closed the door to her apartment. She leaned against it and finally allowed herself to cry. She pressed the back of her hand to her mouth. Why had sending that text been so hard?

"Cait?"

She heard Amy before she saw her. When her friend popped her head around the corner of the living room, her eyes widened and she rushed to Cait's side. "What happened?"

"I'm so humiliated."

"Cait, honey, come here."

Behind Amy, Paul stood in the door frame, his arms outstretched. She hurried into them, his thin limbs enveloping her. So different from Dante's strong embrace, but just as safe.

"Amy, I think this calls for the good stuff," he said.

"Which one?"

"We have tears, Amy. Which do you think?"

The exaggerated disgust in Paul's tone made Cait thankful to be home. She needed her two best friends right now.

Paul led her to the couch and gently pushed her into the cushions. He sat beside her, reached for a Kleenex on the coffee table, and wiped her tears. Concern drew his eyebrows together.

She opened her mouth to spill her guts, but he held up his hand. "We have to wait for Amy. She'd kill me for sending her on an errand then getting all the drama to myself. You know how much she loves the drama."

Cait begrudged a smile.

Minutes later, Amy walked in, carrying three heaping bowls of ice cream. Cait took a bowl. Full-fat Rocky Road. Paul really knew how to wallow.

"Thanks, guys."

"What kind of friends are we if we can't share ice cream when one of us is upset?" He squeezed her hand. "So what happened?"

Cait grimaced. Voicing the humiliation she'd endured would be difficult. Yet she had to, or this night would eat her alive. "A woman asked Dante if I was a pity date."

Paul gasped, his fingers flying to his mouth. "Did you claw her eyes out? 'Cause if you didn't, I sure will."

Amy scooted close and hugged her. "God, Cait, I'm so sorry."

The sympathy in her friend's voice made a fresh wave of tears gather in her eyes. "To be so humiliated, in front of Dante."

Before she could let the waterworks start again, she shoved a spoonful of ice cream into her mouth. The sweet goodness did nothing to relieve her distress.

Paul straightened. "Cait, I know how you think. You will not let some catty bitch come between you and Hercules. Do you understand?"

Cait forced the ice cream past the lump in her throat. "I never wanted anything to do with the fighting part of Dante's life. Tonight's encounter only confirmed that. I let my attraction to Dante cloud my judgment and now I've been rudely awakened."

"Cait, you need to look at this from a different perspective." Amy pinned her with an intense stare. "Dante wanted *you* there. No one else. This woman was jealous. The easy target is to attack the woman he's with. What do women attack first? Other women's looks."

"I *know* Dante wanted me there, but I had women challenging me from the moment I walked in there. I had a woman humiliate me because she wanted the man I was with. I refuse to deal with people like that over an attraction that has no future. I want to go back to life before Dante." Glancing down at the ice cream, she felt her stomach roil. She set the bowl down. Fatigue sapped the last of her energy.

"I want to go to bed."

"Cait—"

She shook her head. "No more tonight. My head is killing me and I'm drained. I just want to curl up in bed, okay?"

"If you need—"

"I know. I'll talk. I promise." She forced a smile, then rose from the couch and went to her room.

Once inside, she closed the door and flung herself across the bed. She'd been a fool. She never should've agreed to the date. She should've concentrated on a safer man, one who didn't make her insides come to life with a smoldering glance. Too many feelings were wrapped up in Dante.

Of course, she would've been embarrassed if the same thing had occurred with any guy, but it wouldn't have been this mind-numbing mortification she felt at Dante witnessing it.

Damn, there were the tears again. She blinked, wiping her eyes on her comforter.

A tapping came from the door. She pulled her pillow over her head. Couldn't her friends just leave her alone? She knew they were worried, but still. The tapping came again. "Go. Away!"

"Open the damned door."

Cait jackknifed into a sitting position, a gasp lodging in her throat at the deep—very angry—masculine voice on the other side.

"Caitlyn!"

The raw authority in his voice made her jump off the bed and hurry to the door. He stormed inside once she opened it, slamming it shut behind him. She backed up to give him room, lots of room, as memories of what happened the last time he was in here came to mind.

She didn't need that. Not now. Not when it would take every ounce of willpower to send him away.

She crossed her arms. "What are you doing here?"

"You can't just leave without a word and think I'm not going to show up."

"I think my text said it all."

"The hell it did. I'm not going to let one incident bring this thing between us to a grinding halt."

Blasted tears blurred her vision and she blinked them away before staring him in the eye. "It's an attraction, Dante. Attractions fizzle out. This one will, too."

"You're scared."

"Oh, I am *so* far outside the spectrum of scared, Dante."

He took a step forward, and she took a step back. He scowled. "Amanda's an ex-girlfriend. You have no idea how sorry I am that you were on the receiving end of her venom. It's why we broke up."

"That's supposed to make it all better? How many other hateful ex-girlfriends do you have waiting out there in after-party land? Better yet, how many women are waiting for their chance at you? From the women I saw drooling tonight, it's one hell of an impressive list."

"I've never claimed to be a saint. Women like me, they always have, and I do have my fair share of exes, but that shouldn't matter when it's *you* I want to be with."

"Shouldn't matter?" She pointed at him. "Let me tell you something, Dante Jones, in all my life, at any weight, with any man I might have been with, I've never been asked if I was a pity date. Why? Because when I did have the occasional date, it was with an average Joe, not someone in the limelight who has every anorexic hussy panting after him—women who have no regard for human freaking emotion."

"What they think doesn't matter."

She stepped toward him. "I've spent a majority of my life beating myself up over my weight. I'm finally getting to a point where I no longer do that, and I refuse to let women who have *you* on their to-do list step in and do it for me." She waved. "This world of yours—I want nothing to do with. So leave."

"No."

She threw her hands in the air. "Why?"

"Because of this."

He grabbed her then, his lips crushing down on hers. Cait pushed at his chest and opened her mouth to protest, but he took the opportunity to slip his tongue inside, caressing, stroking. His fingers worked their way into her hair and massaged her scalp. She wanted to deny him, to turn her head, but couldn't. Instead, she gripped his head between her hands and returned his kiss with passion and a little desperation.

"Caitlyn," he whispered into her mouth. He cupped her bottom and brought her close. The hard evidence of his arousal pressed into her belly. "God, Caitlyn. I can't get enough of you."

Reality crashed over her like cold water. She pushed at his chest. "I can't. It's not going to work. Please…leave." When he didn't budge, the fight left her and she pressed her face into his chest. "Please, Dante, just leave. I can't handle any more tonight. It's all been too much."

He stiffened, his arms tightened around her as he kissed the top of her head. "Fine. But let me tell *you* something,

Caitlyn. I want you. When I want something, I get it. And nothing, *especially* your past, will stand in my way. So get used to it."

CHAPTER ELEVEN

"Three!"

Dante punched the focus pads on Mike's hands with a left-right-hook combination.

"Two."

The snapping sound of glove hitting mitt with a left-right boomed inside the ring. Dante fell back, lowered his hands to mid-chest, and waited for the next command.

"Damn it, Dante, keep your hands up."

Shit. He brought his gloves back up to his cheeks.

"One."

Jab.

"One."

Jab. Dante ducked, weaving back and forth.

"Hands up! Two."

Left, right.

When Dante fell into his stance, a focus pad smacked him on the side of the head. Stunned, he dropped back and stared at Mike.

"I told you to keep your hands up. What's with you this week? Your focus has sucked."

Dante sighed. "Not getting much sleep."

No sleep was more like it.

Caitlyn made a formidable opponent and made it difficult for him to make good on his word that he wasn't going anywhere.

A week had gone by since the Amanda fiasco, and Caitlyn had avoided his every attempt to make contact. After two days of unreturned phone calls, he'd resorted to camping outside the fitness room at the Y waiting for her class to be over. By the time he'd woven through the class, which had tripled in size since the first day, she'd disappeared. He'd toyed with the idea of actually attending a session but knew how important the program was to her and wouldn't stress her out just because he needed to see her.

Unfortunately, the week had taken a toll on his training. He could already hear the big "I told you so" coming from Mike.

"Do you need to take the day off?"

And go back to an empty apartment, where the silence only intensified his thoughts? "No, I need this."

"Fine. Forget the focus pads. Let's move to the bag."

Dante sighed in relief. The intense pain that accompanied bag work was welcome. Anything to numb his racing mind.

"Burn out!"

In quick short punches, Dante hit the bag, over and over again. In less than a minute, fire seared his arms up into his shoulders.

"Two to go. Faster!"

He increased his speed, pounding in swift repetition.

The burning deep in his muscles intensified until he yelled. Pummeling faster, he refused to let the stinging daunt him. Sweat coated his arms and dripped off his elbows. Still he continued.

A loud buzz rang. "Time."

Dante bounced back, hopping from foot to foot as he shook out his arms.

"It's that girl, isn't it?" Mike glared at him.

Dante froze. Damn Mike. Couldn't the man take his lame not-enough-sleep excuse and let it be? He'd depended on Mike to distract him with an abusive session. And his coach had delivered. With one question, all Dante's troubles roared back to life.

"I don't want to talk about it." He shadowboxed around the floor.

Mike came around the bag, scowling. "Whatever happened between you two, push it aside. This has been a wasted week of training. Your timing is off. The strength behind your punches is weak, you're only half here. That's not acceptable." He rubbed his hand over his face. "I warned you not to get involved while you were training."

And there it was—the "I told you so." He really didn't need a nose rubbing right now. "You don't have to worry about that now."

"So she dumped you." Mike grinned. "Good. Maybe now you'll get your head out of your ass."

The tinkle of the bell interrupted Dante's retort. Brad strode in, his gym bag thrown over his shoulder.

Mike held up his hand. "Nope. No work out for you tonight."

Brad paused. "Huh?"

"Take Dante and let him do whatever the hell he's got to do to get this girl out of his system." He pointed at Dante. "As for you, you better come in here tomorrow ready to give me your all. Understand?"

"Yes, coach."

"I know I'm being a hard ass. But you hired me to do a job. When I see something that's interfering with that job, I'm going to address the issue. Do you want to win this title?"

"Yes."

"Then put your personal life aside and focus. The girl will be there after the match. Deal with her then. Now is not the time."

Mike slapped him on the shoulder and walked away. Dante sighed. Deep down, he knew his coach was right. The fight was less than a month away. Intensive training was essential right now. Complete concentration was crucial. He *should* put his personal life on the backburner until after the fight, but the idea soured his stomach.

Memories of Amanda's ugliness and the way that Caitlyn's body shuddered after the insult struck home had haunted him all week. A sane man would probably cut his losses and leave.

But he'd never claimed to be a sane man and he *never* backed away from a fight. The woman who'd held his hand while he spoke about Frank, who opened up about her past to let him see the struggles she'd faced, who'd been awkward and shy but tried so hard to let go for him—she was worth another round.

Brad walked over. "Let's go get a drink."

"Or five."

"Get showered, and we'll go drink ourselves stupid."

• • •

Swaying on his stool, Dante glanced over at Brad. "'Nother one?"

His friend's head swung toward him with a drunken grin. "Yep."

Dante waved to catch the bartender's attention. When he got it, he raised two fingers. The bartender shook his head but pulled out two shot glasses, filled them with vodka, and slid them over. Dante lifted his into the air. Brad followed. "To women. May we survive their existence."

Dante tossed his shot back. The liquor burned his throat as he smacked his lips. He slammed the glass on the polished wood. Two hours ago, they'd walked into the tiny club and bellied up to the bar. They'd been there ever since. Mike was a fucking genius. The alcohol had dulled his senses enough for him to stare numbly into space. And now he was ready to talk.

"We were havin' a fuckin' blast, we'd *connected*, man," Dante slurred. "And it went to shit 'cause of a stupid bitch."

"Sucks, man."

"Bad. Do you know what's like to have a woman kiss you back 'cause she wants *you*, and not the *idea* of you? It's fuckin' hot, bro. Irre-fuckin'-sistible."

Brad studied him. "You fallin' for her?"

Memories from the other night hit him in the chest. Her smiles as they'd danced, her laughter, the *rightness* of having her by his side, how at ease he felt with her. Until it all fell apart. "Possibly. Been a long time since a woman had me this riled up."

"But she's pushin' you away."

Yeah, she was. But he knew why. Dante toyed with the empty shot glass. "You know how we study our opponents before a fight, look for their weaknesses?"

"Yeah."

"I've seen Caitlyn's. Seen how deeply they get to her. She's not pushing me away as much as she is scared out of her mind to be with me. Caitlyn wants me, and I refuse to be a pussy and walk away when she's fighting herself. She doesn't need that kind of man. She needs me. A man not easily deterred. A man who, when she lets her guard down, smiles at him, opens up to him, *kisses* him—" he thumped the area above his heart with his fist— "she gets him right there. I've never had a woman get me there."

"Then why are we here?"

"Good question." He slid off the stool.

Brad held up his hand. "Hold up, man. They're not home."

"Where are they?"

"Amy took Cait to dinner. Where they ended up after, I don't have a clue."

Dante sat back down and waved at Brad. "Find them."

Now that Brad had planted the seed, Dante wanted to get the ball rolling. He wanted to see Caitlyn. Hold her, kiss her, wipe away the memories of that horrible night and create new, more pleasant ones. And she'd let him. He just had to corner her first.

"Okay, hold on," Brad said, pulling his cell out then hitting a number. "It's ringin'."

Brad shifted the phone to his mouth and sat up straighter. "Hey, baby. Where are you?" Momentary silence. "Where are you going afterward?" A pause. Dante could hear Amy's muffled voice but couldn't make out her words.

"Dante wants to see Cait." Brad placed his hand on the receiver. "She had to get away from the table." He removed his palm. "Hey, yeah, I'm here… Paul's? How the hell do I get there? Okay, we'll see you in a bit… Love you, too. Oh, Amy. Don't let Cait know we're comin'."

He chuckled as he hung up the phone.

"What's so funny?" Dante asked.

"She asked if I thought she was stupid."

At that, Dante smiled. Amy was becoming his best ally. Dante jumped to his feet and staggered before he could straighten. "Let's grab a cab."

"Amy's coming to get us. It'll be a few before she gets here. I gotta use the head. Sit down and we'll leave when I get back."

He'd been gone but a minute when a voice sounded behind Dante. "Where's Miss Piggy?"

Dante whirled. His vision swirled before focusing on a green-haired monster. "Fuck off, Sentori."

"Word's spread about the Amanda encounter the other night. Pity date? Ouch."

Dante stiffened. "Don't go there."

"The truth is hard to swallow, eh, Inferno? I wonder how she'd feel knowing she's the topic of conversation in the locker rooms these days, and not because she's the hot piece of ass of the week."

Dante leaned his face close to Sentori's face and poked him hard in the chest. "Listen, prick, it's one thing to play your sick little games fighter to fighter, but to involve outside people is crossing a line. Leave Caitlyn out of whatever mind games you want to play. She deserves better than that."

"Hey. Hey. Hey. Calm the bubbling lava, Inferno. I don't need to say a word. I'm pretty sure she already knows. In fact, I'll bet she wants nothing more to do with you." Sentori studied him, a pleased smile coming to his lips. "My, my. She doesn't, does she? I never thought I'd see the day. You've finally found the one woman you can't have."

· · ·

As soon as Cait stepped into Paul's apartment, she paused and stared at the man sitting on the couch. To keep from smiling, she bit the inside of her lip. She looked at Paul. "Been busy much?"

"Shut up."

Laughing, she walked into the living room. "Jack."

Jack stood, grinning, and opened his arms. She hugged him tightly. They'd only met that one time at the bar, but she'd felt a connection with the man. When they were dancing, he'd asked her about Paul. It pleased her beyond words they'd hooked up.

She pulled free and glanced between the two. "So what's going on here?"

"Nothing to worry yourself over," Paul said. "I want to know how you are."

She sighed. Didn't anyone understand she just wanted to forget? Dinner with Amy had been nice, except for her constant pressure to give Dante a chance. *Cait, you're wonderful together. Dante is so into you. I've never seen you so flustered by a man.*

Blah blah blah.

Amy meant well—she always meant well—but her friend didn't understand Cait was only a challenge for Dante. That hadn't bothered her before, but post-Amanda she refused to be some fighter's entertainment while he was in town, especially if it meant dealing with more women like his ex.

"I'm doing better."

An outright lie. As much as she tried to convince herself to stay away from Dante, she had to fight her yearnings. Every time he called, she wanted to answer the phone. When she'd spotted him coming toward her at the Y, she'd forced herself to make a hasty exit. Her continual struggle to ignore him left her emotionally drained. Why, after all that'd happened, did she still want to hear his voice, want to see him? Wasn't humiliation supposed to cure that?

"What happened?" Jack asked.

By the time Cait filled him in, tight lines pinched his features. "What's wrong with people?"

She shrugged. "It was the wake-up call I needed."

"Where's Amy?" Paul asked. "I thought she was just lagging behind."

"She dropped me off. She had an errand to run, said she'd be back shortly."

. . .

Dante stumbled up the stairs to Paul's apartment. Since when did stairs move? He righted himself and took another cautious step. He'd overdone it on the booze. He'd be lucky not to spend all day tomorrow with his head in the toilet. Yeah, Mike would be real pleased with his performance tomorrow. He cringed to think of his coach's response to his hungover state. It was his own damned fault, though. Mike had said to do what he needed to get Caitlyn out of his head—too bad it hadn't worked.

"Good God, Brad, how much did you let him drink?" Amy asked.

"Coach told me to take him out. I did as instructed."

"I think I regret my decision in driving you here."

Dante whirled, teetered violently, then straightened. "No, I have to see Caitlyn."

Amy arched a brow at him. "At least this should be entertaining."

They made it to the door. Dante swayed and placed a hand on the wall to steady himself. He shook his head to clear the fog. Maybe this hadn't been such a smart idea. Who knew what kind of crap would spew from his mouth in his current condition?

Amy knocked. Too late.

Seconds later, Paul answered. Dante's gaze clashed with the other man's. Paul's eyes went wide before he snapped his attention to Amy. "Have you gone stupid?"

Well, good to see you, too.

Amy shrugged. "Dante wanted to see Cait."

"Muscle Boy can barely stand straight," he whispered harshly.

"Hey, I'm standing right here," Dante said, not caring for the man's disapproving tone.

Paul gave him a dismissive glance. "Girl, I'm glad I'm not in your shoes. Cait's going to be livid."

"Price you pay to help a friend."

"Can we stop the chit-chat?" Dante demanded. "I want to see Caitlyn."

Paul stepped back. "Sure thing, Terminator, come on in."

Dante crossed the threshold then froze. Caitlyn sat on the couch with the jackass who had ogled her at the bar.

Oh, hell no. No man—especially not this one—was going to come between him and Caitlyn. He stormed forward. She turned from the conversation she was having with the guy and glanced at him. Then did a double-take. She jumped to her feet.

"Dante."

He soaked up the image of her before him, twisting her fingers together, her eyes downcast. He wasted no time. He grabbed her around the waist and crushed his mouth to hers.

Excitement shot through him when she wound her arms around his neck and kissed him back. Kissed him with the same fierceness he felt. He plunged his tongue into her mouth. A small moan sounded from her throat. He fucking loved that sound. Dante lowered his hands and grasped her bottom, bringing her closer to the part of him coming to full attention.

In the background, someone cleared his throat. Loudly.

When Caitlyn pushed, Dante released her.

Dante glared at the man sitting on the couch. By the way she'd responded to him, the jerk had better understand she was off limits.

Paul stood behind Jack and slapped him on the back of his head. "Why don't you kiss me like that?"

Huh?

The man looked over his shoulder. "So you like the whole Neanderthal thing?"

Dante frowned. "I wasn't being a Neanderthal."

The man turned mocking eyes toward him. "Really? I was waiting for the club to come out, so you could knock her over the head and drag her away by the hair."

Dante did something he'd never done before: he blushed.

Hot and furious. Maybe he had come in here like a caveman. But once he'd seen Caitlyn, he wanted—no, *needed* to kiss her. Let her know he was making good on his word. He wasn't going anywhere. And he would get what he wanted.

Her.

Paul strolled around the couch, arms crossed. "Seriously, you never kiss me like that."

Jack sighed and got up. He shrugged. Taking a deep breath, he strode over to Paul, grabbed him by the waist, and planted one on him.

Dante gaped at the two men locked in an intimate embrace.

Jack pulled back. "Better?"

Paul's flushed face said it all. "Cait, I can see why you like it. Whew!"

A blush the color of a fire hydrant stained her cheeks. "I don't like it."

"Bullshit," Paul said. "It makes you all hot and bothered, like me." He shoulder bumped Jack. "That was hot."

"Whose side are you on, anyway?" Cait turned and glared at Amy, who stood next to Brad just inside the living room. "That includes you, too."

"Yours, of course," Amy said and stepped forward. "Please believe that."

Seeing a spat about to occur, Dante interfered. "Caitlyn, can we talk?"

She studied him for a moment before she sighed. "Fine."

He grabbed her hand and led her down the hallway toward one of the closed doors. She tugged her arm. "No way. We're going on the balcony."

Dante frowned, but didn't argue.

He opened the cream-curtained French doors and stepped onto the alcove. Paul had made use of the small area. Tall potted bushes lined the walls. A round iron table with two chairs sat in the center.

He pulled out one of the chairs. "Sit."

"I'll stand, thank you," she said, crossing her arms.

Dante sighed and sat down. He propped his elbows on his knees, lowered his face to his hands, and rubbed his cheeks. He had her full attention. Now what was he going to say?

He looked up and was startled to realize Caitlyn was watching him. Normally, she refused eye contact. This time, however, she was staring at him.

The action worried him. A lot.

This wasn't the shy, vulnerable Caitlyn. No, this was the confident, in control, fitness instructor Caitlyn. And she was going to be a harder opponent to topple.

"You wanted to talk?"

Her gaze never wavered. Fuck. He was doomed. "About the other night—"

"Nothing really to discuss there."

"But there is—"

"No, Dante, there isn't. I've made my choice. I'm happy with my choice. Got it?"

Oh, yes, doomed. There seemed to be only one way they could communicate.

He rose and started toward her.

• • •

Cait struggled to stand her ground and not flee into the apartment like instinct screamed for her to do. She tipped her chin up, hoping the gesture would help her feel in control. It didn't.

Determination sounded in his every step as he closed the distance between them. He was going to kiss her. Again. She knew why he used this advantage. When he kissed her, she had the hardest time refusing him. Damn him for playing the weakness against her.

"What are you going to do? Kiss me again?" she blurted.

He stopped. Shock and confusion twisted his features. She stifled a quivering breath of relief. She'd stopped Dante Jones in his tracks. What would happen if she went further? Became the aggressor? Would he believe the chase was over, believe he'd won, and lose interest?

Cait stepped toward him, putting a seductive swing into her hips. "I like your kisses, Dante. They make me hot. Make me think of other ways you can use your mouth to make me even hotter."

What was she doing? This would never work. Dante would see straight through her performance, see the woman who'd never played the part of siren, and call her bluff. What would she do then?

Dante's eyes bulged. Her sense of control increased. He was flustered. Good. He needed a taste of it. She'd been flustered from the moment they'd met.

The gray shirt stretched across his chest. Her fingers itched to skim over the pebbled nipples straining beneath the material. Did she dare?

She raised her hand. Dante froze. The cotton was soft as she ran her palms up his chest and over his shoulders.

Dante shuddered and stumbled backward. "Caitlyn, what are you doing?" The roughness of his voice cocooned her. Drew her in.

"Touching you."

Her fingers trembled as they slid down his bicep and back up. Fire ran through her body and she yearned for more. Her nipples hardened, begging for him to touch them.

Dante groaned. "Fucking. Don't. Stop."

He gripped her hips in his large hands and brought her close, kneading her bottom. Warmth seared Cait, and she suppressed a moan. The feel of him, his scent, wracked havoc on her senses. She wound her arms around his neck, brushing against the hardness of his body.

"Fuck me, Dante." The words felt foreign coming out of her mouth. She hated that the first time she'd said them to a man was a desperate attempt to push him away for good.

He went so still she feared to move.

"No."

The shock of him saying that one word startled her. "Why not?"

"You don't get it, do you?"

"I-I don't."

"Just sex isn't what I'm after, Caitlyn. Been there, done that for years. I can go right now and find a line of women who'd like to fuck." He stepped away from her. "Yes, I want your moans and kisses, but I also want more moments like we had in the truck, hand holding, laughing. I want *more* than fucking…with you."

Stunned, Cait stared at him. He wanted *more*?

"Are we clear on where we stand now?"

She gave a jerky nod.

"Good. You process that." He walked around her and into the house. The front door closed seconds later.

I want more. With you.

How quickly she'd accepted Sentori's warning, wanting to believe that Dante's interest in her was simply a chase, nothing more. *She'd* needed him to be that way. She hadn't wanted to examine why Dante's presence made her happy, why she'd missed him, why her heart jumped every time her phone rang or she got a glimpse at him at the gym.

He wasn't going to stick around, so she'd had to stay detached.

But he wanted more.

With a woman who wasn't sure she could accept his career.

Chapter Twelve

Gritty-eyed, Cait dragged down the hall toward the living room. Sleep had refused to come. She'd finally come to the decision in the early morning hours that she had to face whatever this was between them, which meant facing his career and the possibility of more humiliating encounters with Dante's exes.

Her throat tightened and she swallowed against rising panic.

Pausing in the doorway, she found Amy curled up on the couch, flipping through a magazine. Her friend had crossed a line yesterday. They should've talked last night. But with her emotions in a tailspin, Cait hadn't wanted another confrontation.

But it was time for her and her best friend to have a little chat. She walked into the room. "You're in a boatload of trouble."

Amy froze mid-flip and sighed, laying the open magazine on her lap. "I know."

"Why'd you do it?" Cait came around the couch to sit beside Amy.

Her friend studied the wall, then met Cait's eyes. "Because it's what you want, even if you refuse to admit it."

"These are my dragons to slay, Amy. It's not your place to interfere."

"Cait, how long have we known each other?"

"Fifteen years."

"In all that time, have I ever butted into your business?"

"Are you serious?"

A tiny smile quivered at the corners of Amy's mouth. "Let me rephrase that. Have I ever butted in to this extent?"

"No, which is why I'm so baffled. Why'd you do it?"

"Because you are ruining a good thing. One day you're going to look back and kick yourself for not trying."

"Perhaps. But don't you think that's my decision to make?"

"Let me play devil's advocate. If you saw me being self-destructive, wouldn't you step in?"

"I'm not being self-destructive."

"Yes, you are. You like Dante. Dante likes you. But you're doing everything you can to push him away. Thank God, he's too bull-headed to let you." Amy grabbed Cait's hand and squeezed. "Besides, I'd do the same thing if this had been an unhealthy attraction. Wouldn't you?"

"I wouldn't stop until you dumped the loser."

"That's all I'm doing, Cait. I swear. I'm not trying to be mean or unsupportive. I want you to be happy. You're miserable. And it's because you are denying yourself the one thing you want."

"I have my reasons, Amy. You may not understand them,

but they're very real to me."

"You're right, I don't understand, but it's time for you to let go of the past."

"It's not just about the past any more. It's about the future and what I can live with."

"Be careful with that, Cait. Sometimes you don't realize what you *can* live with until you've lost the one thing you can't live without. I don't want that road for you."

"I don't want that either." Cait sighed. "I'm not going to push Dante away any more. We'll see what happens. Heck, *he* may tell me to screw off when I go talk to him later."

"I don't think that's going to happen."

"We'll know soon."

Amy studied, head cocked to the side. "What are you doing this afternoon?"

"Why?"

"The fighters in Mike's gym are hosting a pool party this afternoon. Would you care to go with me?"

Cait swallowed. Another fighters' function. Great. But if she was going to face this, she might as well start now. "Yeah, I'll join you."

Cait hesitated and stared through the glass doors. Men were everywhere, punching bags, wrestling on the ground, hitting those round thingies on their partner's hands. Yet, the one man she wanted to see was nowhere to be found. Then she caught sight of Dante in the mirror, walking with Mike into an office at the back of the room. She yanked the door open and rushed inside.

When two men stopped to look at her as she entered,

she slowed her pace. She didn't need to disrupt the entire facility in her need to get to Dante, but she wasn't going to stop, either.

"I don't know what to do."

Dante's voice paralyzed her. She pressed against the wall next to the office and listened.

"It's her or the championship," Mike said. "Right now, you can't have both."

"Why not?"

"This goddamn meeting is why not. I know you're hung over, but Jesus, how many times do I have to remind you to keep your hands up? You're a stand-up fighter and you're even distracted from the one thing you do best. At this point, Sentori is going to win the match at your own game."

"That won't happen."

"How many times did I smack a focus glove upside your head this morning?"

Silence.

"How many, Dante?"

"Six."

"Six! Six! Distraction, Dante Jones, is going to cost you the one thing you busted your ass for. And you got no one to blame but your damned self."

Cait pressed her hand to her mouth. She had had no idea she was screwing up his performance. Dante always seemed so cool and collected, so in control. Heck, she didn't even know she had the power to distract him until last night.

Guilt twisted her stomach. This wasn't his fault. It was hers.

"Listen, Mike, things will calm down. I swear it. Caitlyn and I are ironing out some differences. Nothing I can't handle."

"You've lost your mind. What did I tell you weeks ago when I caught you two rolling around on the mat?"

Silence.

"Not going to answer? Fine. She'd be the reason you lose this fight."

Cait stifled a gasp. She couldn't be the reason he was distracted. He wasn't trying to win this fight just for himself, but for Frank.

"Three weeks." Cait heard a slamming that sounded distinctively like a fist hitting a desk. "Three fucking weeks. That's all. Can't you put her aside for three weeks?"

"No."

Her heart stilled. Dante cared so much he was willing to sacrifice his training to be with her. She blinked back tears. And she cared too much to allow him to do that.

"Then you might as well forget training altogether. I don't have time to spend on a man who can't get his priorities straight."

The breath caught tight in her lungs. *No! Oh, please no.*

"What are you saying, Mike?"

She clenched her fist, afraid of what would happen next.

"Need me to spell it out? I quit. Get your shit and find a new coach."

Cait closed her eyes. Guilt weighed her down and she slumped against the wall.

"Mike—"

"No. Out."

Dante muttered something inaudible. Then a chair scraped against the floor. She edged behind a free weight stand as Dante stormed across the gym. When he disappeared into the locker room, she entered the office and closed the door.

Mike's head snapped up. Then his eyes narrowed. "What are you doing here?"

"If I promise to get Dante back on track, will you please not quit? He can't lose this fight."

Mike folded his fingers and placed them on top of the desk. "Do you know what you are agreeing to?"

"Yes."

"I assume you overheard our conversation. So you know he's unwilling to part ways with you," Mike said, his words laced with disgust. "How do you propose to change his mind?"

"I don't know. But I'll find a way. I promise."

Mike studied her for a long minute, then picked up a pen and started writing on a yellow legal pad. "There is nothing you can do. Good day, Ms. Moore."

He'd dismissed her? Hell, no. She stepped forward and slapped her hand on the desk. Mike jumped and looked up.

"I won't be the reason Dante loses the one thing he wants more than anything."

"The title is no longer what he wants." He stared at her pointedly. "He's made his decision, and so have I."

"I can fix this. Just give me the chance."

Mike scoffed and leaned back in his chair. "If your plan is to fix whatever this problem is you're having, then you're wasting my time. I don't need a lovestruck fighter in here. I need you out of the picture. Completely. Unless you're willing to go that far, get out of my office."

Yes, she cared about Dante, but he couldn't lose his dream on a woman who didn't know if she could accept his career.

Cait squared her shoulders. "You have my word. I'll be out of the picture and you'll have your focused fighter back. Please don't quit."

Mike tapped his pen on the pad then nodded. "One chance, missy. I'll tell Dante he has one more training session with me. If I have to remind him to put his hands up once, our deal is off. Got it?"

"You won't regret this."

"You better make damned sure I don't. Right now, I consider you the Yoko Ono of extreme fighting."

• • •

Dante hurled his deodorant across the room. The stick shattered against the wall. What the hell would he do now? Mike was the only coach who could teach him how to take Sentori on the ground. Without his help, Dante *would* lose.

Damn it!

It was only three weeks. Three weeks to throw himself into his training and clinch the title. The title he'd always wanted.

He looked heavenward. "Frank, man, I miss you. I could really use your advice right now."

Caitlyn had thrown a left hook that blindsided him last night. Never had he believed she'd turn the tables on him and become the aggressor. Her one-eighty had to be from her experience with Amanda, some weird tactic to throw him off his game. It had worked.

But he'd recovered, and he'd made it clear exactly what he wanted with her.

He'd expected her to stop him from leaving. Call him

back. She hadn't. And there had been a biting sting he'd been unprepared for at her silence. That sting had stayed with him through the night and into his training this morning.

"Dante."

He twisted on the bench to find Mike striding into the locker room.

"Yeah?"

"I think things got carried away in my office. I'm not pleased with what's going on. But to just cut you off wasn't cool of me. What do you say we give it another go?"

Relief hit Dante. He stood. "I promise not to disappoint you again."

"I'm counting on that. But I warn you, my patience is gone. If you're not in here tomorrow giving me your all, I think it'd be best if we parted ways."

"No problem. I'll give you that and more."

"Good. Meet me here at noon." Mike turned and left.

Dante exhaled as he grabbed his phone out of his duffle bag, then sat and dialed Caitlyn's number. They had to talk. No more kissing, touching, or any other distraction mechanism that could come to mind. A serious lay-out-on-the-line-on-both-their-parts talk. He promised he'd give her time to process what he'd said, and she'd had more than enough time to do so.

She answered on the first ring. "Hello."

"We need to talk."

"I agree."

"How about we meet somewhere?"

"No."

"Why not?"

"Face to face never works for us. Besides, what I have to

say will only take a few seconds."

He scowled. He had a pretty good idea what those few seconds she needed meant. "Scared I'll change your mind?"

"I, uh…what?"

"Meet me somewhere."

"I-I can't, Dante."

"Because you know if you do, you'll never say what you intend to say. You're running scared."

"I'm not running!"

"What was last night about, then? Did you think by coming on to me, I'd lose interest?" Her sharp breath was his answer. "News flash, Caitlyn. It didn't work."

• • •

"So what are you going to do about Dante?"

"I have no idea." Cait glanced at Jack, who sat across from her beside Paul in the booth. She set down her coffee cup.

"Well, let's see." Paul ticked off his fingers. "You tried avoidance. That didn't work. You tried telling him you weren't interested. That didn't work. You had a bitch ask if you were the pity date. That didn't work. You turned whore on his macho ass and even that didn't work." He threw his hands up. "I'm at a loss, Cait."

"Are you sure you want to cut all ties to Dante?" Jack asked.

Cait grimaced. "I don't have a choice. His coach quit because of me, refused to have anything to do with Dante if I was still in the picture. This fight means everything to him. I can't have him lose something he's spent his whole life working toward on my conscience, or his, for that matter."

"Why not talk to him?" Jack asked.

"I tried that. I screwed it up, but I tried."

"What happened?"

"He called me a few minutes after I left the building. I shouldn't have answered the damned phone. I didn't have time to think it through, but if I didn't answer, he would've hunted me down. I didn't want to deal with him in person. I had no idea he could be just as overbearing over the phone."

Paul leaned forward. "What did you say?"

"I didn't *say* much of anything. The stupid man controlled the conversation and then called me out on last night and told me my plan didn't work. I was so flustered, I just hung up. He didn't call back. Why would he? He'd gotten his answer."

Paul grimaced. "Man, you did screw up."

"Thanks, Paul."

He gave her a hey-you-said-it-first look.

"Why didn't you tell him Mike said you had to be out of the picture?" Jack asked.

"I didn't get a chance to think! Besides, I wanted to keep Mike out of it. This training is extremely important for Dante's fight. Dante being furious with his coach wouldn't help anything. I wanted it to come across as my decision, so he could blame me. It totally backfired in my face. Now he's all determined because I'm 'running scared.' " Cait put finger quotes around the last two words. "I have twenty-four hours to convince a man who doesn't listen—"

Paul wagged his finger. "Oh, no. He listens. He just doesn't care. Big difference."

"True. Dante wants what Dante wants. How do you get through to a man like that?"

Jack studied her for a moment. "Sounds like the only

thing you've never accomplished is pissing the man off."

Cait froze. Huh. "Yeah, that's about right."

She'd seen jealousy and determination. What else? But she couldn't recall his anger ever directed at her. Other people, yes. Her? No. How would he react if she finally *did* make him angry? Furious, even?

"Uh-oh. What did I say?"

"Anger's a thought."

Jack held up his hands. "Oh, Cait. Don't listen to me. Pissing that man off might have some serious consequences."

Paul snapped his fingers. "I've got it! Oh, it's so clever. Cait will go on a date with a different guy."

"Are you wishing death on someone?" Jack asked.

"No! It's perfect."

Cait opened her mouth to object, but Paul interrupted. "Hear me out. It's not going to be some random guy. It's going to be his opponent."

"What?" Cait and Jake exclaimed in unison.

"No, no, listen. I swear, it makes sense. You want to piss He-Man off and get him back on track. What better way to do that than to get him pissed off at the guy he's supposed to take down? Really, think about it. Most guys have to bottle up their rage issues. Not this one. He knows he'll have the chance to kick the shit out of this guy. I'll bet my life it'll make him more determined than ever to get beefed up."

It really did make sense. Was she insane for even contemplating the idea?

No, she wasn't. On the first night they'd met, Dante had admitted rivalry could make a fighter train harder. What if she made this his rivalry fight? Would that get him focused?

At the same time, her stomach heaved at the thought of

getting near Sentori. But it wasn't like she'd be dating him or even have to kiss him—God forbid. One outing with Sentori should get Dante enraged and shoved in the right direction.

Jack sighed. "If you do this you might lose any chance of being with the guy. Are you sure you want to risk that?"

Pain twisted Cait's heart, but if Dante won the belt he'd spent years training for, any pain was worth it. "If his training wasn't suffering, it'd be different, but it is—because of me. I can't risk the most important fight of his career when I don't know if I can get past the MMA baggage he comes with in the first place. It's completely unfair to him."

"What if he ends up hating you?"

"I can only hope that doesn't happen, and once his fight is over I can try to make amends, and maybe we can see where things go."

"And if that doesn't happen?" Jack asked.

"At least I didn't cost him his fight. Right now, that's all that matters. I'll face the consequences later." She bit her lip. "There's one problem with the plan, though."

Paul quirked a brow.

"How am I supposed to get a date with Sentori?"

Paul smiled. "Um, I do believe Amy invited you to the pool party the fighters were throwing this afternoon."

"Yeah?"

"Well, honey, grab your swimsuit. We're going to snare us a fighter."

• • •

Dante walked onto the patio. The clear blue sky sparkled off the surface of the pool, inviting him in for a dip. He could use one. A dull ache still resided behind his eyes and his stomach still rebelled at the thought of food. It had taken everything in him to down protein shakes throughout the day.

He glanced around. Pro and amateur fighters alike mingled with girlfriends or wives in small clusters. Some splashed about in the pool, while others sat around large outdoor tables and chairs or leaned against the bar, drinking. No drinking for him tonight. If ever again.

He saw Tommy standing beside his best friend, Julie. Dante ambled over.

Tommy smiled. "Hey, Inferno." He glanced behind Dante and frowned. "Where's that beautiful girlfriend of yours?"

He should have known, drunk or not, Tommy would have remembered Caitlyn. The man never forgot a beautiful woman. "She couldn't make it."

"That's too bad. I wanted to introduce her to Julie." He nodded toward the dark-haired woman next to him. "I thought they'd hit it off."

"Hi, Dante," Julie said. "I hate that I missed the party, it was a huge win for Tommy, but I couldn't get away from the clinic. Tommy told me about Caitlyn. Good to see you settling down."

Her gaze slid over to Tommy. Wistfulness entered her eyes before she blinked and focused on Dante. Any trace of the helpless emotion was wiped from her face as she sent him a bright smile. "I can't wait to meet her."

Dante returned the smile even though he felt bad for her. He'd hung out with the two long enough to know the woman had feelings for her childhood friend. It'd taken Dante a while to see it; she was damned good at hiding her emotions, but every once in a while her guard slipped, like now, and he saw how she truly felt.

Which was sad. Dante knew Tommy didn't return the feeling. The man lived the bachelor lifestyle, and he had no plans to give it up anytime soon. Oh, he loved Julie, would kill anyone who laid a finger on her, but it'd always been in a big brother sort of way.

Tommy was a fool for not seeing what was right in front of him.

Julie was a good woman. One Dante would've loved for Caitlyn to have met instead of Amanda. "Maybe the four of us could get dinner one night."

"I'd like that." Tommy looked over Dante's shoulder and grimaced. "The asshole is headed this way."

Dante glanced back, his grip on his water bottle tightening. Sentori strode toward them. When he reached them, he said, "Dante, my man, where's that gorgeous girlfriend of yours?"

Sentori was smart enough not to make any derogatory remarks in front of other people. Dante wished the man would slip up—just once. Most of the fighters here wanted any excuse to kick his ass, and speaking ill of another fighter's girlfriend topped the list.

"She couldn't make it."

"Ah, well. There are plenty of other delectables to choose from." He swiped his arm through the air. "Take your pick, Inferno."

"The Inferno has a happy woman at home, Sentori. You might want to try it."

"No woman would settle for him, Tommy," Dante said.

Sentori's brows drew together. "I thought you said your girlfriend couldn't make it."

Dante spun around. Caitlyn stood with Amy, Brad, and Paul at the edge of the pool, her red hair flowing around her face. The black bathing suit top plunged low between her breasts, the matching skirt hitting her upper thighs. Now *she* was delectable.

"I'm starting to see your obsession, Inferno. I think it's the confidence. I hadn't seen before. Hmm. I like it."

Sentori was right. She was different again. She stood, sunglasses perched on her nose, head held high, drink in her hand, seemingly unaffected about being around the people she associated with her humiliation. She glanced in his direction but the damn sunglasses kept him from being certain she was looking at him. She turned away and laughed at something Paul said.

"Now *she's* a piece of ass I'd gladly fuck. Think she'll spread those legs for me?" Sentori asked into his ear.

"Not in a million years."

"Sounds like you're speaking from experience, Inferno. Maybe you didn't do it for her, but I will."

Dante's fist popped the plastic of the water bottle. Sentori lifted a brow at Dante and laughed. "I think it's time to catch a piggy."

He sauntered away. Dante breathed deeply, fighting to remain calm. The pig comments infuriated him. Sentori used them to get a rise out of him, but after witnessing how such cruelty had hurt Caitlyn, the words had become even harder to ignore.

Tommy sidled over, watching Caitlyn. "I thought you two were dating."

Dante swallowed. This ugly embarrassment was his own damned fault. Why had he let everyone think things were fine?

Because he'd never imagined Caitlyn would show up to

another fighter function. She was full of surprises.

"We're not seeing things eye to eye right now."

"Does this have to do with the other night?"

Dante shrugged. "That and other things."

"So are you two over?"

Dante glanced over at Caitlyn. She threw her head back and laughed. The musical strum of her amusement engulfed him and he closed his eyes.

"I still have some fight in me."

CHAPTER THIRTEEN

Cait took another sip of the piña colada. The slushy coconut and rum mixture melted on her tongue, leaving behind the sharp taste of liquor.

Dante's gaze drilled a hole into the side of her face and the stare grew increasingly difficult to disregard. Thank God for sunglasses. Her uncooperative eyes sought the one thing they were supposed to ignore. Fortunately, the darkened lenses gave her the ability to watch him without being caught.

He'd mesmerized her, standing there in his blue Hawaiian board trunks, his arms crossed over his impressive tanned chest, the black lines from his tattoo teasing her, begging to be traced. He made no secret about watching her. No surprise there. After all, he was Dante.

Today would be much harder than she anticipated. How could she pretend Dante didn't affect her? Just knowing he was nearby fluttered her stomach and did hot things to her body. She refused to concentrate on his proximity or she'd give up this crazy plan.

She couldn't do that.

"Earth to Cait." Paul snapped his fingers in front of her face.

Cait jumped. "What?"

"You've been staring into your drink for the last three minutes. What's up?"

Amy hooked an arm around her waist. "I'd say it's a certain fighter looking mighty fine in just his shorts."

She didn't know the half of it.

Cait hadn't told Amy about her plan—or rather, Paul's plan. Her friend would blow a gasket, spill the truth to Brad, who'd tell Dante. She wasn't going through all of this for nothing. Yet, Amy and Brad's presence presented a certain complication. How was she supposed to garner Sentori's attention without making Amy go ballistic?

On top of that, what if she couldn't get the guy to notice her?

"One can't help but look," Cait said.

"Girl, you could do much more than look and you know it." Amy nudged her.

"I think I'm going to hit the hot tub." Talking about Dante and his to-die-for body wasn't helping her cause—or her restraint.

"Those things are heated cesspools." Amy grimaced and stepped away.

Cait hid her triumph. "You want to join me?"

Paul glanced at the tub. Two beefy fighters sat on the edge with their feet in the bubbling water. "Girl, I'm supposed to be acting all straight and shit. How am I supposed to do that with such goodies to gawk at?" Then he shrugged. "What the hell?"

Cait laughed and hooked her arm through Paul's. "I'll keep you safe."

"Promise?"

"On my heart." She glanced at Amy and Brad. "We'll catch up with you in a bit, okay?"

"That's fine. Brad wants to go inside and play some poker with the guys, so once you're done with your bacteria-laced soak, that's where we'll be."

Cait strolled to the whirlpool with Paul and stepped down into the hot tub. The churning water tickled her legs as she waded toward one side. Placing her arms along the top, she sank into the bubbles. Paul sat beside her. She could feel Dante scowling at her. She refused to acknowledge him and glanced around the pool.

"Have you seen Sentori?" she whispered to Paul.

"Not since he walked away from your man."

Cait grimaced. The conversation hadn't appeared to be a pleasant one. "What do you think they were talking about?"

"Beats me. But from the tension between those two, I suspect pissing off Thor won't be that hard."

An understatement if there ever was one. If Dante had gripped his water bottle any tighter, the thing would've popped its cap and spewed water like a geyser. "There's a lot of tension already, don't you think?"

Paul shrugged. "These men are OD'ing on testosterone. I figure it only gets worse the closer a fight approaches. That's why this plan will work. I promise." He sent her an encouraging smile.

She hoped so. If this failed, then it might distract Dante more.

"Excuse me, is this seat taken?"

Paul's foot hit hers. Sentori stood at the edge of the tub exuding predatory determination as he stared down at her. The air around him was thick with calculation and coldness. She swallowed her dislike as her doubts ballooned tenfold.

His lily-white skin shone bright in the sun. His green hair cast a sickly glow to his face. Yes, his body was nice. Ripped and trim. But in no way did it compare to Dante's.

She forced a smile. "Come on in."

He lowered himself into the tub, sliding close to her. Too close. His thigh brushed hers. She jumped. To increase the distance between them, Cait scooted away.

Sentori slipped his arm behind her, his fingers toying with her hair. She wanted nothing more than to slap his hand away, but she smiled and feigned interest.

"How have you been, Caitlyn?"

Acid burned her throat. Dante was the only person who used her full name. She liked it that way. It was like an endearment.

"Call me Cait."

His eyes narrowed. "But Caitlyn fits you so much better."

"I prefer Cait."

"But Inferno calls you Caitlyn."

How did he know that?

Her unease tightened, but she pushed it aside. She needed him to believe she wasn't interested in Dante. This presented a perfect opportunity to prove just that. She forced the next words out. "Dante is an arrogant bully who never listens to anything I tell him. I've asked him repeatedly to call me Cait."

Dear God, please don't strike me dead for that lie.

Sentori smiled. "Then Cait it is. I would never want to be

a bully." He nodded toward Paul. "And who's your friend?"

"This is Paul. Paul, Sentori."

Paul gave him a tight smile. "Pleasure."

Silence descended on them. Cait fidgeted. How did she initiate chitchat with someone she didn't want to talk to?

"How's the training going?"

Thank you, Paul.

"Easy enough. The fight will be a cake walk."

That wasn't even cool. "You didn't seem so sure of yourself at the bar."

"I've found humility is overrated. I'm the best fighter in the organization. No reason to pretend otherwise."

She exchanged glances with Paul, whose brows had drawn into a straight line. This man was completely different from the one at the bar. Not that she necessarily liked that one either, but he'd at least seemed humble, legitimately concerned over whether Dante would hurt her. The man before her was overloaded in conceited bullshit.

Sentori's fingers played with the knot at the back of her bathing suit. She whipped her head around and stared at him, jerking away from his touch. His brows rose. Interest gleamed in his eyes. "Jumpy, aren't we, Cait?"

His gaze strayed past her, and his lips twisted in a triumphant smirk. She followed his focus and collided with Dante's furious blue eyes.

"What's going on between you two?" Sentori asked.

"N-nothing."

"Don't look that way to me."

She couldn't turn her gaze from Dante. At any moment, the vein pulsing at his temple would surely explode. She scooted farther away from Sentori. He followed, leaning in close. "I can make you forget him."

She dragged her eyes from Dante to Sentori. "There isn't anything to forget."

"Really? Well then, would you care to join me for dinner Saturday night?" His finger traced the strap of her top, stopping just below her collarbone.

Distaste induced a shiver. She didn't want to go out with this man. She remembered why she was there.

Dante.

"I-I would l-like that."

He lifted her hand from the water and kissed the back of it. "Until Saturday, then." He rose and left the tub.

"I don't like that guy," Paul said.

"Me either." She chanced a glance at Dante. "Oh, shit."

"What?"

"Here he comes."

Paul glanced up. "Oh hell, Cait, he looks ready to do murder."

"God, he does, doesn't he?"

Dante stormed toward them. The fierceness of his expression made it clear he was seconds from exploding. He stopped at the lip of the tub and placed his hands on his hips. "Out," he ordered Paul.

Paul started to scramble out. Cait gripped his arm. "Don't go anywhere."

Her friend glanced between Cait and Dante. "But Cait, The Hulk has requested my absence. I believe it best if I cooperate."

Dante glared at her. "Listen to your friend, Caitlyn. We need to talk."

"He's not going anywhere."

"Scared of being alone with me?"

A challenge. A huge one. She rose, thrusting her chin high in the air. Everything she did from this point forward was vital. A confident woman would never back down. But she felt anything but confident. At any moment, her heart would beat out of her chest or she'd hyperventilate. "Lead the way, Inferno."

"It's 'Inferno' now?"

She shrugged, refusing to answer. She wasn't certain why she'd used his fighter name. It'd gotten a response, though. Perhaps one she didn't want.

Dante stormed to the pool house. She hesitated before following him. Being alone with him, especially in his current mood, was a bad idea. This Dante was dangerous. Unrelenting.

Not good. Not good. Not good.

He opened the door. As she swept by him, her breasts brushed by his naked chest, and her nipples instantly hardened.

Yeah, really not good.

The door slammed shut. The room instantly dimmed with the door closed. She was thankful—the less she could see the better.

"What the hell is going on, Caitlyn?"

She closed her eyes, wishing she could block out the hurt in his voice. "I'm not sure what you mean."

"Sentori." His darkened figure stalked forward. "He's my opponent."

He was going to touch her. And if he did, everything would be ruined. She backed up. "So?"

"So? Why are you getting all cozy with him?"

"H-he seems like a nice guy." And to get it out there and over with, she blurted, "We're going out Saturday night."

He went utterly still, then curled his hands into fists. "You're going out with him?"

"Y-yes."

He pounced, pressing her against the wooden wall and raising her hands above her head. Cait gasped as his chest rubbed against hers.

"Why?" he asked.

She looked into his shadowed face. A mistake. Pain shone there, bright and potent. She faltered, yearning to caress the tension from his clenched jaw. She'd seen so many different emotions clench his jaw: rage, stubbornness, determination. This was the first time she'd ever seen pain—caused by her— and the knowledge of what she was doing to him ripped at her insides.

The championship.

She used the reminder as strength and said, "Why not?"

Oh, that had been the wrong comeback. She knew it the moment she saw his gaze rake over her.

"Because you're mine. That's why."

As if to prove his point, his lips were on hers. Demanding. Dominating. And heaven help her, she couldn't deny him. When his tongue probed her lips, she opened for him, begging for his possession. She tugged at her captured wrists, and he released them, his hands gliding down her arms, the sides of her breasts, before settling on her hips. Cait wound her arms around his neck and pulled him closer.

Dante growled, grabbed the backs of both knees, and wrapped her legs around his waist. Wood bit into Cait's back, but she didn't care. All she cared about was this man's touch.

She rubbed her fingers against the short stubble at the nape of his neck. The rough texture felt exquisite against her skin.

"Caitlyn," he whispered into her mouth.

Desire colored his words. What was she doing? This was wrong. So very wrong. But the darkness in the room allowed her to feel him without worry he'd reach for a light. It felt so good. So right.

His hand skimmed up her leg to her waist, then cupped her breast, lightly pinching the erect nipple. Cait broke the kiss, gasping. Dante's lips moved down her neck, to the vee of her bathing suit where he licked the valley between her breasts. She had to stop him, but couldn't find the strength. This was everything she wanted.

"Dante," she whispered as his fingers fumbled with the tie at the back of her neck.

"That's right. Say my name. *My name*," he commanded.

The cool air touched her nipples as the material fell around her waist. His mouth warmed one as he drew it between his lips. She tightened her grip around his neck, thrusting closer to his suckling mouth.

"Cait?"

The sound of Sentori's voice had her eyes popping open. Dante stiffened. Reality seeped in. She pushed at his shoulders. "I can't do this."

He didn't release her. Instead, he leaned closer, rubbing his cock against her mound. She bit her lip and stifled a moan.

"Groan, Caitlyn."

He rubbed, harder. She bit, harder. His fingers slid down her body to the edge of her bathing suit. "I can check. Do you want me to?"

Without waiting, his finger slipped beneath the material

and grazed her flesh. She closed her eyes and moaned low in her throat.

He moved his finger again, circling her. "You can't deny you're wet. So wet. So ready."

"Cait?"

Dante snarled. "Say you're mine, Caitlyn."

"I-I can't." She took a shaky breath, knowing what she had to do. "It's just sex, Dante."

He released her and jerked back as if she'd smacked him. Cait stumbled to get her footing. She grabbed the top of her bathing suit and covered her breasts, hating herself.

Dante spun then stormed outside.

She secured her bathing suit with shaky fingers.

"Cait?"

Sentori's green hair appeared before the rest of him. She swallowed her distaste. "Yes?"

"I just saw Dante leave. Was he bothering you?"

"No."

His eyes zeroed in on her mouth and he lifted an amused brow. Cait suppressed the urge to hide her swollen lips.

"Nothing going on, eh?" He stepped closer.

She stepped back, not liking his smirk. She straightened. "I don't know what you're talking about."

"Don't you?"

Cait tried to sidestep him, but he blocked her path and backed her against the wall. The same wall Dante had her so passionately pinned to just seconds ago.

She placed her hands on the middle of his chest and pushed. "You're crowding me, Sentori. Back off."

She was relieved he did so without hesitation. But his hand came up and traced her lips. She flinched, and he tsked.

"What are you about, Caitlyn?"

That he used her full name didn't go unnoticed. She opened her mouth to protest, but he continued, "Do you think you can have us both, Caitlyn?" His gaze met hers. "I don't like leftovers, *Caitlyn*."

The taunting way he used her name twisted her stomach in disgust. This man knew exactly what he was doing. What words to use. Did he do this with Dante?

He bent and whispered close to her ear. "Would you like to play a game?"

Revulsion shivered through her.

"Who can fuck with Dante more? You or me?"

She gasped, her eyes flying to his. Her immediate reaction was to deny his implications, but Sentori shook his head, a grin splitting his lips. "You may win."

"What is going on in here?"

At the sound of Paul's voice, relief swept through her. Sentori lazily straightened. "Just having a little chat." He glanced back at Cait and winked. "I'll pick you up Saturday, Caitlyn." Then he strolled from the room.

Paul hurried to her side. "What happened?"

She wrapped her arms under her breasts. "I did what I came out here to do. Dante hates me."

CHAPTER FOURTEEN

Dante hugged his fists to his cheeks, studying Mike's every move. His coach mimicked Dante's stance, fists up, as they circled each other. This was Dante's final chance to prove to Mike he was here to win. He *would not* fail.

Mike shifted slightly to the left. The slight movement was exactly what Dante had been waiting for and he countered. Lunging forward, he thrust a shoulder into Mike's stomach and slammed him to the ground. His coach's shocked "Damn it!" let Dante know he'd taken Mike by surprise. Good. He needed every advantage he could get today, and taking down Mike was a great addition to what had already been a grueling but successful session.

Dante pinned him and lay across his chest. Mike shoved, but Dante braced his knees into his coach's side, preventing any attempt at escape. He surveyed his position. The arm. Perfect. He tightened his grip. With each shove and twist, Mike's efforts to break out of his hold weakened. Dante kept his grip tight, allowing his coach to exhaust out. When

Mike's moves became sluggish, Dante twisted. Clenching his coach's wrist in a powerful grasp, he pried Mike's arm out with his hand and bent it in a ninety-degree angle.

"Ah! Fuck! My arm," Mike yelled. "Stop!"

Dante immediately let go, trying to keep from showing his satisfaction. Mike had no time to tap, just instant pain and the begging to be released. If this didn't prove to his coach he was focused, he wasn't sure what would.

Mike lay on the mat, breathing heavily as he rolled his arm in a circle and stared at Dante. "You're going to fuck Sentori up."

Dante sat back on his haunches and wiped his arm across his forehead. Pride welled in his chest. Finally, he'd done something right. It was about time. "You gave me another chance. I'm not going to disappoint you."

The smile his coach sent him was full of approval. "Glad to see you back, my friend."

Dante rose to his feet and shook out his tight muscles. "Good to be back."

Mike clapped Dante on the shoulder. "That's enough practice. Why don't you go relax in the sauna?"

Now that was an idea. His muscles ached to high hell. The heat would ease the tightness. "Thanks."

Once in the locker room, he changed out of his sweaty clothes and wrapped a towel around his hips then stepped into the sauna. Inhaling the cedar wood scent, he sat on the bench. The eerie silence had a calming effect and Dante closed his eyes, listening to the occasional pop of the heater and creaking of wood.

He was pleased with his performance today. He'd given Mike his all.

He'd refused to focus on the pain Caitlyn's date with his opponent created. Instead, he forced his attention on knowing the woman from yesterday was not his Caitlyn.

Correct that.

The woman who'd melted in his arms, returning his kiss with a passion matching his had been his Caitlyn. The other one? He wasn't sure where she'd come from.

Dante leaned his head against the bench above him.

Why had she agreed to go out with that piece of shit? If this was her way of proving a point, she'd failed. Not only was he an MMA fighter who socialized with the type of people she wanted to avoid, she also claimed she only dated the average Joe. Sentori was anything but average. Flaunting an everyday guy would've had more impact on him than Sentori. Her actions spurred him to uncover her true motivation.

Because one thing was clear: she didn't *want* to go out with his opponent.

It had taken the better part of the night to recall the distaste that scrunched her nose as she'd tried to pretend interest in Sentori. The flinch when he'd toyed with her hair. And the most telling of all, the quick scoot away from the other man after she'd glanced at Dante. She'd known what she was doing hurt him.

So what could possibly be her reason for encouraging his rival?

Sweat beaded on Dante's skin, his face tightening from the heat. He placed a towel over his head.

All the attention from Caitlyn went straight to Sentori's head, giving him another way to taunt Dante. Yesterday, that had worked. Today, it wouldn't. If anything, he was more determined than ever to topple the undefeated fighter.

No, not just topple.

Deliver a crushing, mortifying loss that would leave the arrogant bastard whimpering in his corner, or better yet, completely unconscious. A win so profound any future opponent could smile at Sentori's pathetic attempts at playing mind games and say, *"I'll take you down just as the Inferno did."*

Dante planned to pave the road to the complete annihilation of Richard Sentori.

• • •

Damn.

Cait hung up the phone.

"Well?" Paul demanded.

"Mike said Dante's training has been outstanding this week and for me to keep up the good work."

Paul threw up his hands and groaned, flopping back on the couch.

Her sentiments exactly. Ever since the pool party, she'd called Mike for a daily update. Each day the excitement and pride in his voice grew, much to her consternation. Not that she wanted Dante to lose his coach. She just really didn't want to go out with Sentori. "I guess I need to get ready for the date."

Paul sat up. "Cait, please. I was wrong. Don't go out with this guy."

"What am I supposed to do? It was your plan and the stupid thing worked."

"You picked *now* to listen to me?"

"Nothing is going to happen."

At least not physically. Sentori had backed off far too quickly when she told him to. Mentally, however, she'd have to keep on her toes. After the two encounters with him at the pool party, she knew the man liked to play games—but she had no idea how far he'd go.

Paul stood and grasped her shoulders. "You can't be certain. What if you end up on a dead-end road?"

"Sentori isn't going to hurt me. There's too much riding on the line. For whatever reason, he likes taunting Dante. Having me dead or hurt is not the kind of taunting he's after."

It sickened her to know she aided in Sentori's fun. If she had any clue the kind of man he was, she'd never have agreed to this plan. Now she was in over her head.

Mike had gloated that Dante pinned him in a move Sentori had yet to perfect. He'd finally seen the Dante who would defeat Sentori. How could she quit now?

Paul dropped his arms to his side. "I still don't like this."

"I can't cancel. I'm worried if I do, I'll confuse Dante and ruin the progress he's made."

"He hasn't called you all week, hasn't even been at the Y, so I'd say you've accomplished your goals."

Paul's reminder hurt. Horribly. But she couldn't regret what she'd done, especially with Dante training so well. If fury at her was what kept him focused, then she'd make sure it stayed that way. She still held onto the small chance that once his fight was over, she could tell him the truth and he'd forgive her. "What if I don't go through with the date and Dante shows up wanting to know why I canceled?"

"I doubt creep-boy would admit you stood him up."

"Have you seen how fast gossip spreads in that locker room? Amy isn't talking to *me* because Brad told her about the date, and he'd heard it from one of the other guys at the gym, who'd heard it from someone at Sentori's gym. I can't chance it."

He sighed, which Cait recognized as a sigh of defeat.

"Fine. You *will* call me every hour." He slapped her phone in her hand. "Do you hear me? If you don't, I'm coming after you."

The romantic ambiance on the patio of the Italian restaurant grated on Cait's nerves. Sentori sat across from her. The plethora of plants surrounding them cast shadows across his face, making it difficult to read his expression. She cursed the dark atmosphere, cursed the strands of white lights that emitted only a meager glow.

He'd made her sit with her back to the restaurant. A calculated move, she was certain, to keep her on edge, waiting to hear Dante's voice from behind. What would she do if he showed up? How would she act?

During the last hour, Sentori had been a complete gentleman, making mundane chitchat about movies, books, and anything else that might be of interest. His act didn't fool her. He was trying to make her relax, to become comfortable in his presence. She knew as soon as she did, *boom*.

"How's your chicken parm?" he asked.

Tasted like Styrofoam. "Fine."

Sentori placed his fork and knife on his plate and leaned back with his wineglass in his hand, studying her. Cait struggled not to fidget and held his gaze, positive this was a deliberate attempt at intimidation.

"Tell me, Caitlyn." He paused, taking a long sip of his

wine.

At his use of her full name, her stomach clenched.

He pulled the glass from his lips and sighed. "Why have you dumped the Inferno?"

At some point, she'd known he'd mention Dante and had prepared herself. Her gaze never wavered. "Dante and I never dated. So I didn't dump him."

He rotated the glass between his thumb and forefinger. "Really? I heard different. He brought you to an after-party a week ago, didn't he?"

Cait stiffened. Now *that* she hadn't been prepared for. "That was a mistake."

"I'll say. I heard some woman offended you and he threw her in the pool." Placing his glass on the table, he leaned forward. "Tell me, Caitlyn, what did the woman say that infuriated the Inferno?"

Cait barely heard the question. He'd done that? *For her?*

Warmth spread from her head to the tips of her toes. No man had ever defended her. How freaking sweet could a man get?

"What did she say?"

At Sentori's pressure, her pleasant thoughts turned sour. She saw the twinkle in his eyes, the near giddiness. The bastard already knew what Amanda had said. Cait refused to allow him to upset her. She stared him straight in the eye. "She asked if I was the pity date."

Surprise flickered across his face and he jerked back with a scowl.

Take that, asshole. Cait took a sip of her water to hide her smile. "She's entitled to her opinion."

The scowl deepened, then melted into such sympathy

Cait could almost believe it genuine. Damn, he was good.

"Being known as the pity date had to hurt, embarrassing even. I bet it was a real kick to the stomach."

"People can be cruel. I won't let it bother me. If I did, I wouldn't be out with you, would I?"

A smile twisted one corner of his mouth and he shook his head. "You going out with me had nothing to do with *me*. What did you think? That by accepting my date, Dante would forget what was said? That he would see other men find you attractive regardless of what some bitch said?" He gave her a sad look. "I'll let you in on something. Men don't forget things like that. They might pretend it doesn't matter. But it *always* comes down to the guy wanting to have the hottest girl on his arm. Since that's not you, I suspect Dante will be searching for new options."

Cait's stomach churned. He fed the insecurities she tried desperately to starve. She swallowed them back, determined not to allow them to control her anymore. "If the pity date comment stamped me as undatable, why did you ask me out?"

He shrugged. "To get under Dante's skin. Pity date or not, no man likes another man to succeed where they've failed."

"Failed?"

He reached over and trailed his finger over the top of her hand. She yanked it back.

"Getting you into bed," he said, chuckling.

"I won't sleep with you."

"I have no intention of touching you. I prefer a leaner woman—much leaner." He eyed her with disinterest. "It's called lying, Caitlyn."

"Why do you think Dante will care?"

"An easy lay like you and Dante couldn't get some of the action." Sentori snorted. "Dante hates to lose. Hearing I slammed you will eat him up. Especially when I tell him you begged for it."

She gasped, fighting the urge to smack his arrogant face. "Dante's not going to believe you."

"You, my dear, set this up nicely. I don't know what you and Dante were doing in the pool house, but I'm sure it wasn't innocent. But he wasn't a sated man when he left, was he, Caitlyn?" He paused. "No, he was furious. Was he unable to get into your pants? Did you tell him no? Yet you accepted my date and showed him you wanted to spread those legs for someone, didn't you? Naturally, I'll be the man you spread them for."

Panic squeezed her throat. She hadn't exactly told Dante no. What she had said was way worse. *"It's just sex."*

The plan imploded around her. She needed a reality check. Cait glanced at her watch. A little over an hour had passed since she'd left. Paul was probably waiting for her to call.

"I need to use the ladies' room." She stood and grabbed her purse.

Once inside, she plopped her purse on the counter and dug around. Then dug some more. When she still didn't find her phone, she turned it upside down and spilled out the contents. She stared at the green tube of lipstick rolling across the porcelain.

Oh. My. God. She'd left her cell at home.

Paul was going to freak.

• • •

Dante lay on his couch, his right arm over his head as he flipped channels on the television. It had taken a considerable amount of restraint, but he'd succeeded in not going to Caitlyn's before her date. Letting tonight happen without incident would be a better approach than showing up and making demands like a jealous boyfriend. He'd done that at the pool and it hadn't worked.

A date with the pile of shit should knock whatever sense she'd lost back into place. Or at least make her doubt dating in general. Then he'd have her to himself again.

He groaned, tossed the remote on the table, and ran his hands over his face. Time ticked by. *Tick. Tick. Tick.* Had Sentori been smarter than him and kept Caitlyn away from the MMA crowd? Had he wined and dined her the way Dante should have?

Dante knew the bastard could put on the charm when he wanted. Women loved Sentori. Could he actually win over Caitlyn? She had no idea the vile things he'd said about her, so there was no reason for her not to enjoy the date.

Dante sat up, his stomach twisting. Maybe he should have shown up.

He jumped to his feet and paced the room. It was too late now. She was out with the asshole and he had no idea where.

There was a pounding at his door.

Caitlyn?

He hurried to answer. The sight before him washed away his disappointment.

Paul and Jack spoke in harsh whispers, gesturing wildly at each other. Dante cleared his throat and both men gaped. Then Jack shoved Paul forward. "Fix it."

Paul went white, his eyes huge. Something wasn't right. "Is Caitlyn okay?"

The man's eyes widened further. "Well…"

"Damn it, man, tell me."

Jack popped Paul upside his head. "This was your brilliant idea. Tell the man what you've done."

Paul spun on his boyfriend. "I was just trying to help. You didn't come up with a better plan, so back off."

"What the hell are you two babbling about? What plan?"

Paul faced him and swallowed. "Listen, Wolverine, please don't rip me apart. I was being a good friend. A dumb one, but I swear I didn't know it at the time."

"You need to tell me what's going on."

"Cait is out on a date with that jackass."

Dante sighed and rubbed his forehead. "I know."

"What you *don't* know is why."

Dante lowered his hand, intrigued. "Continue."

"Cait is going to kill me. But I don't trust that man. And since this was my bright idea…"

Dante crossed his arms and leveled the man with his fighter stare.

Paul held up his hands. "Okay! Cait overheard your conversation with your coach."

"What conversation?"

"The one where he quit. She tried to reason with him, but he told her she had to be completely out of the picture or he wouldn't coach you anymore, then she tried to talk to—"

"I'm going to fucking kill Mike."

Paul smacked his hand over his mouth. "Oh, shit. Cait *is* going to kill me."

"Why?"

"She didn't want you to know what your coach said. She didn't want to make things tense between you guys, but I swear when I suggested going out with Sentori, I had no idea the man was scum. I mean really, creepy icky scum. And, *now*, she hasn't called me like she was supposed—"

"Call you?" Dante stiffened. "What do you mean?"

"She was supposed to call and let me know she was okay. But she hasn't and she's been gone for over three hours."

Dante inhaled deeply, calming the sense of alarm. Yes, Sentori was scum. But he'd never physically hurt Caitlyn. The man took too much pride in being the welterweight champion to screw anything up and have his title stripped. That didn't mean he wouldn't play some kind of sick mind game with her.

He grabbed his keys off the counter. "Where'd they go?"

"I don't know."

"You don't know?"

"I was kinda hoping you would."

"How would I know?"

"Isn't that what you beefcakes do? Go after your woman when she's out with another man? So I figured you knew exactly where she'd be."

"Have you called her phone?"

"Only about five thousand times."

"Maybe she left it at the apartment?"

Paul popped a hand on his hip. "What kind of friend do you take me for? I handed it to her as she left. And before you start rattling on about battery power, I charged the damned thing myself this afternoon."

Impressive. But why wasn't Caitlyn answering?

"If it helps, she said the nasty ass mentioned getting

Italian."

"Shit. He took her to Cucina Dell'amore."

"How do you know?"

"It's the new hot spot the fighters have been taking their dates to. The perfect Italian setting for…romance." What if Sentori actually showed Caitlyn a good time? Damn it! And he'd never shown up to interfere. "We have to get there. *Now.*"

Within minutes, the three of them were speeding to the restaurant. Dante had little hope they'd still be there. His fears were confirmed when the maître d' said they'd left an hour earlier.

Outside on the sidewalk, Dante fished out his phone and pressed one on his speed dial. Caitlyn's sweet voice answered with "I can't come to the phone right now—"

Dante snapped the phone shut and growled. Where the hell *was* she?

Chapter Fifteen

"Take me home."

Sentori glanced away from the road. "Not yet."

Cait muttered a curse. In hindsight, she should've called a cab. Or called Paul from the restaurant phone. No, not her dumb ass. She *had* to come off strong and unfazed by his games. So instead of leaving him sitting there in the restaurant, she'd marched out of the bathroom and demanded he take her home. He'd simply shrugged and said okay. She should've known it was a lie. Lying and taunting was what the man did best.

Now, over an hour later, she sat in the passenger side of his Jeep watching the same buildings pass by—over and over again. Paul had to be a basket case by now. One day she would actually memorize the phone numbers and stop relying on her contact list in her *phone*.

"How much longer are you going to drive around town?"

He peered at his watch. "At least another thirty minutes. If I take you home too early, the Inferno won't believe me." He gave her a sorrowful look. "I can't have that, can I, Caitlyn?"

Finding the question unworthy of an answer, she glanced back out the window. Unfortunately, she could still see his reflection illuminated by the green glow from the dashboard.

Disgust knotted her insides. She despised this man. If one positive came out of this godawful night, it would be watching Dante kick Sentori's face in. Seeing blood gush from his smug nose would have been a welcome sight.

Cait closed her eyes.

Dante. Her heart twisted.

He was never going to forgive her.

"What are you thinking over there, Caitlyn?"

She scowled. Even his voice disgusted her. "None of your damned business."

His chuckle sparked her anger. Whipping her head around, she stared at his profile. "You're low-lying slime, do you know that?"

Sentori glanced at her, amusement twisting his lips. "Now, now, no reason to get hostile. The person you should be mad at is yourself. You started this game."

"It's not a game."

"Isn't it? You have an agenda and so do I."

"Take me home, Sentori."

"In due time, my sweet."

Cait huffed, contemplating jumping out the damned door. If her life had been in immediate danger, she would have.

Another hour of tense silence passed before Sentori finally stopped in front of her apartment complex. Flinging open the door, Cait hopped out and started across the asphalt. Footsteps fell into step behind her. She whirled and almost slammed into Sentori. She stepped back. "I don't need an escort."

"Night's not over yet."

Before she could so much as gasp, he yanked her into his arms. One hand was locked on the back of her nape, keeping her head immobile as he kissed her, a bruising, aggressive kiss that cut her teeth into the back of her lips. The metallic taste of blood tinged her tongue. Cait shoved at his chest. After he ground his mouth into hers one last time, he released his hold on her head and jerked her wrists behind her back. Skin twisting against bone made her cry out.

When Sentori buried his head into her neck, followed by a sharp pain as he bit and sucked, the shock of what was happening wore off and fury filled her.

Her knee jerked up, hard and fast, connecting with vulnerable flesh. He stiffened, his eyes wide in surprise.

"You disgusting bastard." She kicked him before walking away.

"Try explaining that to Dante."

Sentori's words froze her.

She touched her lips. Swollen. Bruised. With her tongue, she traced the cut on the back of her lip. The bottom one would still be puffy tomorrow. Proof of a night of rough sex. She had little doubt Sentori would claim she'd been a wildcat.

The side of her neck throbbed. A bite mark marred her skin. Furious, she spun around and marched back over to Sentori. She kicked his hip. She started to leave, but then she paused. Giving into her urges, she whacked him upside the head with her purse.

"Asshole."

Sentori laughed.

She strode across the parking lot to her apartment and fished her keys out of her purse, muttering obscenities the entire way. She thrust the door open and slammed it behind her.

Flicking on the light, she went to the mirror hanging on the wall. As she suspected, her bottom lip was swollen, giving her the kissed-senseless look. She inspected her neck and found a bruise—no, a fucking hickey—forming. She flung her purse on the table, and noted the red marks marring her wrist.

Damn it!

Muffled footsteps sounded from the hall. She froze. His scent enveloped her and she closed her eyes. She wouldn't have time to rectify the damage. He'd see it fresh.

"Dante."

"Where've you been, Caitlyn?"

Shoulders rigid, she stood with her back to him, unable to face him. He'd believe she'd slept with Sentori. Tomorrow when the rumors started flying, he'd have his beliefs confirmed. She wanted nothing more than to confess everything, but she couldn't.

For him, for his fight, for his future, she couldn't.

She slowly turned, prepared for his concern to switch to scathing accusations as he took in her disheveled appearance.

His eyes narrowed on her lips then traveled to her neck, to her wrist, and he went ramrod straight. "He hurt you."

Cait inhaled sharply. That'd been the last thing she'd expected him to say. "Dante—"

He rushed by her, flinging the front door open.

She grabbed his arm. "Where are you going?"

He jerked away from her, looking at her with an expression of such murderous rage, her breath caught tight in her lungs.

"He's fucking dead."

He started out the door. Fear for him and what he was capable of in his current state scattered her thoughts. "Dante, it's over. Let it go."

"It's not over! He put his hands on you. Hurt you. He'll bleed for that. I swear it."

As he stalked down the breezeway, she hurried to intercept him at the stairs. He stopped, his nostrils flaring, fist clenching and unclenching at his side, his eyes not seeing her even though he stared at her.

"Don't leave me," she blurted. She'd say anything to keep him with her, make sure he didn't wind up in jail.

"Did he—" He ground his teeth. "Did he—"

"No! Oh God, Dante. No. He didn't. He wants you to *think* we slept together. It's evidence, that's all."

"Evidence?" He grabbed her hands and lifted them up. The red on her wrists had faded to purple. "He did this to you as evidence. He's going to pay, Caitlyn. Tonight."

When he moved to walk around her, she shuffled back in front of him. "He already has. I have a great self-defense teacher. I left him rolling in the parking lot clutching his crotch."

Even though he didn't even crack a smile, she sensed some of the tension creep out of him. Cait stepped closer, wrapped her arms around his waist, and rested her head on his chest. "Dante, don't leave. Stay with me."

He held her tight, his arms around her, as he kissed the

top of her head. "I won't go anywhere, but it kills me to know he touched you like that, Caitlyn."

She leaned back. His jaw was tight, eyes closed. She rose on her tiptoes, kissed his cheek, and whispered, "Then erase his touch."

Eyes popping open, Dante stared down at her as if battling indecision. That he faltered surprised her. A thread of panic weaved into her chest. Now that his knee-jerk reaction had calmed, was he second-guessing her words? Thinking she lied?

Before she could contemplate why he wavered, his lips claimed hers.

Cait opened to him as his tongue slipped into her mouth, caressing. A gentle, hesitant kiss. She wrapped her arms around his neck and pressed closer. The ugliness of the night melted into the background. The only thing that existed was her in Dante's arms.

He scooped her up, never breaking their kiss. He carried her so effortlessly, as if she were the lightest woman on earth. Cradled against his chest, she truly felt small. Vulnerable.

Once inside the apartment, he kicked the door closed behind him and strode to her darkened bedroom. As he lowered her to her feet, he reached for the light. Panic engulfed her and she grabbed his arm. "No, please. Keep it off."

Dante shook his head. "Not happening."

As light flooded the room, every monstrous insecurity roared with a vengeance. She wanted to cry. To scream. She'd freely offered herself to this man. Finally. She'd been ready, willing, wanting to feel his skin against hers. With one flick of the switch, all she could focus on was knowing he'd see her naked body, see every flaw.

"Please, Dante."

She despised that she begged. Pathetic.

Dante gripped her hips and kissed her. "I want to see you, Caitlyn. All of you."

Horrible images of her rounded belly, stretch marks and plump thighs flew into her mind. "I can't let you see me."

His brows drew together in a deep scowl. "I *want* to see you."

They stared at each other. A battle of wills. Hers driven by fear, his by determination. Cait wanted to run from the room, ashamed she'd let her mind ruin this moment, but unable to rise above her ugly thoughts.

Dante sighed and dropped his hold on her. "Fine," he said, and walked out of the room.

Cait stared after him. He'd left? Just like that?

The room closed in on her. She had her answer. Her inability to make love with the lights on had disgusted him.

Crossing her arms, she sat on the edge of the bed. She should go after him, but her legs were incapable of holding her weight. She waited for the slamming of the front door. It never came.

Instead, Dante strode back into the room. She jerked to her feet. He was still there. Then her eyes settled on the crimson piece of fabric hanging from his hand, the sash from the curtains in the living room.

"Turn around, Caitlyn," he said.

The determination in his voice mesmerized her. Dante placed his hands on her shoulders and rotated her. She didn't fight, too curious as to what he was about to do. The fabric covered her eyes and blocked the light.

"You can have your dark, Caitlyn," he whispered in her ear, "and I will have my light."

She shivered as his breath fanned her cheek. "Dante—"

"Shh, it's dark, Caitlyn. Embrace it and just feel."

His lips brushed her neck. Goosebumps rose on her skin. Then the heat from his nearness was gone. The area around her felt empty, cold. A click echoed in the room. She turned toward the noise, knowing it was her bedroom door closing.

"Dante?"

"I'm right here."

Warmth returned as two light kisses were placed on each of her wrists before his hands claimed her hips and his chest brushed hers. Cait swallowed and concentrated on the dark, trying to ignore the knowledge that he could see her clearly.

"Relax."

Easier said than done. The makeshift blindfold gave her the darkness she craved, but her mind refused to play along. She envisioned Dante before her in all his naked splendor. Tanned, muscular, perfect, staring at her plump body. Tears welled in her eyes. "I can't do this."

"You're thinking too much. I'll have to put a stop to that."

Next thing she knew, her shirt was over her head. She gasped as the air touched her stomach, and her hands flew to conceal herself. Dante's warm palms covered hers and pulled them away. "Never hide yourself from me."

His lips touched her belly, trailing kisses up to the curve of her breast.

"You're beautiful," he murmured against her skin.

Cait shuddered and placed her hands on his shoulder for balance. The cotton of his shirt was soft against her palms. A reminder he was still clothed while she stood half-naked.

As if sensing she was thinking again, Dante sucked an aching nipple into his mouth through the fabric of her bra. Gasping, she fisted the material of his shirt in her hands.

His fingers fumbled with the clasp. The lace gave way and slid down her arms. Dante breathed in sharply. "Lovely."

Embarrassed heat flushed her skin. But the sincerity in his tone gave her the strength to stand still and allow him to look.

He cupped her breast, rubbing his thumb over the sensitive nipple. Cait moaned and pressed into his hand.

"You fill my hand. Perfect." He paused. "Perfect for me."

Perfect. He found her perfect.

Moisture gathered between her legs, a slow throb pulsed. She ran her hands along his shoulders and up his neck. Wet heat encased her breast as his mouth closed around her, sucking deeply.

Electricity ran from her nipple straight to her core. Throwing her head back, she moaned as she laced her fingers around the back of his head to hold him close. He switched to the other breast and gave it the same treatment, inflaming her desires to a new level. Her awareness of the light faded with each touch.

Dante skimmed his lips over her shoulders and neck to her mouth, taking her in a deep kiss. He cupped her bottom and brought her close. His jeans-restrained erection pressed into her belly. So very hard and impressive. Rubbing against him, she fell completely into the darkness, her need taking control.

Cait searched for the hem of his shirt and tugged. Dante broke the kiss. Material rustled momentarily, then she was back in his arms. The contact of his naked chest touching her breasts made her tremble. No hair. All hot skin.

He buried his face in her neck and lightly bit the area Sentori had marked, then licked it. She tilted her head back and allowed him to remove every trace of the other fighter from her body. Allowed Dante to make his mark.

"You're mine, Caitlyn."

"I'm yours," she whispered.

Dante growled. Shivers of excitement raced through her. His fingers grasped the button of her jeans. Reality stepped back in with the speed of a freight train and she stiffened.

"No," Dante said. "Just feel."

He popped the button. The sound of the zipper lowering ricocheted around the room, tightening Cait's tension.

"Shh," Dante breathed against her stomach as he pushed the jeans to the ground.

She waited to feel the air hit her bottom, a harsh reminder she stood before this man naked. The coolness never came.

Cait hiccupped a quiet sob as gratitude lifted her heart. He'd left on her boyshorts. He understood how hard this was for her, that each step was a new milestone. He allowed her the opportunity to adjust, to enjoy, before moving on to the next step.

God, this man was wonderful.

His fingers grazed their way up the inside of her leg, stopping just inches from her core. As if her body pleaded for him, the throbbing intensified. Cait shifted her legs further apart. His open mouth replaced his fingers.

At the change in sensation, Cait gasped. The wetness of his tongue lapped at her inner thigh before slowly moving up. He nuzzled the front of her panties. She shuddered, grabbing his shoulders for support as her legs begged to crumble and spread for him. "Oh, God."

"Do you like that?"

"Y-yes."

His tongue traced the waistband of her panties, scorching her stomach.

"Dante, please."

Gone was all inhibition, all insecurities. Need for him consumed her. In one swift movement, her panties were gone. Dante took her into his arms and laid her on the floor. Soft carpet cushioned her back as he covered her body with his. His weight pressed into her, exuding his raw power. The power he had over her.

He claimed her lips then shifted, the sound of his zipper filling the air. Moments later, he settled between her legs. His hardness pushed against her. She arched toward him, but he backed away. "Not so fast, Caitlyn. I'm not done loving you."

With his mouth, he raked a line from her lips down her body until his breath blew on the area screaming to be touched. He paused and she knew he was viewing her in all her naked glory.

She didn't care. She just wanted. Wanted to see him. To watch him love her. Yanking off the blindfold, she looked at Dante, who knelt between her thighs.

He smiled, a lopsided smile. "Hey, baby."

The raw desire in his eyes erased any lingering doubt. She widened her legs. "Please."

His smile turned wolfish. "My pleasure."

Dante's head dipped down and he nuzzled the curls with his nose. Cait watched, awed at the sight the darkness had denied her. His tan skin contrasted with her paleness. His broad shoulders dominated the space between her legs, the muscles rippling as he positioned lower.

Their gazes met across the length of her body. Cait's heart tripped. She'd never shared this kind of intimacy with anyone. The impact stunned her.

"Thank you," she whispered.

Another crooked grin stretched his lips, then she felt the first touch of his tongue. She gasped as he worked his magic. He teased, licked, sucked, and curled the ball of desire tighter and tighter until she exploded. Arching off the floor, she screamed her climax.

Dante straightened and took a shuddering breath. "Beautiful."

Cait drifted back to the here and now and glanced at him. He'd watched her as no man ever had, in the grip of her release. His expression spoke volumes—he'd enjoyed every second of it. Dante rained kisses over her belly. Cait stroked the back of his head. Content. Complete.

No, not complete. Yet. "I want you inside me."

Dante's head snapped up. Cait smiled. He'd been unprepared for that. It was his fault. He'd released her inner vixen and she wanted to embrace it.

He straightened and hooked his hands behind her knees. Dragging her forward, he draped a leg on either side of his waist. "I want to be inside you, too."

He reached for his jeans and grabbed a condom from the back pocket. Ripping the foil open with his teeth, he quickly sheathed his erection. Anticipation coiled deeply. Soon, so soon, she would know what it was like to be taken by Dante Jones. The Inferno. Fitting, since that was the sensation he created within her.

He gripped her hips and brushed against her. Still

sensitive from her orgasm, Cait moaned and closed her eyes. Once more, he brushed against her.

"Open your eyes, Caitlyn."

She did as he commanded and his heated gaze seared hers. Dante probed the folds of her center. He slowly pushed inside her. Cait arched, her body stretching to accept him. Dante closed his eyes, his jaw tightening, breathing deeply.

She marveled at him. This strong warrior fought for control. She wiggled closer. His eyes snapped open. "Don't move, Caitlyn. I've been waiting a long time for this and my body knows it."

She stilled, watching him regain control. When he climbed up her body and pressed her into the carpet, she knew he had regained control. He combed the hair from her forehead, fanning kisses over her face, and he took his sweet time thrusting into her. Cait grasped his butt, encouraging him to increase his speed, but he denied her, setting the lovemaking at his pace.

He moved his head to the curve of her neck. "You feel so good around me. So warm. So tight."

Cait's breath caught. She turned her head and took his lips. He groaned and rose, ravishing her mouth with deep, purposeful flicks of his tongue. She met each swipe with her own demands. Inviting him to abandon his slow progression and take her. Hard and fast.

He must have sensed her urgency because his thrusts increased. Dante tore away from her lips and buried his head in her shoulder, his plunges faster, rougher. Cait moaned, scratching her way down his back to grab his butt, helping him pump into her. Her need was unbearable. Their short, choppy breaths melded in the air.

"Caitlyn, Caitlyn," he repeated.

Hearing him chant her name pushed her over the edge and she shattered around him. "Dante!"

One more thrust and Dante stiffened against her. He lifted up, his eyes squeezed, teeth bared. He gasped sharply as his body jerked with tremors. Then he collapsed against her.

She gazed over Dante's shoulder and stared at the ceiling, enjoying each little aftershock quaking her body. A smile tugged at her lips. She'd done it. Made love to him, in the light, no less, the most amazing experience of her life. His gentleness, his understanding, did the one thing she'd never been able to accomplish on her own—obliterate the last barrier of her insecurity.

Cait held him close and drew lazy circles over his shoulder blade. Who knew letting go of the past would be so powerful, so freeing?

The skin twitched under her fingers and Dante shivered. She chuckled. "Sensitive, are we?"

He rose up on his elbow, a wicked gleam in his eyes. He moved his hips. She gasped. "Sensitive, are we?"

"Touché."

Dante's expression softened. He bent and placed a swift kiss on her lips. He opened his mouth then shut it.

"What?"

A small smile crept along his lips. "Later. Now's not the time."

What was that supposed to mean?

He stood and lifted her into his arms with ease. Gently, he laid her on the bed. He walked around the bed oblivious to his nudity. He was magnificent.

Cait waited for him to look at her. When he did, she deliberately stretched, slow and long. Lust flared to his eyes. Oh yes, this man liked what he saw. That knowledge gave her the confidence to rise from the bed and saunter to him. His gaze never wavered. She smiled when she reached him.

He wanted her. Had taken her. Exactly as she was.

CHAPTER SIXTEEN

Last night had been a mistake.

Dante propped up on his elbow and watched Caitlyn sleep with her back nestled against his chest. She exuded peace, the opposite of the angst churning inside him.

Why had he made love to her?

Too many unanswered questions lingered between them—the most important being how she felt about him.

Cait had to care for him. Her foolish plan to keep his coach from quitting said as much. Unfortunately, what she'd said to him—twice—sat like a rock in his stomach and put a damper on what should have been a great morning.

It's just sex.

Her blatant invitation set off warning alarms in his head. He'd come close to refusing her last night, hesitated when she'd asked him to erase Sentori's touch. But the desire in her eyes, mixed with her vulnerability, so enticed him he'd crumbled and taken what he'd wanted since they'd first met.

This morning he regretted his moment of weakness. Regret and sex should never mix.

His chest tight, he slid back a strand of red hair from her cheek then trailed the back of his fingers along her soft skin. From day one, he'd known she was special. Time had only proven what his gut had known. He loved her.

He'd believed when he finally fell in love, it would be a wonderful thing, a simple thing. On his end, it was. He longed to hear her voice, to be in her presence. Just the thought of her made him smile.

Did she love him?

It's just sex.

He should shove her comment aside. Forget it. Her skittishness proved she wasn't the sex fiend her statement intimated. Still, he couldn't banish the words festering in his mind.

Cait stirred beside him. Dante drew his hand back and watched her eyelids flutter open. His heart raced. How would she react to his presence in her bed?

She tensed, then tentatively glanced over her shoulder. Green eyes met his, and a timid smile lifted the corners of her mouth. The sleepy, shy expression stole his breath.

"Morning," she whispered.

"Morning." Relief hit him. She hadn't shut down. She appeared pleased to see him.

He kissed her forehead and pulled back. At his quick retreat, her brows furrowed. Damn it, he should have kissed her senseless like he wanted to. But her drowsy, disheveled look was a massive turn on and one kiss would lead to more. They needed to talk first.

Frowning, Caitlyn sat up and pulled the sheet over her

breasts. "Did you sleep well?"

"Well enough."

Her frown deepened. Dante sighed. He could almost hear the *chink, chink, chink* of her barriers falling into place.

Next time, kiss her, idiot.

He rubbed the back of his neck. "We need to talk."

Her fingers tightened around the sheets, but she held his gaze. "Okay."

Dante swallowed. He remembered all too well two other times she'd held his gaze with such determination. Both times she'd told him the same thing.

"Paul told me everything. Why'd you do it?" he asked, wanting to hear the reason from her.

"I couldn't let Mike quit because of me. I know how important this fight is to you."

Dante raked a hand over his face. *Tell me you care for me.* But she didn't. Instead, she watched him with narrow, guarded eyes. It unnerved him.

He inhaled deeply. "*You're* important to me."

"I can't come between you and your dreams."

"You're not. I can have both."

Caitlyn raised an eyebrow. "Apparently not, since Mike quit."

Ouch. No comeback to that. He changed tactics. "Do you care for me?" *Love me?*

"Of course I care for you."

There was a "but" behind those words, he was sure of it.

Just sex. Just sex. Just sex.

"Why'd you sleep with me?"

She jerked back. "What kind of question is *that*?"

"I want to know, Caitlyn. Why did you sleep with me?"

She opened her mouth, closed it, then opened it again. "I-I've wanted you from the moment I laid eyes on you. I'm pretty sure you felt the same. Isn't sleeping together the natural progression to those feelings?"

"It is, but what happens after we leave this bed?"

"God, Dante, what do you want me to say? I'm here. I *want* to see what happens between us. What more do you want?"

As he opened his mouth, the doorbell rang.

She flung back the covers. "I've got to get that. It could be Paul. I never called him. He's probably worried sick."

She grabbed her robe and was out the bedroom door in two seconds flat. Dante followed more slowly, pulling on his jeans along the way.

He came out of her bedroom as she opened the door.

"Good morning, Caitlyn. I trust you slept well," a masculine voice purred.

Fury exploded. *No one* called her Caitlyn but him. He charged forward.

"What do you want?" she asked.

"I found your—"

Dante flung the door wide and brushed past a gasping Caitlyn. He took momentary notice of the pink cell phone Sentori dangled from his fingers before he grabbed two fistfuls of his shirt and shoved him up against the opposite wall. The cell clattered to the floor.

Sentori smiled and glanced over Dante's shoulder. "Well, well, Caitlyn. Been a busy night for you. First me, now him."

Dante's grip tightened and he lifted Sentori off the

ground.

"Shut up, Sentori," she said.

She stepped beside Dante. The movement drew his eyes to the bruise on her neck—the bruise left by this man. He thrust his opponent higher into the air. "If you ever lay a hand on Caitlyn against her will again, I'll kill you."

"Can't handle that your woman asked for me to touch her?" Sentori grabbed Dante's fist with a slimy grin on his face. "I told you I'd get the pussy first, Inferno. I'm disappointed she gave it up to you, too. It makes my victory less sweet."

Dante growled and lifted Sentori higher. Caitlyn placed a hand on his arm. "Let him go. He's not worth it."

He hesitated, but he knew she was right. He released him.

Sentori stumbled but caught his balance, then reached down and plucked the phone off the floor. "I found it on the floor by the couch at my place."

Dante stiffened.

"We didn't go to your place, and you know it." She snatched the phone away. "What did you do? Steal it from my purse when I wasn't looking?"

Sentori tsked. "You've been caught, Caitlyn. Too late trying to cover your tracks now."

"Caitlyn, go back in the apartment." When she hesitated, he added, "Please."

She glanced past him toward his rival. "I'd rather stay."

The panic in her voice grabbed his attention. What was she afraid of?

"Scared of what I might tell him, Caitlyn?" Sentori asked.

So he'd heard her hesitation, too. What had gone on between these two?

"Never."

"Then go inside like a good little girl."

Dante spun on him. "Shut the fuck up."

The other fighter laughed. "I can do this all day. Your choice, Caitlyn. Have us stay out here in a standstill or go inside so Dante and I can do this like men."

Silence followed his statement before she said, "Fine."

The slamming of the front door marked her exit.

Dante stepped forward. "Leave her alone."

"Don't want to hear the truth, Inferno?" Sentori asked, leaning against the wall.

"Nothing that comes from your mouth is the truth."

The other man smirked. "Did she beg for the lights to stay off?"

Dante froze.

"Oh, she did." Sentori tsked. "Not a smart game plan for a chick, huh? If she's going to take on two men in one night, she should at least change her performance."

"How about this? Did she play all vulnerable at first, but when things got going, turn into a wildcat?"

A buzzing filled Dante's ears and he stood rooted to the ground.

"She did with me. I licked every inch of her plump curves. What's it like knowing you took a body I claimed not an hour earlier?"

Dante stopped listening. She hadn't done it. Period.

"Leave," he ground out.

"Fine, fine. I'm gone." He started to walk away then turned. "But not for long." He winked and went down the stairs.

Rage shook his body, anger at Sentori and anger at

himself for allowing the asshole into his head. Even for a split second. It was all lies. Nothing more. With a cleansing breath, he entered the living room.

"Whatever he told you is a lie," she said the moment he stepped inside.

He studied at her. Her words were too defensive. Too quick. She stood in front of him, wringing her fingers together.

Just sex. Just sex. Just sex.

Another split second of doubt rose. He muttered a curse. He refused to believe Sentori over her. Not now. Not ever. If she said it was a lie, then it was a lie. End of story.

She wanted to see where things went with them. That was enough…for now.

"I know. He's playing mind games."

She crossed the room and grabbed his arm. "Just remember that about anything he says."

"What happened last night?"

"Nothing I didn't somewhat expect."

"Tell me." When she faltered, he cupped her cheek. "Please, I want to know."

"Where do you want me to start?"

"From the beginning."

She eyed him, then sighed. Taking his hand, she led him to the couch. "You're not going to like it."

"I'm prepared for that." Anything spoken with the words "Sentori" and "Caitlyn" in the same sentence would bother him. He gathered every ounce of strength he had and prepared not to react.

She began her tale and Dante realized he didn't have enough strength after all. He'd known Sentori had touched her, and he'd wanted to kill him for that, but her plea for him to stay had eased the anger. Now the rage was back with a vengeance. With each excruciating detail, his jaw clenched tighter, his teeth ground harder until he thought they'd shatter. It took considerable restraint to sit and listen to how Sentori had held her against her will, bit her, kissed her. Her. Caitlyn. The woman he loved.

He shot to his feet.

"Dante."

He stiffened. "I've got to go."

"*Dante*," she repeated. The warning in her voice made him stop.

"I'm not going to do anything, Caitlyn. But I need to hit something. And if it's not Sentori's face, I need a bag. I don't want to punch a hole in your wall."

"Okay. Good." She gave him a timid smile. "Just take it easy on the poor bag."

"Not a chance in hell."

His gaze lowered to her neck, the purple bruise glaring. If it weren't for him, she never would have gone on a date with Sentori. But she had. For him. He had to make it up to her.

"Dinner Wednesday night? Just you and me. I know it's a few days away, but Mike—whom I have to have a very long talk with—has me training sun up to sun down for the next two days. When I train like that, I'm exhausted."

She held up her hand and smiled. "No explanations, Dante. The championship comes first. Just don't be mad at Mike, okay? He was only looking out for your best interests."

"He crossed a line."

"Maybe he did, but I heard the pride in his voice when

I talked to him this week. He knows you can beat Sentori, you just need to focus. Just don't lose that focus now that you have it back."

Dante caressed the bruise on her neck. "You don't have to worry. I have an all-new reason to beat Sentori's ass. I'll pick you up at seven on Wednesday?"

"I'd like that. Just save it for the cage, okay?"

He gave her cheek a quick peck before dressing and leaving her apartment.

Images of Caitlyn struggling in Sentori's arms while he buried his head in her neck flooded his mind. Dante squeezed his eyes closed.

Sentori would regret the day he ever laid his hands on Caitlyn.

• • •

He believed her.

She'd worried Dante would believe Sentori and had wanted to stay outside to hear exactly what the slime said. Whatever he'd said hadn't worked. Thank God.

The morning had taken its toll, but at least she'd never have to suffer Sentori again. Instead, she could focus on Dante and figure out what the hell he expected now that they'd slept together.

She sighed and flopped on the couch, his question heavy on her mind.

Why did you sleep with me?

What had he expected her to say?

Cait had strong feelings for him. How could she not? But something in the way he'd acted this morning made her believe he was ready for more. *She* wasn't ready for more.

And she wasn't ready to talk.

Since when did men want to talk, anyway? About feelings? About caring?

Last night had been a huge step forward for her. Why rush into more? Couldn't they just enjoy each other, see if they were compatible, and if she could accept his occupation?

A rapid succession of knocks sounded on the door before it banged open and Paul burst in. Cait straightened on the couch.

"Oh, thank God!" His hand flew to his chest. "Your knight in shining armor never called, so I've been frantic." Then his gaze lowered to her neck, and he smirked. "Well, not so frantic I was willing to interrupt."

She covered the bruise with her palm. "That's not from Dante."

Paul's eyes narrowed. "Creep boy?"

"Yep."

"Have you sicced the rabid Inferno on him?"

Cait's heart stuttered as she remembered Dante's fury. "I had to talk him down."

"Why in the hell would you do that?"

"Do you want me to date a convicted murderer?"

"Oh." Paul grimaced. "That bad?"

"Yeah, that bad." She paused. "I slept with Dante."

Paul's brows rose. "Well, that has been a long time in coming. Literally."

"Does everything have to have an innuendo with you?"

"Of course. Talk would be boring otherwise." He plopped beside her on the couch and took her hand. "So tell me, is G.I. Joe's thingy a teeny-weeny or thicky-wicky?"

"Paul!"

He sighed. "Fine, don't tell me. I'll let my imagination run wild." His expression turned serious. "What's got you spooked?"

"How can you tell?"

"Worry shouldn't be on your face after a night of sex with Macho Man."

"He wanted to talk this morning."

"The bastard."

She smacked his arm. "Stop it. I know it's stupid. But I'm terrified."

"Of what?"

"How many boyfriends have I had?"

Paul winced. "Ah, Cait, let's not go down that road."

"How many?"

"What's your definition of 'boyfriend'?"

She jerked her hand from his. "See! That right there is why I'm terrified. I've never had a relationship with a regular man, much less a man who's a panted-after MMA star in a sport I find appalling."

"Forget about his career right now."

"How can I do that? It *is* a huge part of him."

"Yeah, but he's not asking you to marry him. Enjoy the man who wants you, Cait. Let him help you learn the things you've missed out on all these years. Nowhere does it say that just because you've slept together everything has to be serious now. Enjoy his fine ass and let what may come, come."

He was right. So Dante had wanted to talk. It easily could've been a last-night-was-fantastic chat, because it had been. His questions this morning shouldn't make her panic. But even as she tried to convince herself, a voice in the back of her mind told her she was wrong. Very wrong.

Chapter Seventeen

Dante's grip tightened on the steering wheel. For the last hour, the Atlanta skyline had been silhouetted against the darkening sky, teasing him. Once again he fiddled with the radio before clicking it off with a disgusted grunt.

Beside him, Caitlyn sighed.

The longer they sat in standstill traffic, the angrier he got. He glanced at his watch.

8:27.

They were supposed to be at his apartment a half-hour ago.

She shifted in her seat. "Why don't we get off at the next exit and go back to my place?"

He continued to stare out the window. "No."

"Where are you so bound and determined to get to?"

"It's a surprise." He glanced at her, his jaw tightening. "I don't mean to be an ass, Caitlyn. I just had everything planned and now it's ruined."

Ruined with a capital R. Tonight was supposed to be

about wooing and impressing, not sitting in his truck on an Atlanta highway.

The click of a seatbelt sounded. He turned his head as she slid across the tan leather seat. Dante sat up. She leaned into him, holding his cheek as she rained kisses along his face.

His breath caught and he swallowed. "Whatcha doing?"

"Trying to make you relax. Is it working?"

He chuckled. "Not really."

Definitely not relaxed. More like rigid and throbbing. He closed his eyes.

"Anything I can do to make it better?" She kissed down the front of his shirt.

Damn it. He wanted it in the car. Hell, he wanted it everywhere. But he'd promised himself tonight would be about romance. What little he knew about romance. He hoped some old-fashioned courting would sway her into opening up. A hot blowjob in the middle of traffic was not the way to start a night of courting.

God, he was being such a woman.

One area definitely *not* woman pressed painfully against the fly of his jeans. Her lips lowered. Dante took a deep breath. "Caitlyn, not here."

She froze.

Why did he have to be so damn rational?

"What?" She sat back and tucked a strand of hair behind her ear.

He really couldn't blame the shock in her eyes. He was shocked at himself. Talk about self-discipline. Sheesh.

She scooted away and blinked. "Sorry."

"Not so fast." He reached over, grabbed her around the

waist, and slid her back to his side. "You have no idea how much I want that. But not here, not now. I don't want tonight to be about that."

Confusion puckered her brow. "About what?"

"Just sex."

Her color faded two shades. "What do you want it to be about?"

"Just us."

Caitlyn swallowed. "I-I can do that."

"Good." He leaned back against the seat and wrapped his arm around her shoulder, tugging her against his chest. She sat stiff in his arms.

Frowning, he toyed with her hair. Seconds ago, she'd been more than relaxed, she'd been ready to make *him* more than relaxed. Now that he'd uttered the "us" word, she was tense. What the hell?

"Did you have a good class today?" he asked.

She glanced over with worry in her eyes. Damn it, *why?*

Cait nodded. "It went great. We weighed in today. Every member had lost at least three pounds. You could practically see the pride."

He didn't need to see it—he could hear it in her voice. She relaxed against him. Dante breathed. She was letting go. Some.

"You know I'm proud of you."

She shot him another glance. "For what?"

"For what you're doing."

Amusement twisted her lips and she cocked a brow. "I seem to recall a certain fighter expressing his opinion on the matter when we first met."

He chuckled. "I was wrong."

Gasping, she sat up and turned. "Do my ears deceive me? Did Dante 'Inferno' Jones admit to being wrong?"

He liked hearing her say his full name. Liked it so much he captured a quick kiss on her lips. When he lifted his head, he said, "I can admit when I'm wrong."

"Good to know."

She relaxed into his chest and grabbed his arm, bringing it around her shoulder to play with his fingers. The quick gesture of ease surprised and pleased him at the same time.

"What about you? How did training go the last couple of days? How are things between you and Mike?"

"It was strained at first, but he did feel horrible about what happened with Sentori, so I was able to let it go. My training afterward has gone really well. Mike thinks I'm ready. Which is nice to hear, since the fight's a little over a week away."

"When do you leave?"

"Two days."

"I'm going to order the fight on TV, you know."

Dante laughed. "Do my ears deceive me? Is Caitlyn Moore going to willingly watch an MMA event?"

"What can I say? I want to see Sentori get the snot beat out of him."

Dante clenched his teeth. Why couldn't she have said she wanted to watch him? To support him? He craved her support something fierce. He craved to know she was in his corner, cheering him in both wins and losses. Not because of his scum opponent.

The car ahead of him rolled forward. Dante unhooked his arm and sat up. "Traffic's moving again."

She scooted over, put on her seatbelt, and clapped her

hands. "Yay! You have me so curious."

Dante glanced at her and released a breath.

At least she was willing to purchase the fight. That had to account for something.

He returned his attention to the clearing road ahead and pressed the gas pedal. Twenty minutes later, they pulled in front of a high-rise building.

Caitlyn's eyes rounded. "Are you kidding me?"

"What?"

"You live at the Paramount?"

"No, my roommate lives at the Paramount."

Her eyes rounded even more as a doorman opened her door. Pleasure rippled through him. He was the first to give her the five-star treatment. She deserved it, plus more. He got out and tossed the keys to the approaching car valet.

Going to her side, he gripped her elbow. "Now for your surprise."

• • •

As they walked into the lobby, Cait felt considerably underdressed in her jeans and blouse. Really, she shouldn't have since Dante wore his signature jeans and T-shirt. But she did. The place oozed money.

The primped woman at the front desk nodded. "Good evening, Mr. Jones."

"Good evening, Charlotte," he said as he led Cait to the elevators.

"They know your name?"

Dante grinned. "Yeah. I imagine they learn all their tenants' names."

That made sense. She wasn't used to five-star treatment.

Her landlord had never gotten her name right and still called her "Payton" every month when she dropped off her rent payment. Not a big deal, if she hadn't lived there for three years.

The elevator chimed and opened. Dante stepped inside with her, then pressed forty.

It kept getting more unreal. "He lives on the top floor? How much do you fighters make?"

"Depends on your level. Beginners don't make much at all. Once you've been in, won some fights, and gotten a fan base, though, the money gets better."

She desperately wanted to ask how much he made. Not that she cared. She was curious, though. From the truck he drove, she would've said he made a comfortable living. It wasn't a Lexus or Mercedes, just a simple Ford without any bells and whistles. Yet, Mike had called Dante a big name, so he had to make more than most.

His eyes twinkled. "Go ahead. Ask."

"Ask what?" Embarrassed he read her so easily, she felt her face heat. She wouldn't. It was just too rude.

The elevator chimed again and the doors opened again. Cait started to get off, but Dante grabbed her elbow and whispered in her ear, "I can afford all this and more."

Holy hell. She shot him a glance and he winked. Nope, she'd never guessed it. He didn't seem the rich type.

They went to an apartment door and Dante unlocked it. Cait gasped as she stepped inside. *Luxury.* Simple as that. Rich cherrywood floors stood out against cream-colored walls. They walked into the living room where a huge plate-glass window looked down on the city. The miles of lights amazed her.

"Where's your roommate?"

Dante glanced at his watch. "He left about an hour ago." He reached out for her hand. "Come here, I want to show you what I had planned."

She weaved her fingers through his. She liked the ease she felt right now. He led her into a small room, and she gasped again. Before her was the most elaborate dinner placement she'd ever seen. Dante released her hand and lit the two white tapered candles flanking a gorgeous centerpiece of daisies. Two plates, covered with a domed metal lid, sat on a crisp white tablecloth.

"Oh, Dante."

He watched her, his disappointment evident. "It's ruined. We were supposed to be here forty-five minutes ago. I didn't factor in traffic. I'm sorry."

"Sorry?" She wrapped her arms around his neck. "This is the sweetest thing any man has ever done for me. Thank you."

She rose to her tiptoes and kissed him. His arms went around her waist and drew her close. He deepened the kiss with gentle swipes of his tongue against hers. Low in her belly, her insides twisted and she clung to him. She loved the way he took his time when he kissed her. No rush, no intensity, just a thorough gentleness that made her knees weak.

He broke the kiss and stared down at her. "Only the best for you."

Her heart thudded. This man wanted to please her, to awe her. He had, but not with this fancy-shmancy display. Her pleasure came from simply being with him. Her awe came from the way he gazed at her and made her feel beautiful.

Dante Jones was the best thing that had ever happened to her. A huge admission. Because of him, she'd finally believed she was as beautiful as he said she was. Losing the weight, alone, had never done that.

"Let's eat," she said, needing to get away from the seriousness of her thoughts.

"It's ruined, Caitlyn."

"Nah, it's only been out for about an hour. It's still edible."

"Should I try to nuke it?"

"No, it's perfect the way it is."

"Okay," he said as he pulled out her chair. "Please have a seat, my lady."

She lowered her lashes and smiled demurely. "Thank you, kind sir."

Dante swallowed and she fought a smile. Maybe she'd get the hang of this flirting thing, after all.

After he placed a white linen napkin across her lap, he grabbed the wine bottle and popped the cork. He poured the red liquid into their glasses, then sat down opposite her.

"To a wonderful evening," he said, lifting the glass into the air.

She tapped her glass against his. "With a wonderful man."

The flames from the candle danced off his cheek as his eyes flashed with warmth. She couldn't draw her gaze away from his. Everything seemed to stop around her; there was only him and the eyes that had mesmerized her from the moment she'd met him.

"God, you're beautiful," he said, his voice husky.

Her breathing quickened. "Thank you."

Dante cleared his throat and glanced down. He lifted

the lid off his plate and gestured for her to do the same. She removed the lid and gasped. The presentation alone was impressive. This wasn't food simply slopped on a plate. Béarnaise sauce artistically covered filet mignon in yellow curls then trailed to the edge of the sage plate in sporadic dots. Almonds were sprinkled on five spears of asparagus. A rosebud sat on one corner of her plate.

She picked it up and laughed in delight. "It's a tomato."

Dante chuckled. "Mac has talent."

To say the least. The skin had been shaved off the tomato then rolled to form a mock rose. Shockingly realistic, too. "Mac? Your roommate?"

"Yep. Besides being a class A fighter, he's a three-star Michelin chef."

"You're kidding."

He placed his hand over his heart. "I swear. He moved from Kansas to focus on his fighting so he doesn't cook anymore, but the man makes a killer dinner."

She cut into the meat. Really, she didn't need to use the knife. It sank easily into the perfectly cooked beef. She took a bite and closed her eyes. Heaven. The food melted on her tongue.

She opened her eyes to see Dante grimace. "What?"

"Did sitting out ruin it?"

"If it tastes this good sitting out, I can't imagine what it would taste like straight from the grill."

"Thank God. I wanted this to be perfect."

"This could've been the worst meal ever and it would've been perfect."

A pleased smile tilted his lips. There was that quiver in her belly again. As a distraction, she took another bite of food and changed the subject. "Mac has cooking to return to when he retires. What about you?"

He took a sip of his wine. "I'd like to one day open my own facility, and do for another upcoming fighter what Frank did for me."

That made sense. "At what age does a fighter usually retire?"

"It depends. If I don't receive a career-ending injury, it's possible for me to still be battling it out in the octagon into my forties."

Forties? That was a long time.

"Have you ever had a serious injury during a fight?"

He smiled at her. "Believe it or not, injuries don't just happen in the ring. A friend of mine had to cancel his fight two days before the match because he tore his ACL during training. Took him months to recover, too. As for me, nothing serious yet. Can't say it won't happen, it does come with the territory, but so far I've been lucky. Just some pulled muscles."

"I didn't realize the training was so brutal. I guess that's why you always seem to have some kind of bruise or cut on you somewhere." Like the tiny purple bruise at the corner of his eye right now. "What would you do if you got hurt and had a long recovery?"

"I've prepared for that that. I took a percentage of winnings from each fight and put it aside. I don't believe in squandering my money."

"That's smart."

Dante shrugged. "I knew going in there was a high probability I'd get injured. Even a broken arm could lay me out for a year, depending on the break."

She didn't like thinking about him getting hurt like that—or worse, watching it. Could she stand by the sidelines and watch someone hurt him? The idea of witnessing one of his bones snap appalled her. Someone else's, maybe. Sentori came to mind. But Dante's? No way.

"Explain MMA to me," she said. Knowledge was power. Maybe if she understood it better, she could see why he did it.

"What would you like to know?"

"Everything."

She saw the delight in his eyes as he leaned forward. He truly loved what he did, and wanted her to be apart of it. Could she?

Every part of her still hated the violence of his profession. How would she feel having Dante's face looking like Brad's had the night she met him? All bruised and swollen. What if things got serious between them and kids came into the picture? How would their children feel about seeing Daddy all banged up?

Whoa! You're getting way ahead of yourself there, Caitlyn. There's time to figure all this out. No one's talking marriage, kids, or even a serious relationship.

Once this fight was over, it would be months before she had to face another one. She needed that time to get to know the man behind the fighter. She'd seen glimpses of him. What would it be like to have that man to herself for a couple of months? No excessive training, no upcoming matches, just them being them. She hoped by the time he was ready to fight again, it'd no longer matter to her that he fought. Only time would tell.

She focused on the animated man before her. Over

the next thirty minutes, she listened intently while Dante explained training, conditioning, the importance of breathing, and terminology. It was a lot to digest, and most of it she didn't understand.

"I should be taking notes."

Dante laughed. "It sounds like a lot, but you'll be surprised how quickly it sinks in."

Oh, it had sunk in all right, right along with panic. Pushing her plate away, she said, "I'm stuffed."

He wiped his mouth with his napkin, then threw it on his plate and stood. "Stay here. I have something for you."

He strode from the room, only to return seconds later, carrying a thin, rectangular box wrapped in silver paper with a red bow on top. He handed it to her. "Here."

"What is this?"

"Open it and find out." He positioned his chair in front of her then sat down, bracing his elbows on his knees.

"Dante, you didn't have to buy me anything."

"Just open it."

He twisted his fingers together. Surprised by his sudden refusal to look at her, Cait studied him. Why was he nervous?

Curious, she slid her nail underneath the tape and peeled back the paper, revealing a white box. She placed it on her lap and lifted the lid. She stared at the contents, her stomach churning. She didn't know what she'd expected. A necklace, maybe. A scarf. Anything but this.

She picked up the airline ticket. "What is this?"

He grabbed her free hand and finally made eye contact. "Come to Vegas with me. I leave in two days. I'd like you to be on the plane with me."

She jerked her hand away and held it up. "Wait a minute.

You want me to go *where*?"

"Vegas. Be by my side."

He wanted her there, with him. So much for wanting it to be just them for a while. He wanted to plunge her headfirst into the spotlight, straight back amid the vipers who went to any length to get what they wanted: Dante. "I can't just up and leave. I have a job."

"Taken care of."

She blinked, her mouth popping open before she choked out a startled laugh. "Pretty sure of yourself, weren't you?"

He gave her a strained smile. "Actually, no. I just knew that would be the first excuse you'd come up with not to come."

The panic twisted tighter, but the hesitant hope in Dante's eyes gave her pause. How could she deny him?

Maybe this was for the best. If she spent too much time ignoring the part of him that scared her, she might get too comfortable and fall flat on her face when the time came to enter his world. If she accompanied him now and couldn't get past the limelight and fear of humiliation, or worse, see him take a fist to the face, it was early in their relationship and their hearts could be spared before deeper feelings came into play.

What if she had a great time?

Then she and Dante might have a chance. A win-win situation—a possible future with this wonderful man, or cutting him free to find someone who could handle his lifestyle.

She inhaled. "Yes."

Dante straightened. "Yes?"

She nodded. "I'll go to Vegas with you."

The pleasure that lit his face lifted her anxiety. She would make the best of this trip and enjoy their time together. She owed him that much after everything she'd put him through.

He grabbed her into his arms and swung her around. "Thank you, Caitlyn."

She hoped he'd still be thanking her at the end of the week.

Cait folded another shirt and placed it in the suitcase, trying to keep the butterflies from overtaking her stomach. This was the worst case of jitters she'd ever had.

Second-guessing her decision had sunk its sharp claws into her mind, but she refused to stop packing. She wouldn't allow her reservations to rule her. She would get on that plane tomorrow. She would fly across the country by Dante's side and she would face this hurdle.

For herself and for Dante.

If this week turned into a complete disaster, she'd know they weren't meant to be and move on. And Dante could find someone else to treat as sweetly as he'd treated her last night.

Cait frowned. She didn't like the idea of another woman getting the full Dante experience. Not one bit.

He hadn't touched her, like he'd promised. What he had done had been so much more. After dinner, he'd turned the air-conditioning up until it was completely frigid in the condo. He'd lit a fire in the fireplace, turned out all the lights, and they'd slow danced for hours. He'd held her tenderly, swaying back and forth, whispering some of the sweetest words she'd ever heard.

Dante never pressed her to talk, making the evening relaxing and enjoyable. They'd ended the night curled under a blanket on the couch watching the fire crackle, wrapped in each other's arms with the occasional kiss and touch. He'd been completely there, completely hers. Just the two of them. And how she'd wished it could stay that way.

She felt herself falling deeper and deeper under his spell. Another reason this trip was a good thing. If she weren't careful, she'd find herself hopelessly in love with the man. Then where would they be?

"How did it go last night?" Paul asked as he walked into her bedroom.

"Good."

He rolled his eyes. "'Good'? Jeez, Cait. Is that the best you can do? Learn to be a little more creative. How about 'Oh, Paul, it was the most orgasmic night of my life. He made me come'—"

"Okay! I get it!" she said, laughing.

"So? How was the sex?"

"We didn't sleep together."

He shook his head. "I know I didn't hear that right. So I repeat, how was the sex?"

"You heard me right. We didn't sleep together. I even took your advice and initiated a blowjob, which he stopped."

"He. Stopped. It."

"Yep."

"Lord, that man is full of surprises."

She folded another shirt. "He asked me to go to Vegas with him."

Paul's brows arched. "Well, now we're getting somewhere. I take it that's why you're packing."

"I'm surprised that wasn't the first thing you asked."

"Come on, Cait. Juicy sex stories or a boring suitcase? Which would you have picked? So when do you leave?"

"Tomorrow at ten."

"Is Amy going?"

"She couldn't get off work."

She'd learned that this morning when she'd found Amy in the kitchen. Brad was going, but not fighting. It would've been nice to have her friend along so she wouldn't be utterly alone, but at the same time, she needed to face this week *utterly alone.*

"Are you going to be okay?"

She sighed and sat on the edge of the bed. "I'll have to be, won't I?"

"If you want, I'll go with you."

"What did you call yourself? My beard?"

Her friend studied her. "You've shaved, Cait. Not a quick half-assed job either. We're talking clean-shaven, smooth-as-a-baby's-butt, not-a-stubble-in-sight, shaven."

"You're giving me more credit than I deserve."

"No, I'm not. Over the last two months, you've transformed. Not just in your appearance, either. Your confidence is a force to be reckoned with. Hell, you took on Rocky's scary coach without batting an eyelash, went out on a date with that piece of trash opponent, all on your own. I am no longer needed."

"You'll always be needed, Paul."

"Oh, I know that. Your life would be dull without me in it. But you no longer need to hide behind me because you no longer hide."

"What if I revert?"

"Hmm. What would your Superman think if he heard you say that?"

Failure and Dante never mixed. "He'd be disappointed."

"Exactly. You won't fail."

He was right. If she went into this thinking negatively, she would sabotage the week. She had to go in with a sense of purpose. And that purpose was to do everything she could to fit into Dante's life.

"If you need to talk, I'm a phone call away. And if you need me, it's only a four-hour flight."

"I can do this alone."

"I'm certain of that. But if anything were to happen, I'll be there in a flash."

The only thing of consequence she hoped would happen was having the time of her life with a man she could easily love. She held onto that thought as she finished packing.

CHAPTER EIGHTEEN

Dante draped his arm along the back of the booth, smiling as Caitlyn and Julie chatted about Julie's veterinarian clinic inside one of the cafés at the MGM Grand Hotel and Casino.

Caitlyn threw her head back and laughed. About what? He had no clue. He was too captivated by the happiness brightening her face, the life shining in her eyes, to register the exact words of their conversation right now.

Love constricted his chest as he twirled a strand of Caitlyn's hair around his index finger. She glanced over at him, then scooted closer to him with a soft smile on her lips. The same smile she used after they made love and were wrapped in each other's arms.

She was here, and she'd been completely his.

In the four days since they had arrived in Vegas, everything had been downright perfect. Caitlyn had left her insecurities back in Atlanta. She'd been completely open and supportive, except for the times he caught her muttering pep talks to herself. Those whispered "You got this" pump-up sessions were usually right before a fighters' social function. Considering the way Amanda and Sentori had treated her, he couldn't blame her for being wary about meeting more people in the industry. But she faced each one like a champ, with her head held high and a friendly smile.

Afterward, they'd go back to their room and make love and spend the night holding each other tight.

He couldn't have asked for this trip to turn out any better. The more time he spent with Caitlyn, the more she awed him. She'd faced so many internal obstacles in her life, and she'd fought back like any man would in the cage. Pride and love clogged his throat.

"I told you these two would hit it off," Tommy said, draping his arm behind Julie. "This one loves to run her mouth."

Julie nudged his side, lips pursed. "Hello pot, meet kettle."

Tommy laughed, wrapping his arm around her shoulder and hugging her to his side as he kissed the top of her head. "That's why I love you. You don't put up with my shit."

The amusement faded from Julie's face before she recovered and poked him under the arm. "Someone has to keep it real for you, or that ego of yours would go to your head."

Dante studied Julie. Would she ever tell Tommy how she felt?

He wasn't sure how long she'd sat on her feelings for her best friend, whether the childhood love they shared had morphed into an adult love somewhere in the last few years, or if it'd always been there for Julie. Either way, Dante was amazed at how well she kept her desire for Tommy in check.

He didn't want to be like Julie. Spending time with Caitlyn, laughing together, cuddling, and enjoying her company made it almost impossible for him not to tell her he loved her.

But he had a plan. After he won the championship, they wouldn't attend the after-party. They would go back to their room, where he'd arranged for candlelight, roses, the whole romance ambiance package, and he would confess his love for this woman.

"You ready for the weigh-in?" Tommy broke into his thoughts.

Dante lifted his glass. "There's a reason I'm only sipping water."

"Did you have to cut weight?"

"No, but I'm right at limit, so no eating until afterward." He glanced at his watch. "In fact, I probably need to be getting back to the room. The press conference is in a few hours and then I have the weigh-in tonight. I'd like to rest for a bit."

"Sure you would…with that sweet lady beside you."

He glanced at Caitlyn to see a blush spreading across her cheek, but instead of looking away, she chuckled. "You're bad, Tommy."

"That's what all the ladies tell me. That's why they love me." He winked at Caitlyn.

Dante watched Julie, who'd ducked her head, then fiddled with the fork by her salad plate. How did she put up with Tommy's womanizing?

He could almost go insane with jealousy thinking about Caitlyn with another man. She belonged to him. "You ready, baby?"

When she met his eyes, there was a wicked gleam in them. She no longer fought her desire for him; she displayed it freely now. "More than ready."

After they paid and said their good-byes, they hurried up to their room. As soon as the door closed behind them, Dante pulled Caitlyn back against his chest, nuzzling the skin behind her ear. The scent of her green apple shampoo teased his nose.

He tightened his hold and nipped her neck. Caitlyn tilted her head to the side to give him better access and Dante smiled against her skin.

God, he loved her. And he wanted so badly to say it.

"I know you've got more than that, Inferno." The breathless challenge charged him with lust.

Whipping her around, he grabbed her by the hips and hauled her closer, bringing them pelvis to pelvis. "Oh, I'll show you what I got."

She pulled from his embrace and ran her finger along his chest. "You've got to catch me first."

He lunged for her. Caitlyn squealed and ran into the living room area of the penthouse suite. Dante gave chase. Halfway to the bedroom, he caught up with her and scooped her against his chest, carried her to the bed, then tossed her there. Standing at the edge of the bed, he watched the woman who'd stolen his heart curl into a ball and giggle.

Her delight tightened his chest. The real Caitlyn. Carefree and full of life. Not the troubled soul he'd met two months ago.

He climbed over her body, and Caitlyn smiled. Desire flashed in her eyes as she stretched beneath him and rolled on her back. She slid her hand under his shirt and caressed his chest, scorching his skin. He loved how uninhibited she'd become. No more worries about the light. No more coaxing and being patient. She devoured him with the same frantic need that he devoured her.

Dante braced his arms on either side of her head and gazed down at her. Her tongue flicked out to wet her lips. Dipping his head, he nipped her lower lip then licked where he'd bit. "I'm glad you're here."

"Me, too." She looped her arms around his neck and feathered her fingers across his skin. The touch sent shivers through him. With his hand, he seized her hip and positioned himself atop her as he took her mouth. He didn't tease, he didn't entice. He took. Caitlyn clung to him and met his tongue with hers, her nails digging into his back as she pulled him closer.

He ran his palm down her thigh, then hooked his hand behind her knee, drew it up, and rocked against her. The friction made him groan and he increased the intensity of his kiss. Caitlyn returned his passion with a ferocity of her own.

He yanked her shirt over her head. Black satin greeted him. His breath caught and he slowed his lovemaking to outline her cleavage with his finger. The bra pushed her lush breasts up and together, creating a tantalizing valley, perfect to play in. "You need to wear lower-cut shirts."

"You like?"

"Very much." He replaced his finger with his tongue.

Caitlyn shivered. Her ragged breaths made his cock tighten even more. The need to take her—now—hit him.

He flicked the front clasp and freed her breasts, their pink tips hard and pleading. Not one to deny, he sucked one into his mouth while lightly pinching the other. Mewling, Caitlyn arched toward him, her fingers gripping the back of his head. He rolled his tongue around the nub, making her whimper and shift closer. He loved the way she responded to him.

Sliding an arm behind her shoulders, Dante lifted her upper body and peeled the bra down her arms. As he laid her on the mattress, her eyes never wavered from his, trust shining from them. His heart stuttered as he placed a kiss on her belly.

"You need to lose your shirt," she said.

He glanced up. "What?"

"You heard me. I want to explore you."

His shaft hardened to painful. To relieve the pressure, he rubbed against her.

"I said," she gasped out, "lose the shirt."

"As you wish." He grinned and pulled his shirt over his head.

"Lay back," she demanded and pointed to the head of the bed.

Dante immediately obliged. Excitement raced through him. She was taking the lead.

She crawled toward him, her breasts swaying provocatively with each movement. Dante gulped—he might not be able to wait much longer. Every nerve ending demanded fast and hard. By her lazy movements, she planned to do the exact opposite.

She placed her first kiss on his belly button. Dante shuddered. His gaze never strayed from the erotic vision she made kissing her way up his chest. Her lips trailed over his abs, his nipples, his shoulder, until she straddled his lap and rocked against him.

Dante grabbed her waist, pushed her on his throbbing cock, and ground upward. Caitlyn gasped, moving faster. He gritted his teeth to prolong the exquisite torture.

Half her clothes missing, her head thrown back, her breasts jiggling as she moved, she drove him mad. He had to have her. Now. "Kiss me," he ordered.

A saucy grin twisted her lips and she pecked his mouth.

He growled. "That's not what I meant."

"I know."

Her grin widened with mischief as she leaned forward, her erect nipples a hair away from caressing his chest. One deep breath and their flesh would touch. Dante prepared to do that, but stilled when her mouth hovered over his. He waited, wanting, needing to feel her lips. But the little minx barely touched his mouth before backing away.

"Caitlyn," he groaned.

The plea was his release from her teasing, because she took his mouth the same way he'd taken hers minutes earlier. Hard and demanding, her tongue boldly invaded his mouth. The moment her nipples scraped across his chest, Dante's fragile control shattered. He crushed her to him and rolled her beneath him.

If he had to endure one second more, *premature* would have a whole new meaning. He fumbled with the snap of her denim shorts as he ravaged her mouth with purpose and promise, oblivious to anything except being inside her and sating the unbearable arousal she elicited.

Suddenly, she shoved at his shoulders and turned her head away from his kiss. Dante stilled.

"Do you remember the song we danced to the night we met?" she asked.

She was *thinking*? He blinked. "Umm…no. Can't recall that right now."

He couldn't recall anything except the feel and taste

of her.

"I do."

"Okay." This wasn't a great time for chatting. It irked him she hadn't reached oblivion with him. He'd have to rectify that. He bent to kiss her. She placed her hand on his lips. He groaned. "Caitlyn!"

"It was 'Save a Horse (Ride a Cowboy).' Do you know what I thought?"

She wasn't going to drop it, so he might as well listen. She pushed at his shoulders again and he allowed her to roll him onto his back as she climbed on. "I thought I'd like to take a ride on this man."

Dante's eyes widened. Good God.

"What do you say, Dante? Can I take a ride on you?"

The erotic words made his heart gallop. "Ride away, baby."

The smile she sent him dazzled his senses.

Caitlyn rose to stand beside the bed. With slow movements, her fingers clasped the button of her shorts. When she popped it open and lowered the zipper, his cock jumped.

"A man can only take so much, Caitlyn. I won't be held accountable for my actions if you keep it up."

A wicked grin tilted her lips as she lowered her shorts and panties. At the provocative strip, Dante panted. God, he wasn't going to last. One sweet touch of her wet center welcoming him, and he'd be done.

"Your turn." She climbed onto the bed, and rested on her knees.

She unsnapped his jeans and tugged the zipper. The back of her fingers grazed his rigid shaft, sending shards of need through him. Dante inhaled and closed his eyes.

"Commando? How very naughty of you."

Her scolding pushed him to the edge. He squeezed his eyes closed tighter.

"Condom?"

"Wallet, nightstand," he grunted and forced his eyes open.

She leaned across him, her nipples grazing his chest.

Dante stiffened, so turned on that the soft touch was painful.

She ripped the foil and placed the rubber on his tip. When she slowly rolled it down with her lips, shocked excitement ran through him. Although she fumbled with the task, it was the most sexual thing he'd ever seen. Fascinated, he watched her mouth work around him, her hair flowing around her face. As she withdrew, she pressed her tongue against him, driving him wild.

"How can you make putting on a condom erotic?" he gritted out.

Pink stained her checks as she straddled his hips once again. "I read that once in a dirty book. With you I can do the things I've read about. I like it."

Masculine satisfaction spread through him. He *was* the first. Yes, she'd had other lovers. In the dark. But he'd shown her the pleasure of true lovemaking. And no other man would ever have the honor.

She took him into her hand and positioned him. The pressure of her palm made him groan. "Do not move your hand."

If she did, he'd spill himself right now. She chuckled and he growled in response. She was enjoying this a little too much. Her warm heat encircled the tip of his shaft before she stopped.

"Caitlyn," he moaned, desperate to drive into her. To end the agony that gripped him.

"Shh, patience," she said, placing her hands on either side of his head as she lowered herself with excruciating slowness.

Captivated by her movements, Dante watched, his breathing quickening.

"Hmm…" She closed her eyes, sighing in pure ecstasy.

Fisting the bedspread, he inhaled between clenched teeth. She lifted only to take him back in at the same sluggish speed. Inches from his lips, hers parted in a silent gasp.

"God, Caitlyn. You're gorgeous," he croaked.

Her eyes opened. Desire heavy in her gaze. "And you're all man."

She picked up the pace. Up and down in quick succession. Dante helped her, the coil low in his stomach ready to explode. He gritted his teeth, his gasps harsh. He would not come until she did. And she was close. Her tight center gripped him, her movements desperate. He moved his hand between her legs, circling the swollen nub. Caitlyn gasped and thrust down. "Dante!"

He pressed harder, needing her release *now*, unable to hold his back any longer. She sat straight, her fingers digging into his chest, and she tensed. "Oh, God."

As soon as she squeezed around him and shuddered, he let go. Using her hips as leverage, he pumped into her, her body milking him as he groaned through his orgasm.

Shuddering once more, she collapsed onto his chest. Their ragged panting danced in the air. Caitlyn nestled her head into his neck and he wrapped his arms around her sweat-coated body. They lay like that, neither moving, still joined, enjoying the exquisite aftermath of mind-blowing sex. At least he was.

"God, I can't even find a word to describe what we just did."

He chuckled. "I was just thinking 'mind-blowing.' "

"Hmm. I like that."

As he feathered kisses along her face and shoulders, he rolled them onto their sides. When she caressed his cheek with her hand, he glanced up. The warmth in her eyes stopped his heart.

"You're good for me, Dante."

His chest expanded. Emotions clogged his throat. Unable to speak, he kissed her. She responded with such trust and adoration, love flooded through him.

"I love you." The words spilled out against her mouth. And he knew at once he'd made a huge mistake.

Her lips stilled, her body tensed, then she shoved away from him. "Damn it, Dante."

She jumped out of bed and grabbed her clothes, yanking them on with jerky movements.

The pure fury she sent his way froze him. Did she truly not feel the same way? It wasn't possible he felt this way about this woman and she didn't return it.

"Damn it, Caitlyn, that wasn't the reaction I was hoping for." He tried to keep the hurt out of his voice, but he couldn't. It rang loud and clear.

"Why do you rush everything? Haven't you heard of taking things slow?"

He sat up. The pain of her not saying she loved him back was nothing compared to those words. He loved her, wanted to openly love her. How was that rushing?

"Why couldn't we just enjoy each other? Take our time and see where things went? Why did you have to bring feelings into it?"

Enjoy each other? Anger replaced the pain as her words hit him full force in the gut. He shot to his feet and yanked on his jeans. "What is this week to you? Some kind of sex fest? If that's what you want, then you're fucking the wrong man. I made it clear sex wasn't what I wanted."

She flinched but he wouldn't back down. Everything he said was true.

"I don't want just sex either."

"Then what do you want?"

The anger eased from her. "I don't know."

"You don't know? Well, isn't that just peachy keen."

She dropped her gaze to the floor.

"Look at me."

She kept her gaze averted.

"The least you can do is have the guts to look at me when you reject me. You've had no problem with that in the past."

She finally met his gaze. Tears brightened her eyes. Remorse?

"Dante, I care for you, *immensely*, but your career scares the hell out of me. All I wanted was to get through this week, see the fight, and make sure I could accept the violence. Why couldn't you give me that?"

"So this week was a *test*? You were going to dump me if the week didn't meet your fucked-up expectations?"

She swallowed, but held his gaze. "I'm not going to apologize for believing you deserve someone who can accept all of you, Dante."

"What I deserve is to be loved by the woman *I* love."

"I didn't know you loved me," she said in a tortured whisper.

He stormed past her to the picture window overlooking the Vegas Strip. She hadn't known he loved her. What a load of shit. He might not have said the words, but no man chased a woman for as long as he had without feelings involved.

"Damn it," she muttered from behind him.

He spun to find her sitting on the edge of the bed, cupping her head in her hands.

He glared at her. "I've never told a woman I loved her. Never. I finally do and what do I get in return? A woman who *doesn't know*."

Caitlyn lifted her head. "I'm trying to be honest, Dante."

He needed to get out of here, needed to think. He walked toward the door, hoping she'd call him back. When he grabbed the knob and she still hadn't said a word, he turned. She hadn't moved.

"You know something, Caitlyn? Going out with Sentori to get me refocused was a waste of your time. This is the biggest distraction ever thrown at me. Thanks for that."

He stomped out the door.

Dante kicked the bag once more. The leather swung high into the air then spun as it slowed. Over the last hour, his anger still churned in his chest.

What was he supposed to do now?

He sure as hell couldn't pretend he hadn't said the words. He had and he meant them, with his whole heart. How was he supposed to go back up there and lay in the same bed with her, knowing she didn't feel the same?

He punched the bag with a left hook, the loud *pop* echoing in the hotel's gym. He ran his forearm across his sweaty forehead.

She was terrified of his career. Man, if that didn't burn. Fighting was a huge part of him. Of all the women he could have fallen in love with, it had to be the one woman who despised his sport. What were the fucking odds?

He ripped off his gloves and wraps.

"What's Miss Piggy up to?"

Dante spun. "Get the fuck out of here, Sentori. I don't have time to deal with you."

His opponent stepped closer. "Man, she really puts the oink in boink, doesn't she?"

Without thinking, Dante swung out with a right hook. Sentori dodged, then grabbed Dante around the waist, took him to the ground and pinned his arms down.

"Break it up!" Mike yelled as the sound of running feet came toward them.

Sentori sprawled across Dante's chest, his weight bearing down on him. Dante bucked and twisted, but Sentori held on as if Dante were a kitten instead of a raging inferno. He bent close to Dante's ear. "This is just a taste of what will happen tomorrow night. Did you see, *feel*, how easy it was for me to take you down?"

Dante shifted. His opponent's weight lifted as Mike pushed him back. "That's enough. Get the hell out of here, Richard."

Sentori sneered. "I'm not the only one you have to worry about. Your girlfriend was in the lobby, suitcase in hand. Can't keep her satisfied?"

Sentori chuckled before sauntering out of the gym.

What the hell did Sentori mean?

Dante shoved past Mike and sprinted from the room, forgoing the elevator and taking the stairs two at a time. Once he got to the right floor, he ran to the room and glanced around.

Gone. Not a trace of her. Not even a goddamned note.

She'd made her decision.

She'd left him.

CHAPTER NINETEEN

Cait aimlessly walked around the busy Vegas Strip. A little over an hour and a half ago, Dante had stormed from their room. She'd been left with deafening silence and the horror of what she'd done—what she'd said.

How had it gone so wrong?

She'd enjoyed every minute of this trip with him. Every. Single. Minute.

Over the last few days, she'd started to wonder what a future with Dante would be like. The whole package. Love. Marriage. Kids. But a future with Dante wouldn't just those three things. The MMA came with him.

The people who surrounded him no longer mattered. She'd put that fear to rest days ago. Yeah, there were some bad apples like Amanda and Sentori, but for the most part everyone she'd met had been warm and welcoming.

The problem was he willingly entered a cage and put himself in harm's way. And the brutality hung over her head like a dark ominous cloud, terrifying her that come Saturday, no matter what she felt for him, watching him take a beating, possibly hearing a bone snap, would be too much for her to handle.

She'd wanted to embrace everything about Dante, give herself over to him completely, with no hesitation or distaste over what he did for living. She'd wanted to accept all of him.

Dante deserved a woman who loved every aspect of him, especially his sport. A woman who would stand in his corner and be the image of love and support when the cameras panned to her. Not a woman cringing in horror. If she couldn't give him that, she didn't deserve *him*, and she'd been willing to walk away if she couldn't make it through his match.

But Dante had changed everything with three beautiful words.

Words she hadn't found beautiful at that time but had induced a panic so overwhelming she'd reacted without thought. She hugged herself tight as she remembered those expressive blue eyes of his shattering in pain. Pain, because all he'd wanted from her was her love.

She wished she could rewind time to when she and Dante had been wrapped in an embrace, enjoying the aftermath of their lovemaking. When he'd said those three precious words. Unfortunately, hindsight wouldn't transport her back to fix her stupid response.

But she wasn't stupid any longer. She *loved* Dante.

As much as she fought to deny it or convince herself that *she* had to be perfect for *him*, it hadn't stopped her heart from loving him. It'd taken the slamming of the door for her mind to accept what her heart had known. His leaving had brought forth a fiercer panic that terrified her more than his fighting ever had.

He was gone.

Amy's warning, about not realizing what she could live with until she lost the one thing she couldn't live without, finally made sense. Cait could live with the fighting. She couldn't live without Dante Jones.

Her realization might have come too late. She might have lost him, but she'd learned one thing from Dante since he'd come into her life: never go down without a fight.

She'd give him time to cool down, let him blow off his anger and hurt on a bag.

The MGM Grand towered in the distance, and she inhaled a calming breath as she squared her shoulders.

She was going to win her man back.

Cait quickened her pace. She was no more than a half a block down when she noticed a man striding toward her. Beefy. Tall. Determined. She tensed, but then he smiled and said, "You're Dante's girlfriend, right?"

She relaxed. "Yes."

"I thought so. I'm Blake Prowler. I've seen you two around the last few days but haven't had a chance to introduce myself." He offered his hand.

Blake Prowler. She'd never heard Dante mention him. She took his hand. "It's nice to meet you, Blake."

A black car pulled up beside them. The back door opened and before she could say a word, Blake had latched onto her upper arm and shoved her into the car beside another burly guy.

"What the hell?" She immediately tried to climb out, but the other guy grabbed her around the waist and yanked her back as Blake slipped in beside her and closed the door. The car sped off.

"Let me out!"

Blake shot her an annoyed look, replacing the charming man he'd been seconds before. "Chill. You're safe. We're just going on a little trip."

Caitlyn sat rigidly on the couch, arms crossed tight over her chest, foot shaking with building fury as she glared at the three goons who were watching a movie on a large, flat-screen television hung over a marble fireplace.

Since Blake had told her they were going on a little trip, which had been a fifteen-minute drive to a wealthy gated community, they hadn't spoken one word to her, other than to laugh at her feeble attempts at escape. The big bullies. Anytime she'd tried to run, a massive, muscular arm would wrap around her waist then chuck her back on the couch. After the fifth time her tush had bounced on the expensive leather cushions, she'd taken to glowering at the thugs. Like they even noticed.

"This is kidnapping, you know."

"Technically it's an intervention," a deep voice came from her left.

Sentori stood in the doorway between the living room and gourmet kitchen, with a smirk on his face and newly dyed purple hair.

"You!" She launched herself across the room. Not five feet later, a beefy appendage scooped her up again and dropped her back on the couch. Furious, she blew her hair off her face. "Screw you, asshole."

Blake had the audacity to chuckle as he went to sit down.

"Welcome to my humble abode, Caitlyn. Isn't it gorgeous? I bought it just a few months ago. I love Vegas and I'm thinking of relocating permanently. Atlanta has become such a drag."

"I should've known that this pretentious monstrosity of a house was yours."

Sentori laughed. "I really do bring out the worst in you, don't I?"

She crossed her arms over her chest and glared. "What's the point of taking me hostage?"

"To fuck with Dante, of course." He sat on the arm of the couch, leaning his elbows on one knee. "You see, I heard some disturbing gossip about Dante's training. Everyone believes he's going to beat me. I can't let that happen, can I?"

"So you're going to make him worried sick about where I am?"

"Oh, no. I don't want the cops involved. I'd been wracking my brain trying to figure out what I could do to really fuck him up. Ya'll have been so cozy and cute this week, I'd all but given up hope in using you." He grinned. "But then there you were, storming through the lobby, crying. And Dante was nowhere to be found. I caught up with your man at the gym. The way he was hitting the bag was all the confirmation I needed that you two were fighting, and my plan was a go. I could never let a moment like this pass without really getting into his head."

"W-what did you do?"

"Let's just say Dante now knows who dominates this fight. But I have to keep the momentum going. A make-up session between you two wouldn't help my cause. So I have to keep you two apart until after the match."

"How is this not going to involve the cops? When I don't return or answer my phone since your goons took my purse, he's going to worry."

His smile was cold and calculated. "Blake, go to my car. I have a gift in the passenger seat for Caitlyn."

Blake went outside and returned a few moments later with a piece of luggage in his hand.

A roaring filled her ears.

Her luggage.

"H-how?"

"You underestimate my charm and conniving, Caitlyn. You should be impressed. Dante won't be looking for you, because he's going to believe you left him."

Dante thought she'd left. That he'd told her he loved her and she'd fled.

"I hate you," she whispered, nausea churning her stomach.

He shrugged. "Not the first time I've heard that and it sure as hell won't be the last." He glanced at his watch. "I need to get back to the hotel. The press conference is in an hour. I just wanted to stop by and make sure you were getting settled in."

Yeah, she was sure that was exactly why he'd stopped by. He'd wanted to mess with her just as much as he wanted to mess with Dante. "Go to hell."

He tsked. "Such hostility and Dante kisses that filthy mouth." He stood. "Blake, make sure she watches the conference and weigh-in. I don't want her to miss a thing."

"Yes, boss."

She glared at Blake's back.

"You're not even fighting tomorrow night, are you?"

He looked over his shoulder. "Nope."

Assholes. The whole lot of them.

The door closed behind Sentori, and she was left with the significance of Sentori's plan and all the weeks she'd pushed Dante away. When he returned to the room to find her clothes gone, he wouldn't even be surprised. He'd assume she'd run from him again.

Except this time she hadn't. She'd gone for a walk to clear her thoughts. To prepare to fight for the man she loved.

And he would believe she'd abandoned him—right before his fight.

There was no way in hell that was happening. She *would* find a way back to Dante.

"I need to go the bathroom." Maybe there was a window she could crawl through.

Blake stood, took her arm, and led her down a hallway. He opened a door to a half-bath the size of a closet. A toilet and sink but no windows. She sighed.

"You think he was going to let you escape through the bathroom?" He gave a scathing laugh. "You really do underestimate Sentori."

All right, so getting out of there wouldn't be as easy as she thought. But if they were confident she couldn't escape, then their defenses were down. Eventually, she'd be able to use the weakness against them. She just hoped that time came soon.

An hour later, Blake flipped to the sports channel. Dante popped onto the screen. He sat on the left side of a podium between two long tables. A black banner with the MMA logo decorated the backdrop, bringing focus to the seven other fighters at the table with him. Sentori sat on the right side of the podium, his championship belt in front of him.

She could only see Dante from the chest up, but he wore a pressed white buttondown shirt with a navy blazer that made his blue eyes pop, but their usual sparkle was missing. Deep lines bracketed his mouth.

Her heart tightened as she pressed her fist to her mouth, silencing a horrified cry.

What ugly thoughts were going through his head right now? How many unsavory names was he calling her? Was he regretting he ever met her? Wished he'd never come to Atlanta?

Sorrow sliced through her. It took everything in her not to weep about her part in his pain, but she refused to give the goons or Sentori the satisfaction of knowing they caused two people needless grief.

A man with graying hair crossed behind the fighters and came to stand behind the mike.

"It's my pleasure to introduce the competitors of the most anticipated match in MMA history. Two undefeated fighters and one belt on the line. The man sitting to my left has an impressive record and one hell of a punch. Dante came into MMA six years ago and plowed his way through one fighter after another. His blinding hand speed and rock-solid chin has shocked some of the most seasoned professionals in the industry, leaving him with an astounding seventeen and zero record. He is the most respected, heavy-handed knockout artist in MMA today, please welcome Dante 'Inferno' Jones."

Claps sounded as the camera panned to Dante, who approached the podium.

He cleared his throat before he bent forward. He didn't glance up, seeming focused on the microphone. "Thank you for this opportunity. This is the biggest fight of my career. Tomorrow's fight will be anything but easy. Richard Sentori is a dangerous fighter. But I'm ready. I've trained hard, studied my opponent's movements. I go into the cage with every intention of victory."

Dante lifted his head and he glared straight into the camera. Cait's breath froze as she stared into the intense blue eyes filled with so much anger and hurt. Even with a television between them, she knew those emotions were directed at her.

"And for those of you who *don't know* what outcome you want, your message has been clearly received."

Murmured confusion rippled in the background. She couldn't blame them. He'd said the words so intensely, with such fury, it was clear there was an intended recipient for the message.

Her.

Cait ground her teeth together to prevent the sob from exiting her mouth, her body quivering from the effort.

Your message has been clearly received.

Dante was telling her that he was done.

A thousand stabs with a knife would've been less painful. When she noticed Sentori's men watching her closely, she stared straight at them and lifted her chin. "I hope you burn in hell."

The three men exchanged glances, but she returned her attention to the TV, to Dante.

"Thank you," he said then stepped back from the podium.

The speaker returned, his brows drawn together. "Er.

Thank you, Inferno." He flipped the top index card and stacked them. "Now to our champion. Richard Sentori has dominated the MMA world, defending his title successfully four times. Considered the best pound for pound fighter in MMA, Richard is lethal in his groundwork. Out of his twenty wins, fifteen were won by submission within the first round. Please welcome the undefeated and current welterweight champion, Richard Sentori."

Sentori approached the podium exuding his usual cockiness. For Cait, rage swooped in and replaced the pain. She curled her hands into fists, her nails biting into her palms.

"Thank you." Annoyance swept Sentori's face. "Everyone has been yammering about this fight for months. I'm here to set the record straight. Saturday's fight will be no different than any of my previous bouts. This is just another fighter wanting to take a stab at fighting the best."

Sentori turned his head to the left, and the camera zoomed out to include Dante, who stood to one side.

"I've already proven I can take you down, Inferno." Sentori shifted so he was right in Dante's face. "Tomorrow will be no different. So go ahead and face the facts. Only when *Miss Piggy* flies will you beat me."

Dante's nostrils flared. His lips fused together in a tight line. A muscle jumped in his cheek. He looked ready to snap. Then Sentori poked Dante, once, hard in the chest.

Cait could see Dante's long fingers curl into tight fists.

The commentator stepped between them. "Fight's not 'til tomorrow, guys."

Dante rolled his shoulders, sneered one last time at Sentori, and sat down.

After everyone was reseated, the speaker returned to the

podium and laughed. "Whoa, boy! Can you feel the tension? We won't be disappointed with this event."

The people in the background cheered, but Cait was anything but cheerful. Dante was clearly ready to explode. Anything that came out of Sentori's mouth from this moment on only messed with him more. If he lost this fight tomorrow because she'd given Sentori the means to get further inside his head, she'd never forgive herself.

• • •

Dante paced behind the curtains waiting for his name to be called for the weigh-in. Hours had passed since the press conference and still he could barely contain the flood of pain that engulfed him every time he thought of how Caitlyn had upped and left him.

A day before his fight.

Who did such a thing?

A woman who was so wrapped up in herself she gave no thought to others. Man, he'd thought Amanda was bad. He'd stood by Caitlyn, practiced unwavering patience, kept telling himself she needed time and understanding. When he'd stepped on the plane headed for Vegas, holding her hand, he'd believed all his support had finally been rewarded.

How fucking wrong he'd been.

The message he'd delivered during the press conference hadn't given him the peace he'd craved. He'd hoped by finally telling her he was done, that he would no longer wait for her to get her shit straight, his mind would clear.

It hadn't. Saying good-bye to Caitlyn with those cryptic words had been agonizing, and he'd cursed the weakness.

And then Sentori had stepped up to the podium,

referred to Caitlyn as Miss Piggy, and his vision went black. He wasn't sure how he'd refrained from punching the fucker, but somehow he had.

"Next up in the welterweight division, Richard Sentori versus Dante 'Inferno' Jones."

The crowd hollered. Dante stifled his thoughts as he climbed the stairs.

"First up on the scale and still undefeated, Dante Jones."

He stepped onto the stage and grimaced at the bright lights. He hated this part. The spectacle. It'd only been recently that MMA had brought the weigh-in into the public eye for marketing and publicity purposes. Not a bad thing, but stripping down to his skivvies in front of a bunch of howling women was not his idea of a good time. But if Caitlyn was watching...

Letting her see one last time what she'd rejected appealed to him.

He stopped beside the huge scale in the center of the platform and glanced around. The cameraman stood about fifteen feet away. Dante motioned him closer. When the man took a few steps toward him, Dante held up his hand for him to stop. Not breaking eye contact with the lens, he peeled his T-shirt over his head and tossed it aside.

The girls in the front row screamed. Dante ignored them, concentrating solely on the one person he hoped was watching. Would she be able to look away? Was she full of regret?

He unbuttoned the snap to his jeans and lowered the zipper. He sent the camera a cocky grin and winked, then lowered his pants until he stood only in his boxer briefs.

"Miss this?" he said to the camera, a hard smile pulling

at his lips. "Good."

He spun and stepped up on the scale and the commentator marked his weight.

"One hundred and seventy pounds for the Inferno," the commentator yelled into his microphone.

Dante flexed his arm in a muscle man pose. He stepped off the scale.

"And his opponent, the welterweight champion of the world, Richard Sentori."

Sentori sauntered onto the stage and stripped down to his boxer shorts, his white skin almost blinding under the lights. Just seeing the man made Dante's anger pulse to life, reminding him of Caitlyn's hurt and humiliation when Amanda spewed her hatred.

Sentori stepped on the scale.

"One sixty-nine for the champion."

His opponent flexed his arms, then stalked over to Dante. The media always wanted a picture after weigh-in of the fighters squaring off. They came nose to nose, staring into each other's eyes. Neither moved. The crowd hushed as if sensing this was no ordinary photo op. The tension crept higher and higher.

Sentori smiled then whispered, "Oink."

"Fuck you," Dante whispered back.

Sentori shoved Dante. When Dante raised his arm to strike out, Mike Cannon jumped between them and dragged him off the stage, away from the cameras. Having had enough of Sentori's shit, Dante flung off Mike's grip and headed back to the stage. Mike grabbed his bicep and bent in close to Dante's ear.

"Calm down," Mike said. "He's gotten into your head.

You can't react. It gives him the power."

"He needs a face full of my fist."

"Dante, you have to focus."

"I *am* focused."

"No, you're not, and you haven't been since Cait left. I'm worried about tomorrow. You're going into this fight half-cocked. You're going to make a mistake and you're going to lose."

CHAPTER TWENTY

Oink.

The word had revolved around her head for the last twenty-four hours while she waited for the prime opportunity to escape. So far, the goons had made it impossible. They took shifts sleeping. At all times, two stood guard in the room. Time was running out. It was already a little after nine and the third fight was under way. Dante was the main event and wouldn't go on before ten, and that was quickly approaching.

At some point *Miss Piggy* had to fly.

It hadn't been until Sentori's whispered oink, and the three gorillas had looked at her and snorted, that she'd put two and two together.

Humiliation at their taunts hadn't been anywhere on the radar this time. Just rage.

She'd kept her calm, though. She'd smiled sweetly and then given them two middle-finger salutes. The shock on their faces had been satisfying but hadn't stopped her racing mind.

She now understood what mind game Sentori had used to get to Dante.

Degrading cruel words about her weight. Probably tossed out during their entire relationship. Yet Dante had never wavered. He had stood solidly by her side.

And now she had to get to his side.

But first, she had to get away from these assholes.

She *had* to get alone.

But how?

And then it hit her. A plan so devious even Sentori would be proud. A slow smile came to her face. The one thing that made men squirm.

She pulled a throw pillow over her lap and made a surprised noise, covering her mouth with her hand, eyes wide. Blake glanced at her. "What?"

She averted her gaze. "I need to go to the bathroom."

"Fine. Come on."

"No, you don't understand. I *need* to go to the bathroom."

"*Okay*. Come on."

She blew out a fake frustrated breath and glanced back at him, hoping her expression came off as mortified. "You're going to make me say it, aren't you?" She inhaled. "I-I just started my period."

Blake jerked back. "H-how can you tell?"

"I gushed." The bluntness had the intended effect. Blake recoiled. Now to really freak him out. She gestured to the pillow. "It's all over me. I need a shower and a change of clothes, or I'm going to get *blood* all over the couch."

Blake shivered. "Okay…okay. Just…you can use the bathroom down the hall."

She stood, keeping the pillow in front of her. "I'll need

my purse. My tampons are in there."

He made a gurgling noise and hurried across the room, grabbed her blue bag, then all but tossed it at her.

Men. So easily freaked out over a woman's menstrual cycle.

After he escorted her to the bathroom, she bit her lip and looked helplessly up at him. "I'm going to need a change of clothes."

"Yeah. I'm on it." He hurried down the hall and back into the living room, she assumed, to retrieve an outfit out of her suitcase.

She waited for him to return. When he did, she took the jeans, noticing he'd skipped a clean pair of panties.

Wimp.

After she closeted herself inside the bathroom, she turned on the standalone ceramic tiled shower. Once the sound of running water filled the room, she climbed into the Jacuzzi tub and opened one of the windows. Within seconds, she was outside and sprinting for the neighbor's backyard.

She didn't stop running.

Her only goal: get to Dante.

. . .

Dante slouched in the leather chair while two teammates taped his hands. The fury that had fueled him yesterday still burned deep in his gut. He was ready to face Sentori. He had had weeks of bitch-talk and cruel comments about Caitlyn built up until it raged inside him. Now the inferno was ready to be unleashed.

But Sentori was where his rage ended.

The anger he'd had toward Caitlyn had faded, leaving

him with a dull ache thumping in his chest. Sleeping in that bed without her had been torture. Multiple times he'd woken up, searching the empty spot beside him. Then he'd roll over onto his back and stare at the ceiling until he'd fall into a fitful sleep again.

Two months ago, he'd met a woman who had presented a challenge. He hadn't been searching for love or even a relationship; he'd just wanted to have some fun with a girl who wasn't impressed by his celebrity status. He had no idea that same girl would still his heart and then stomp all over it.

Why couldn't he stop thinking about her? Wondering if she got home safe?

A pathetic part of him had waited all day for the phone to ring. Waited to hear her voice. Wanted so badly to hear her apologize, tell him she'd made a mistake, that she loved him…and wish him good luck.

She never called.

Reggie ripped the tape and patted it down, then placed four-ounce gloves on Dante's hands. He flexed his fingers, loosening the leather around the black padding.

The roar of the crowd grew louder, forcing him to focus on the here and now. Focus on his championship fight. The apprehension he felt before every fight clenched his gut. He inhaled, then released a controlled breath. In just a few short minutes, he'd be in the cage, ready to battle Sentori.

Mike entered the room and jerked a pair of focus pads onto Dante's hands. "Time to warm up," Mike said.

Dante slowly got to his feet. With soft punches to the pads, he warmed up his muscles, but kept the power out of his thrusts. He needed to conserve his energy for his opponent. Even with his anger as fuel, he wasn't fool enough to believe this would be an easy fight, or that he'd come out unscathed.

Perhaps it wasn't a bad thing Caitlyn had left. She'd made it clear she hated this sport. There was no telling what he'd look like at the end of the match. He didn't know what would've been worse—her refusing to say she loved him back, or her saying she loved him, then seeing revulsion in her eyes when he came out of the ring.

Didn't matter now. What was done was done. She was gone.

Thinking that, he hit the pad with more force than necessary and knocked an unprepared Mike back a few steps.

"Whoa!" his coach said. "Take it down. We're just warming up here."

"Sorry." Dante went back to soft taps.

The door to the waiting room opened and a young man with a headset on poked his head inside. "It's time."

Dante moved his head side to side to work out the tension in his neck, and let out an anxious breath.

Mike clapped him on the shoulder. "The championship is riding on this. The anger isn't going to help you, Dante. Let it go before you step into that cage or you're going to make a mistake. Okay?"

Mike was wrong. The anger helped, but Dante nodded anyway. His entourage ushered him out the door as he pulled the hood of his sweatshirt over his head. While they waited for their cue at the entrance to the arena, Mike popped in Dante's mouth guard.

Darkness fell in the arena and the crowd fell silent. A loud roar blasted from the speakers and beams of red light ricocheted across the audience. A guitar solo ripped hard, hurtling the crowd into a screaming mob.

The untamed energy fueled Dante's determination and he strode toward the cage, his body humming with adrenaline. His team shielded him from the grasping hands of the crowd as he bounced and hit the air with an onslaught of short punches. Ready to fight. Ready to win.

When he reached the cage, he kept his gaze away from the empty spot where Caitlyn would have sat. No negative thoughts. Not now.

He pulled his sweatshirt over his head. The official smeared Vaseline over his forehead, cheeks, and chin to keep the gloves' leather from ripping his skin and then patted him down. Once prepared, Dante climbed the stairs and entered the cage, the canvas under his bare feet welcoming him. He ran a lap around the perimeter of the mat and jumped high into the air a couple of times to warm his muscles.

The arena went dark as his song faded, then colored lights zipped around the room again. The beat of drums and the squeal of an electric guitar sounded. Then a booming voice chanted, "Shout! Shout! Shout!"

Dante ground down on his mouthpiece. This wasn't Sentori's normal entrance song. No doubt the asshole had handpicked this one as a final attempt in his pathetic mind games. His opponent, purple hair glowing, strolled toward the cage as if he weren't about to defend his title.

"Shout! Shout! Shout!" came from the speakers.

"Shout at the devil," the fans yelled in unison.

Dante shook out his arms. The song irritated him. Sentori would love to be considered Satan himself, but Dante wouldn't give him the satisfaction. His opponent was nothing more than a nuisance in need of squashing.

When Sentori reached ringside, he went through the same prep then entered the cage, his gaze trained on Dante, who held his glare. Dante knew the game well. Intimidation. Who would shrink the quickest? It wouldn't be him. The direct challenge enflamed him, bringing forth the raging inferno of his namesake.

The announcer came into the middle of the ring. "Ladies and gentlemen, this is the main event," he yelled into his microphone.

The crowd screamed.

"And the moment of truth, live from the MGM Grand Garden Arena in Las Vegas, it's tiiimmmeee!"

The ground shook from the thundering applause. Dante fed off the atmosphere and held Sentori's gaze, listening to the people who chanted "Inferno."

"Five, five-minute rounds for the undisputed welterweight championship of the world." The announcer pointed to Dante. "Introducing first, in the blue corner, this man holds a record of seventeen wins and no losses, standing six feet one inch, weighing in at one hundred and seventy pounds, fighting out of Atlanta, Georgia, presenting the challenger, Dante "Inferno" Jooones!"

The noise level increased to deafening as the fans stomped and shook signs of support in the air. The adrenaline inside Dante grew to bursting.

The announcer pointed to Sentori. "And now introducing the champion, fighting out of the red corner, this man holds a record of twenty wins and zero losses, standing five feet eleven inches, weighing in at one hundred and sixty nine pounds, fighting out of Atlanta, Georgia, the reigning, defending welterweight champion of the world, Richard Sentoriii."

Loud boos mingled with Sentori's supporters' yells. Hearing the negative response from the fans energized Dante more. Even the spectators wanted to see Sentori fail. He would give them what they wanted.

The referee came between them. "All right, gentlemen, protect yourselves at all times, listen to my instructions, and we'll have a clean fight. Touch gloves."

Dante lifted his hands toward Sentori's. Instead of reciprocating the show of respect, his opponent threw a short, quick punch toward Dante's jaw. He snapped his head back before the fist made contact and the referee dove between them.

Sentori jumped back, raising his arms.

Dante tensed, muscles flexed, jaw locked.

The referee stood as a barrier between them, then pointed to Dante. "Are you ready?"

He nodded.

Ref pointed to Sentori. "Are you ready?"

Another nod.

"Let's do it!" the ref yelled and backed away.

Dante met his opponent in the middle of the cage and they circled each other, hands up, chins down. Watching for any sign of an attack, Dante focused only on the man before him. Sentori wouldn't allow this fight to stay on its feet for long.

Judgment time. Two months of improving his groundwork came down to this moment. Sentori weaved from left to right, searching for a way to take him down. Wouldn't happen. Not yet. He needed to get a few shots in before they went to the mat.

Unwilling to allow his opponent to control things, Dante

charged, threw a jab, and caught Sentori on the cheek. His head retracted as he jumped out of Dante's reach. To finally feel Sentori's face under his fist released the aggression he'd stored over the months. He wanted to feel more. For him. For the fans. For Caitlyn.

He faked a jab but in the last second came around with a right hook, landing it on the side of his opponent's face. The force of the hit stung Dante's arm as Sentori stumbled and revealed a gash above his eyebrow. Blood crept down his face.

Taking advantage of his staggering opponent, Dante snapped his leg around, catching Sentori high on the left thigh. The loud pop surged satisfaction through him. His opponent hopped back, favoring his right leg for a moment before he wiped his glove across his face and settled back.

Exhilaration pumped Dante up. The kick had hurt. That wasn't the only pain he planned to inflict. They circled. Dante kicked out, catching Sentori on the leg again. As soon as the crack sounded, Dante lunged, planning to deliver another brutal blow. To finish it.

But Sentori dodged the punch and wrapped his arms around Dante's waist, driving him against the cage. The wire mesh dug into his skin, but he grabbed the back of his opponent's head and brought a knee up into his gut. For a second, Sentori's grip loosened, but it was enough time for Dante to take the advantage in the clench and hit him with another blowing knee.

He had to get out of this position. Against the cage with a seasoned jujitsu artist was dangerous. If he wasn't careful, Sentori would take control.

Dante tried to maneuver out of the clench and take the

fight back to the middle of the cage, but Sentori lifted one of Dante's legs, knocked him off balance, and slammed him to the mat. The air whooshed out of Dante's lungs. He grabbed one quick breath before Sentori landed a heavy right hand to his temple. The power behind the punch stunned Dante and his head jerked to the side. Sentori had seized control and Dante was in deep shit.

He brought his gloves up to protect his head when Sentori went to deliver another punch. Desperate to get back to his feet, Dante made a fatal mistake. He rolled and gave his opponent his back. One moment of instinct shattered his game plan as Sentori took advantage of the submissive position.

Sentori latched on behind him, his legs wrapped around Dante's waist, his fists delivering side blows to his temple. Then Dante felt it. The setup. His opponent was going for it.

His signature hold.

The rear naked chokehold.

He twisted, refusing to lose this fight in the first round. Not to this man. And not by submission.

Even as he thought it, the arm snaked around his neck.

· · ·

"Can't you go any faster?"

The cab driver looked over his shoulder at her. "Listen, lady, I don't have any control over traffic. We're still two miles from the arena. Be my guest to walk it."

Cait groaned and flopped back against the seat. She dug out her cell phone again. She'd tried Dante's number three times but hadn't received an answer. She wasn't sure if it was because he didn't want to talk to her, or he was unavailable.

She prayed for the latter.

It was after ten now. No reason to try his number again. He was already in the cage. She pressed two on her cell phone and waited for Paul to answer.

"Girl, the Mighty Grape Ape is...why don't I hear any screaming?"

"I'm not at the arena."

"What the hell do you mean you're not there? Your man is fighting."

"It's a long story, but I'm trying to get there now. What round is it?"

"Second. Hercules almost lost at the end of the first round, but he held out for the bell to ring."

He'd almost lost? And she hadn't been there? Her stomach twisted. "How's he doing this round?"

The taxi finally jolted forward and Cait sighed in relief.

"Slimeball Sentori has taken a few impressive hits to the face."

She would love to see that.

"And Dante?"

There was a moment of silence. "He's taken some, too."

"Cait, what the hell is going on? Why is Paul giving you a play-by-play?" The feminine voice that suddenly filled her ears let her know that Amy had yanked the phone out of Paul's hand.

"Like I said to Paul, it's a long story. I'm trying to get there now."

"You're not going to be able to just walk into the arena, Cait. The fight's almost over. The box office is closed."

She'd been so focused on her goal, she hadn't thought of that.

"Shit." Cait rubbed her eyes.

Dante was going to go through this entire fight thinking she didn't want to be there. All she could do was go back to the room, wait for him to return, and hope he'd believe her when she said she'd wanted nothing more to be standing in his corner, supporting him.

"How far away are you?"

She glanced up. The arena was finally coming into view. "Down the block."

Screams of the fans poured through the phone and she clenched the phone tighter. What was happening?

"Second round is over!" Paul's voice came back on the line.

"Where's Amy?"

"She's on the phone. Wait a sec." Her two friends talked back and forth. "Hey, Cait, Amy says Brad will be waiting. Come through the hotel. He'll take you ringside."

Brad! She'd forgotten he'd flown out for the fight.

"Amy said you need to hurry. These fights can end in seconds."

"I just pulled in, tell Brad I'm coming." She ended the call and stuffed the phone in her purse.

Before the cab had pulled to a full stop, she'd tossed the money for the fare into the front seat and shot out the door. She raced through the hotel then the casino, weaving around the crowds, throwing "Sorry" over her shoulder every time she bumped into someone.

The fight could end any second.

Please, not before I get there.

When she reached the entrance, Brad handed her a badge. "Put this on."

As she pinned it to her shirt, she asked, "What round?"

"Fourth. We've got to hurry."

After they flashed their badges to a security guard, who waved them in, she followed Brad into a hall, then a pair of doors.

The boisterous stadium greeted her. Everyone was on their feet, their attention glued to the ring.

That was when Cait noticed she wasn't in the thick of the dense crowd but walking in a clear path between the seats. Her heartbeat picked up. She was headed straight for the octagon without anyone in her way.

Hallelujah!

She stopped just outside of view, not wanting to make her presence known while Dante was in the middle of a round.

She gazed at her fighter in all his glory. Even coated in sweat and blood, he took her breath away. Both men were on their feet, dancing around each other. Dante swung out and caught Sentori in the face, who stumbled back but righted himself. Next, the butthole swung out and caught Dante on the chin. Her heart froze as Dante's head jerked violently to the side. Then she saw it. The true testament of how hard this fight had been. Blood oozed from above his eye, his nose, and the corner of his mouth.

Sentori didn't appear any better with one eye swollen, and a gash across his nose and brow—served the bastard right. The two had beaten the absolute crap out of each other. And the fans ate it up. Her? Her stomach rolled instead and she swallowed her distaste.

Sentori lunged, lifted Dante high into the air, and slammed him against the mat. Cait slapped her hands over her eyes. "No!"

She spread her fingers to see Sentori press Dante into

the mat, chest to chest. Her fighter struggled underneath. "Kill him, Dante!" she screamed.

God, had that just come out of her mouth? Maybe she had a fighter's spirit after all.

The bell rang. End of round four. Dante crossed to sit on a stool in his corner. His team immediately surrounded him, squirting water in his mouth, pressing gauze over his wounds, rubbing his muscles, yelling instructions all the while he sat there dazed and breathing heavily. More than likely he was completely exhausted.

Cait made her way around the octagon to his corner. He was right there, his back toward her. She shouldn't speak to him, distract him, but couldn't help herself. He had to know she was here.

"Dante," she yelled.

He stiffened. Mike whispered in Dante's ear and he whipped around on the stool. He stared at her. Shock and pleasure swam in his eyes.

Right there, in front of his team, and all the eyes that had followed the fighter's sudden interest, she yelled, "I love you."

His eyes widened, then he smiled a big black mouth guard smile.

"Beat him," she mouthed.

He nodded then turned back to the octagon. The bell rang again and he was up. This Dante was pumped, so different from the exhausted one a moment before. Liveliness flowed off him in waves, determination in his every move.

The men tapped gloves, then Dante swung a right hook, making his mark on Sentori's left jaw. The man's eyes widened as he fell back onto the mat. Without hesitation,

Dante covered him. Limbs bent in awkward angles, and so many fists flew that at times she wasn't sure whose was whose.

One moment Dante was on top, the next Sentori was, then vice versa. Back and forth they went. Cait stood with her hands held to the side of her face, ready to shut out the view at any moment, cringing at each pop and crack, avoiding looking at the blood-stained canvas. And the canvas was stained. So gross.

So much for wanting to be a top-notch corner supporter. It took every bit of willpower not to close her eyes and cover her ears. But she forced herself to watch each movement, even if it was at times through squinted eyes.

The two men grappled until Dante got an edge. Or at least she thought it was an edge. She really wasn't sure. But the hold Dante had Sentori in—behind him, legs wrapped his waist—and the sudden fear on his opponent's face told her this was a good position for Dante.

Sentori grabbed Dante's wrist as his arm came around his opponent's neck. With his free hand, Dante punched the side of Sentori's face until his grip loosened.

Mike screamed at him from outside the ring with a bunch of lingo she'd never heard and hit the top of the canvas three times. Breath held, she watched, mesmerized. Something was happening. Something big. She just wished she knew what.

Dante's arm slid under Sentori's chin as he continued to pound at his opponent's head. Mike screamed louder, hitting the canvas harder. Good God, what was happening?

The grip around Sentori's neck was so constrictive, as though Dante was trying to pop his head clean off.

Teeth bared, Dante leaned back, cranking the grip tighter.

If that was even possible. Sentori's eyes snapped open in his beet-red face and he slapped Dante's forearm.

Oh my God!

She knew what that was. A tap. Sentori had tapped!

Cait screamed, jumping up and down.

The crowd roared as the referee leapt in and separated them. Dante shot to his feet. Arms raised high, he yelled and ran around the ring. His team stormed the cage, all taking their turn hugging the new champion.

As his gaze met hers, he ripped his mouthpiece out and grinned. Pride for this man filled her to overflowing. She kissed her fingers and blew it to him. His eyes twinkled with triumph and delight.

The announcer walked into the middle of the cage while the ref stood between Dante and Sentori, holding one arm each. "Ladies and gentlemen, this fight has ended fifty-five seconds into the fifth round by tap out, declaring the winner by rear naked choke and the new welterweight champion of the world, Daaante 'Inferno' Jooones."

The ref held up Dante's arm as another man wrapped the gold belt around his waist. The pleasure on Dante's face caused her chest to tighten. He'd worked so hard for this, had wanted this so badly. Now he had it. Her champion.

The announcer came to stand by Dante. "This was the biggest fight in MMA history and the biggest fight of your career. You beat the toughest guy in the sport tonight with an incredible performance. How does it feel?"

Dante's gaze met hers again. "It is the most wonderful feeling in the world."

Heat rushed into her cheeks, and she smiled. She knew he wasn't talking only about the fight. She wouldn't have missed this moment for anything. He'd wanted her here. And this was exactly where she wanted to be.

The next few minutes were chaos. Dante finished his interview, and then he and his team huddled in the middle singing some song she'd never heard. As things died down, they exited the octagon and Dante walked over to her. It was the first time she'd seen him up close and she gasped at what she saw.

A huge gash was taped over his forehead, his right eye swollen and starting to bruise. Another cut sliced across the bridge of his nose. He looked awful and she couldn't have found him sexier. A man, fresh from battle, exiting the ring and walking straight to her…oh, she liked it. A lot.

When he reached her, she grabbed his hands and held them to her chest.

"I never left. I need you to know that. I *never* left."

Confusion clouded his eyes. "But your stuff was gone."

"I'd gone on a walk to think. That's all. Sentori took care of the rest."

"What the fuck do you mean Sentori took care of the rest?" His head snapped up, jaws clenched as he surveyed the area. "I'll fucking kick his ass a second time."

She cupped his cheeks and forced his gaze to hers. "I was on my way back to tell you I love you. That was what I wanted you to hear. I love you, Dante Jones. I am so sorry for the pain I caused you, but I am completely, irrevocably, *desperately* in love with you. *All* of you. And I am yours if you will have me."

His eyes full of love, he grabbed her in his arms and whirled her around, squeezing her tight. Cait laughed as he lowered her to her feet. The air left her lungs as she gazed at him. She loved this man so completely it hurt.

"All was forgiven the moment you said you loved me. I needed to hear that. I needed you here," he said and pressed his forehead to hers.

She ran her hand over his tattoo, tracing the lines with her finger. He kissed her gently then pulled her to him. Cait laid her head on his chest, enjoying the sound of his heartbeat against her cheek.

Cameras flashed, but she didn't flinch. *Ahhs* came from the fans who remained, and still she didn't flinch. She held onto her warrior, intent on never letting him go.

He pulled back. "Think you can get used to waking up to this ugly mug every morning?"

Gazing up into his battered face, she smiled. "I think I can handle it."

As long as she had him, she could handle anything.

EPILOGUE

Cait squealed and slapped her hands over her eyes. It didn't matter how many times she watched, seeing Dante eat a fist never got any easier. She peeked through her fingers and relaxed. The punch hadn't fazed him. He was still on his feet, defending his title for the first time.

After a long break, she'd been thrown back into his world. With another huge fight on the horizon, the interest in them as a couple had increased tenfold. Surprisingly, she'd found it wasn't the horrible place she'd thought it would be.

The pride she felt for Dante as he interviewed and signed autographs surpassed any residual panic she still battled. But with each day, this became her world, too. Hell, she'd even been interviewed on occasion, letting the fans know the trials and tribulations of being an MMA star's girlfriend, the weeks of barely seeing him as he trained hard. But she didn't resent the time away from him. She spent those long weeks submerged in her program, which had taken off and spread throughout the South at record speed. Dante proudly stood in *her* corner and supported her dedication to helping others lose weight.

And she supported him, wanting him to achieve every goal he set out to win.

Loving Dante had taken her far outside her comfort zone, and she couldn't be happier.

The bell dinged, signaling the end of round one. She fidgeted in her seat while Dante sat in his corner, Mike barking out orders. When the bell sounded again, he shot out of his chair and ended the fight with one punch. His poor opponent crumbled to the ground.

Cait jumped to her feet screaming and clapping. The octagon filled with people and when the announcer came to Dante's side, her man took the mike from him. The announcer's eyes widened but he didn't protest.

"Caitlyn, come here." Dante motioned for her to come forward.

She froze. She wasn't supposed to enter the cage. Her place was right here, supporting him.

Mike, with a look of defeat, sighed. "Go on up, Cait."

She glanced at him. Their relationship had gotten stronger; she now considered him like an uncle. "What's going on?"

He rolled his eyes. "Just go."

She hesitantly climbed the stairs and entered the ring. It felt so weird to be on this side of the action, among the flood of people, the cameras, the bright lights. She shuffled to Dante's side and smiled shyly at the lens thrust in her face.

He took her hand. "I wanted to win this fight for you."

"Why?"

"Because I wanted to do this."

He bent on one knee and Cait's eyes widened. Everything around them faded. Only Dante existed.

Mike appeared at their side and handed Dante a black velvet box.

"Caitlyn Moore, you are my life, my future, my love, and I want you in my corner always. Will you do me the honor of becoming my wife?"

As the fans screamed, he popped the box open to reveal a teardrop diamond ring with a white gold band. Cait pressed her free hand to her mouth, tears filling her eyes. "Yes."

Dante slipped the ring on her finger and rose, taking her in a long kiss. As the cameras flashed and the crowd whistled, she smiled against his mouth and held him tight.

She'd slain her dragons and her reward was a lifetime of happiness with this man.

Her warrior. Her champion. Her love.

ACKNOWLEDGMENTS

This book has been six years in the making and there are so many people to thank. *Extreme Love* was a very long road that started with me needing a catalyst for my own weight loss journey. There have been multiple revisions to this story, and each one has brought it closer and closer to the book it is today. I'm very proud of the book it has become, and I thank everyone that had even the smallest part in helping me create it.

First off, I want to thank Entangled Publishing and Liz Pelletier for believing in the story and truly getting it. Your excitement as we spoke on the phone means more to me than you will ever know. And thank you for the freaking hot cover! It screams Dante and I love it!

To Robin: You kicked my butt during edits, and I appreciate it. The ending is more than I could have ever imagined it to be now. Thank you for holding me accountable and making me dig deeper. I may have muttered a few curses and lost some hair in the process, but even at my most stressed, I knew you had the books best interest at heart, and you really helped me bring this book together. Deeply, I thank you.

To my publicists, Morgan and Babs: You guys rock! Thank you for being a kickass publicist team and helping me get *Extreme Love* out there into the world!

To my CP's: Alison, Angie, Christina, Christyne, and Tina, I love you!

To all of writeromance: The support this group gives is like none other. You girls are seriously the best.

To JJ: Dude, you're awesome. Thank you for being my special CP during this project. Yeah, I know you had to suffer through some "girly" scenes, but thank you for toughing it out. Your vast knowledge of MMA helped me bring the sport to life in the way I wanted.

To RHEK: Thank you for allowing me to come and sit in on some training sessions. I learned a lot by seeing things firsthand.

And as always, to Ophelia and Rupert: Mommy loves you.